WITCH FOR HIRE

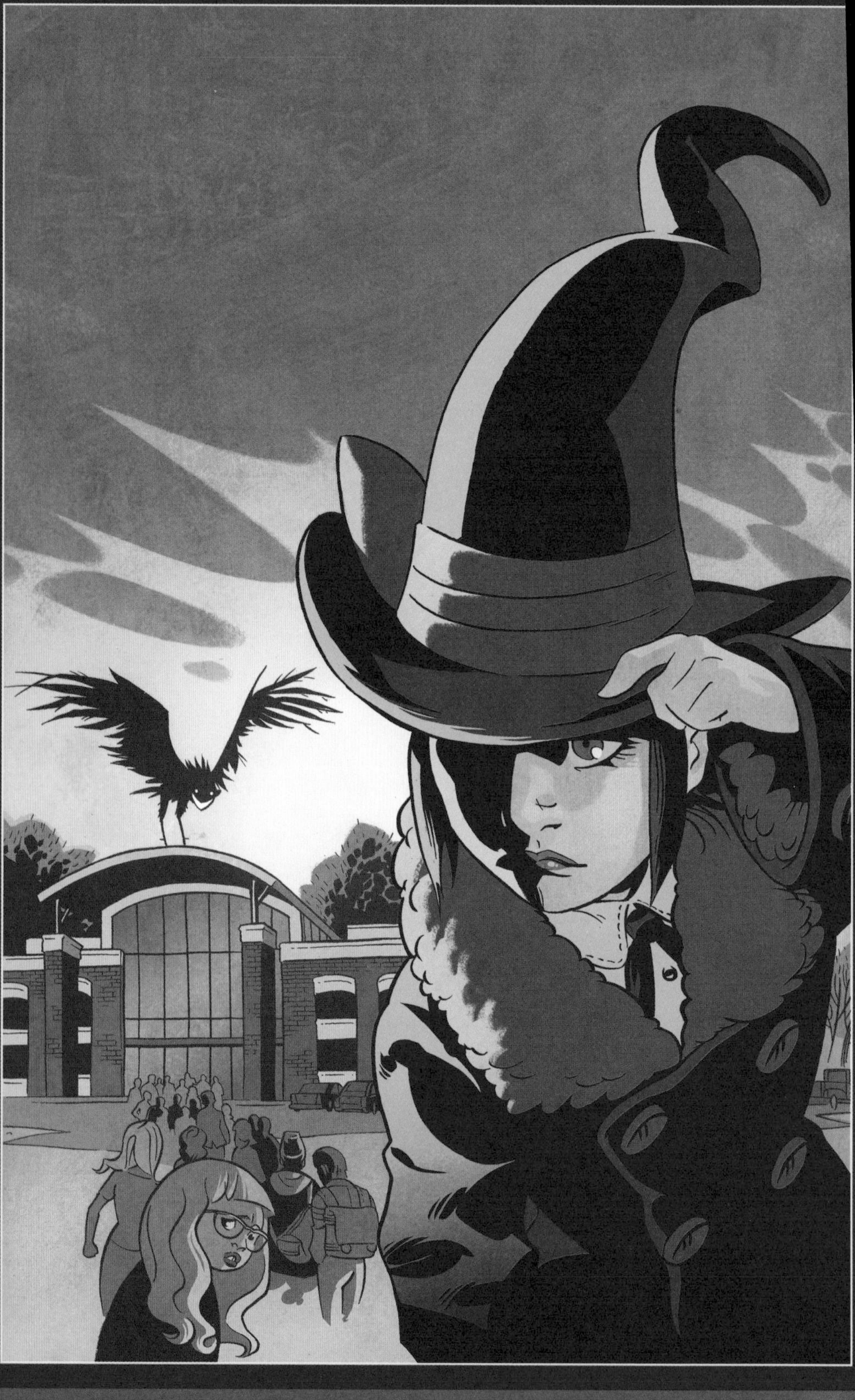

WITCH FOR HIRE

TED NAIFEH

AMULET BOOKS • NEW YORK

Library of Congress Control Number: 2020952012

Hardcover ISBN 978-1-4197-4810-3
Paperback ISBN 978-1-4197-4811-0
Text and illustrations copyright © 2021 Ted Naifeh
Book design by Kay Petronio

Printed and bound in China
10 9 8 7 6 5 4 3 2 1

Amulet Books are available at special discounts when purchased in quantity for premiums and promotions as well as fundraising or educational use. Special editions can also be created to specification. For details, contact specialsales@abramsbooks.com or the address below.

Amulet Books® is a registered trademark of Harry N. Abrams, Inc.

ABRAMS The Art of Books
195 Broadway, New York, NY 10007
abramsbooks.com

For Charlotte, whose
guidance and
support have been
a revelation.

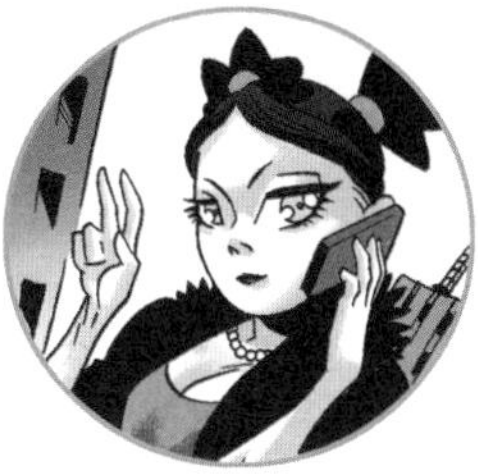

shy__shelbi

3k post | 2,3 mil followers | 5 following

Do you dream of changing your life? Me too. I tried it all: fitness, fashion, universal one-ness through yoga and healthy bowels . . . but I realized I needed to #transform who I was on the inside. If you want to do what I did, leave weakness behind and become your best self, I can help. Message me up now! I respond to EVERYONE.

Follow | **Message** | **Email**

5-step program | rules | prizes & penalties | more

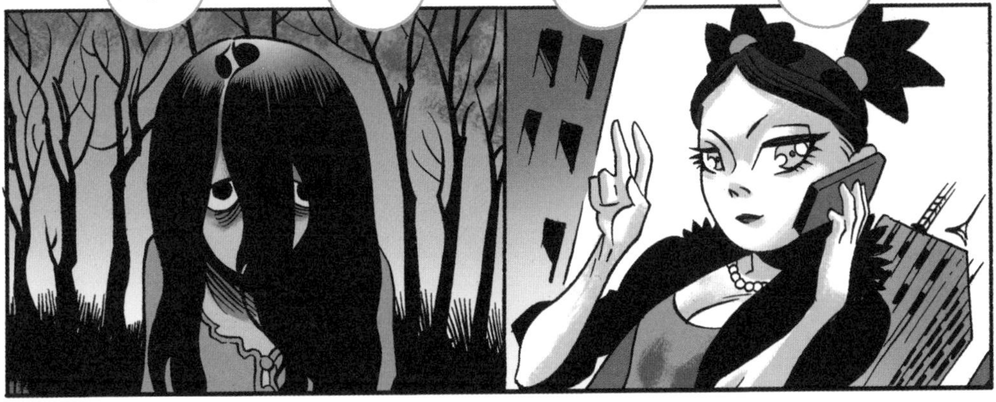

Check out my before-and-after photos! It's easier than you think to shed your worries, fears, regrets, and become stronger than you ever dreamed. Meet people just like you who #selfactualized through the shy__shelbi 5-step program.

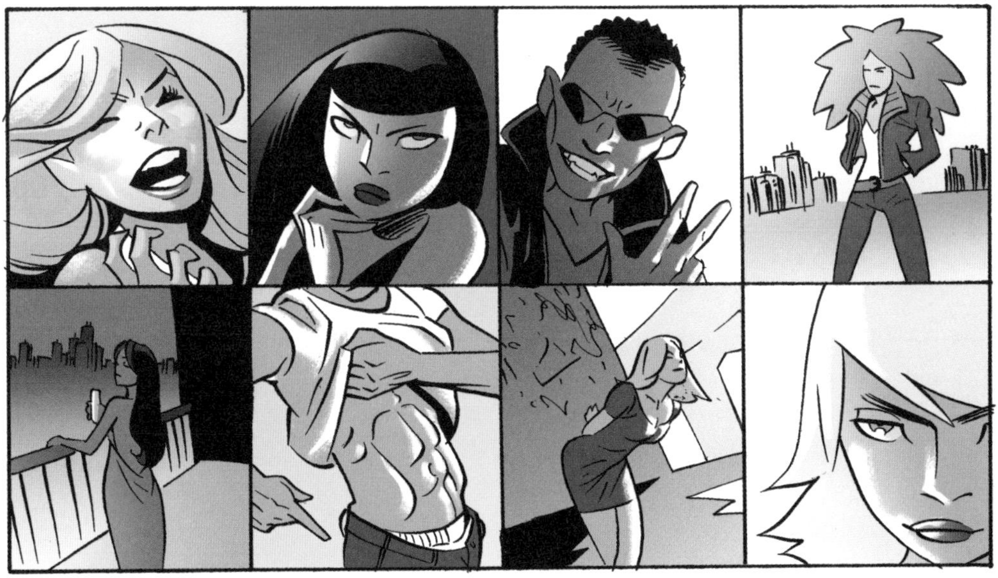

ting-a-ling

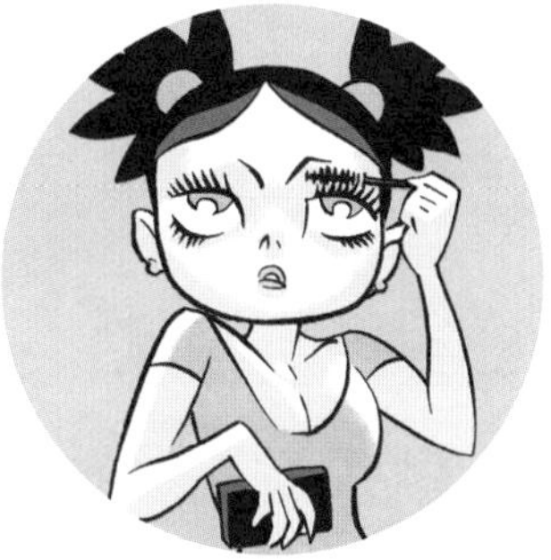

the shy_shelbi program

Step 1: I'm not here to make friends

The world will constantly tell you how much you need people's approval. Don't listen. You don't want to need them, you want them to need you. So step 1 is learning to dominate your social group . . . more

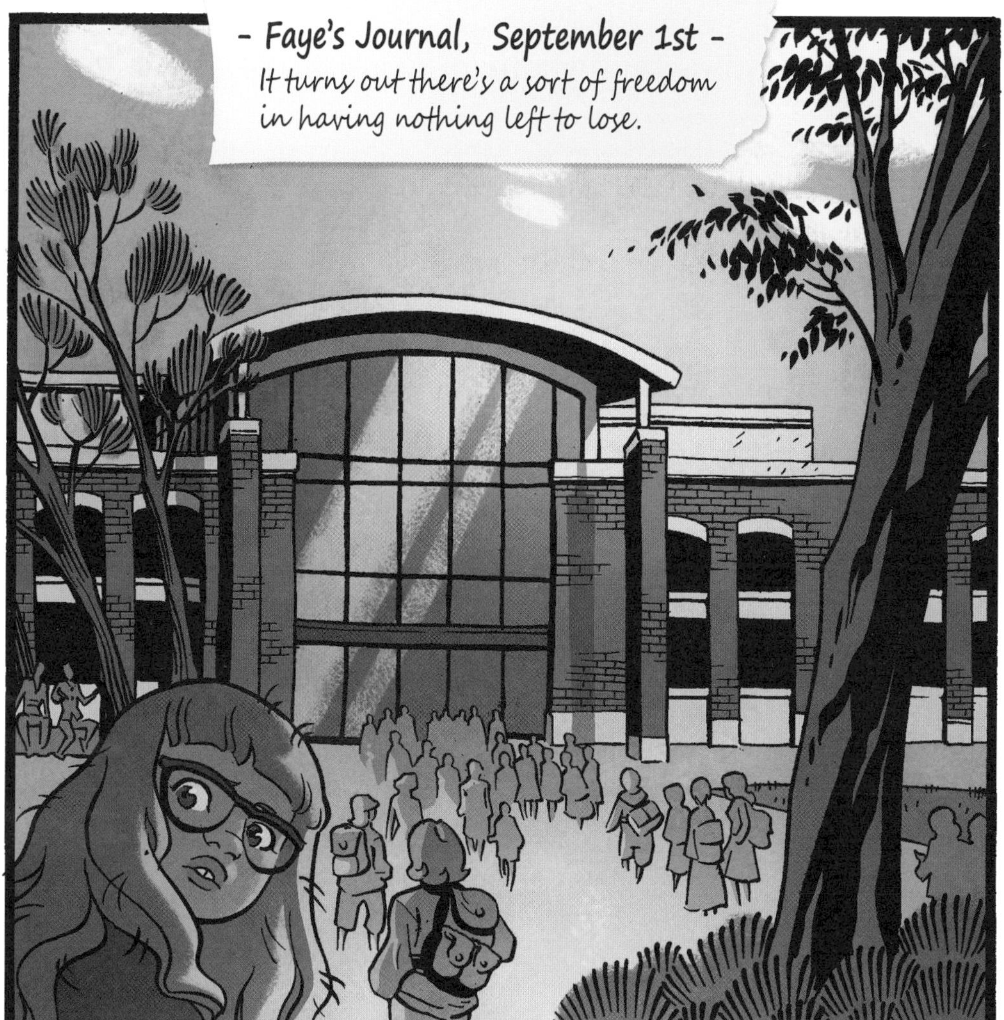
- Faye's Journal, September 1st -
It turns out there's a sort of freedom in having nothing left to lose.

It's kinda like wading into icy water . . .

SO **MACKENZIE** DID FOUR **PHOTOSHOOTS** OVER THE SUMMER. GUESS HER SO-CALLED **MODELING CAREER** IS REAL AFTER **ALL.**

YEAH, I **HEARD.** KNOW WHAT SHE'S **SAYING** ABOUT IT?

Every inch you sink is agony. Knowing there's more to come makes it worse.

"IT'S NO BIG **DEAL.**"

ugh!

SHE'S LITERALLY THE **WORST.**

umm, HEY, **BRYCE?** CAN I, uh . . .

4

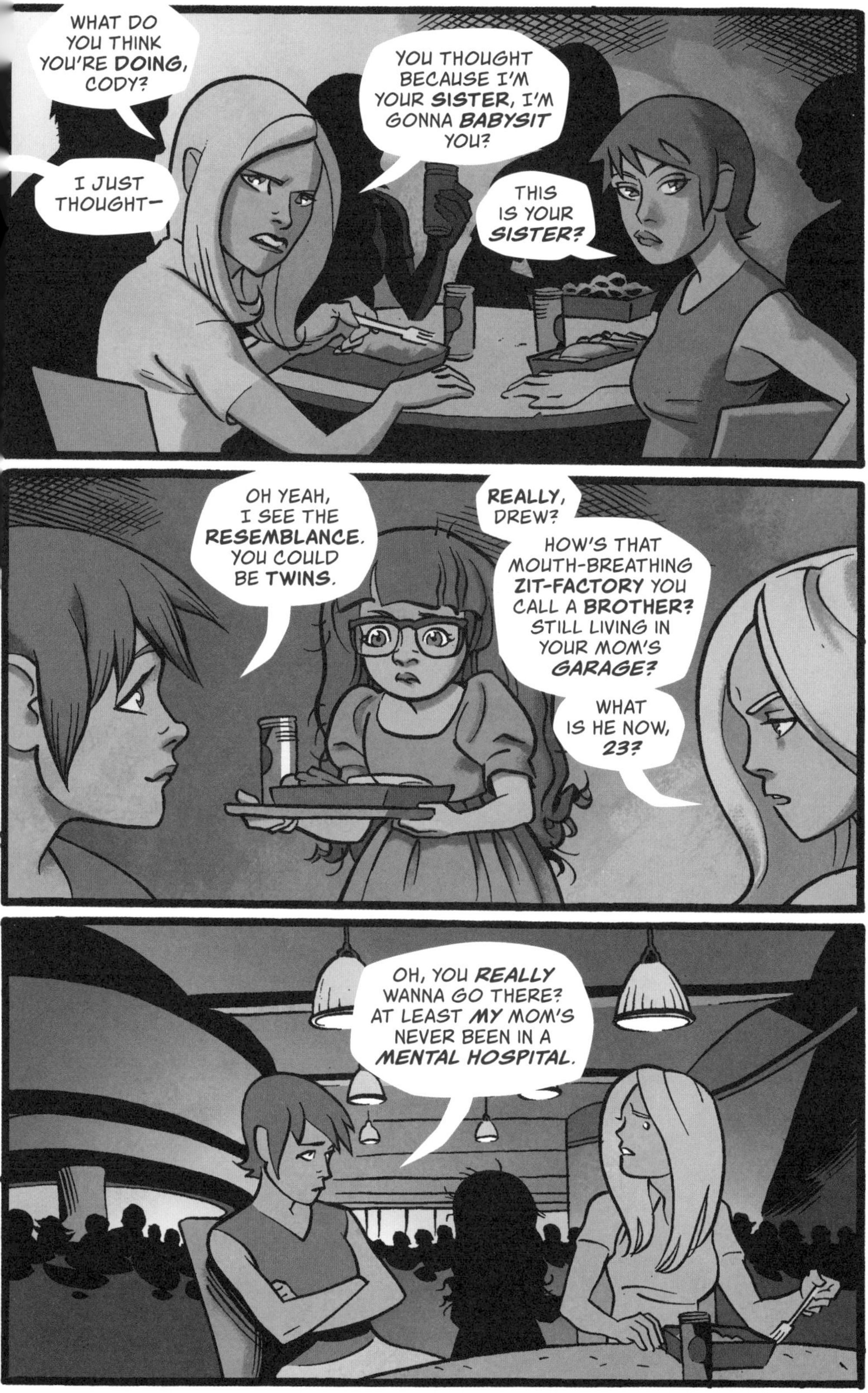
WHAT DO YOU THINK YOU'RE **DOING**, CODY?
I JUST THOUGHT—
YOU THOUGHT BECAUSE I'M YOUR **SISTER**, I'M GONNA ***BABYSIT*** YOU?
THIS IS YOUR ***SISTER?***
OH YEAH, I SEE THE **RESEMBLANCE**. YOU COULD BE **TWINS**.
REALLY, DREW?
HOW'S THAT MOUTH-BREATHING **ZIT-FACTORY** YOU CALL A **BROTHER?** STILL LIVING IN YOUR MOM'S ***GARAGE?***
WHAT IS HE NOW, ***23?***
OH, YOU ***REALLY*** WANNA GO THERE? AT LEAST ***MY*** MOM'S NEVER BEEN IN A ***MENTAL HOSPITAL***.

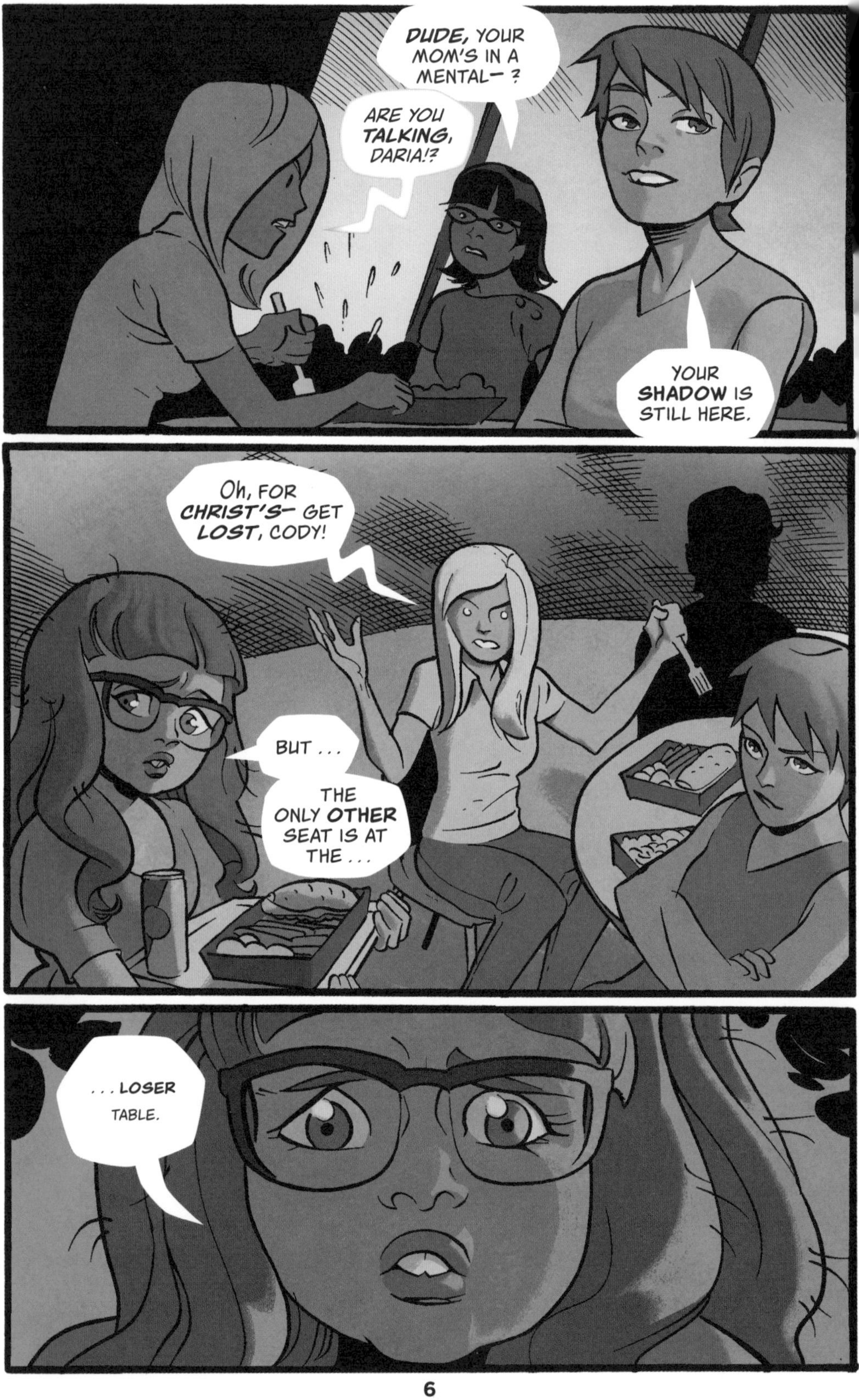
DUDE, YOUR MOM'S IN A MENTAL— ?
ARE YOU TALKING, DARIA!?
YOUR SHADOW IS STILL HERE.
Oh, FOR CHRIST'S— GET LOST, CODY!
BUT . . .
THE ONLY OTHER SEAT IS AT THE . . .
. . . LOSER TABLE.

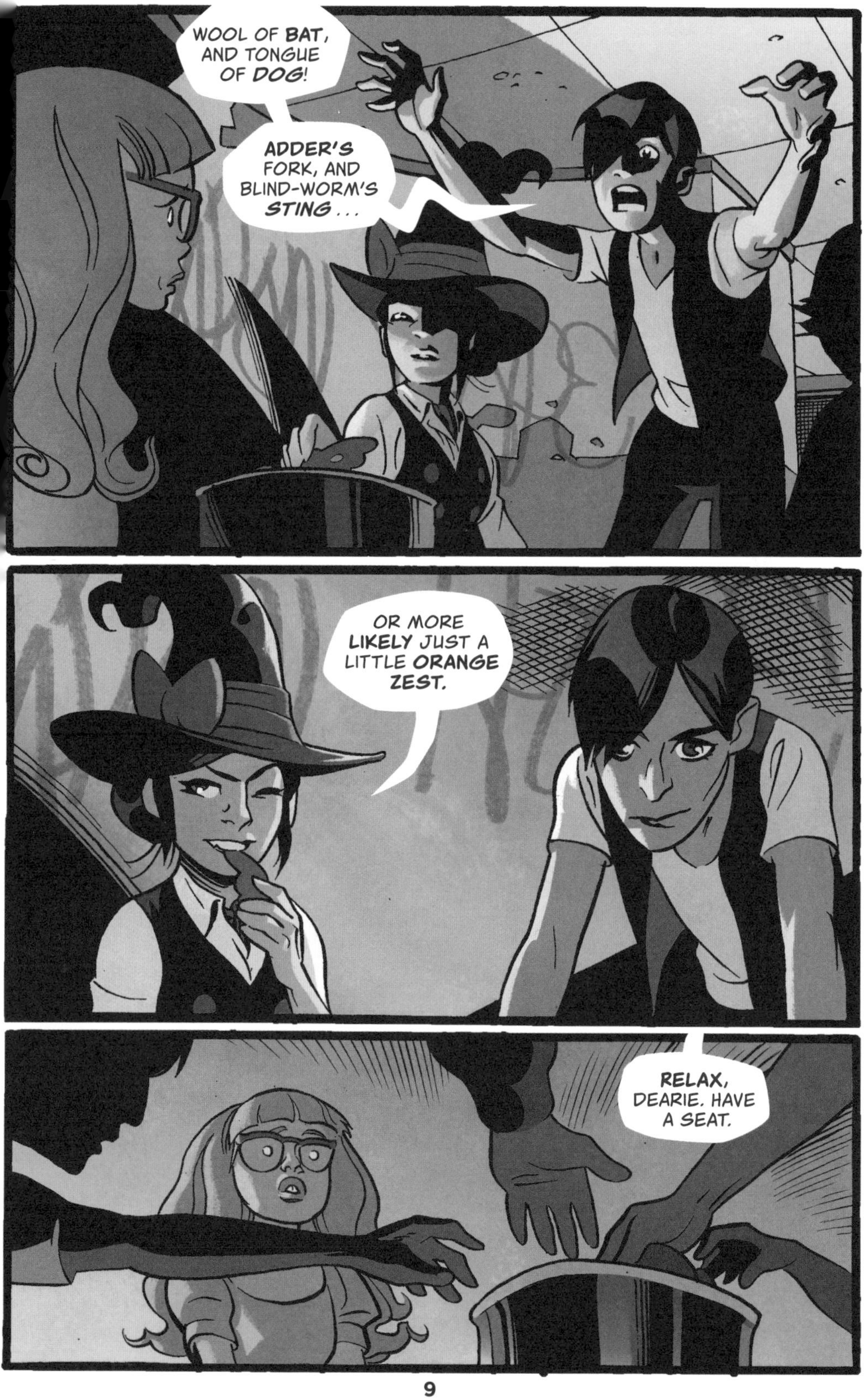
WOOL OF BAT, AND TONGUE OF DOG!
ADDER'S FORK, AND BLIND-WORM'S STING . . .
OR MORE LIKELY JUST A LITTLE ORANGE ZEST.
RELAX, DEARIE. HAVE A SEAT.

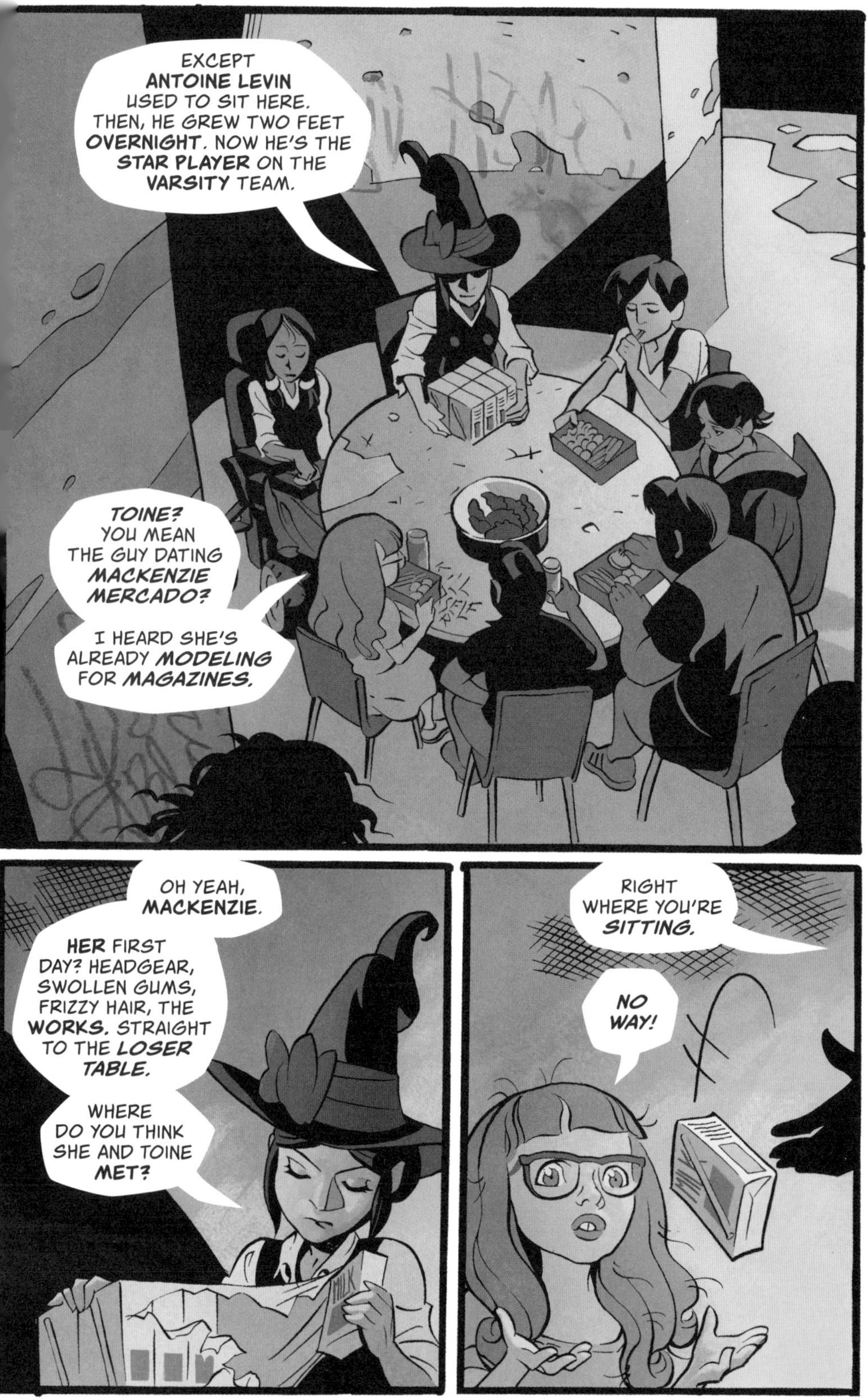
EXCEPT ANTOINE LEVIN USED TO SIT HERE. THEN, HE GREW TWO FEET OVERNIGHT. NOW HE'S THE STAR PLAYER ON THE VARSITY TEAM.
TOINE? YOU MEAN THE GUY DATING MACKENZIE MERCADO?
I HEARD SHE'S ALREADY MODELING FOR MAGAZINES.
OH YEAH, MACKENZIE.
HER FIRST DAY? HEADGEAR, SWOLLEN GUMS, FRIZZY HAIR, THE WORKS. STRAIGHT TO THE LOSER TABLE.
WHERE DO YOU THINK SHE AND TOINE MET?
RIGHT WHERE YOU'RE SITTING.
NO WAY!

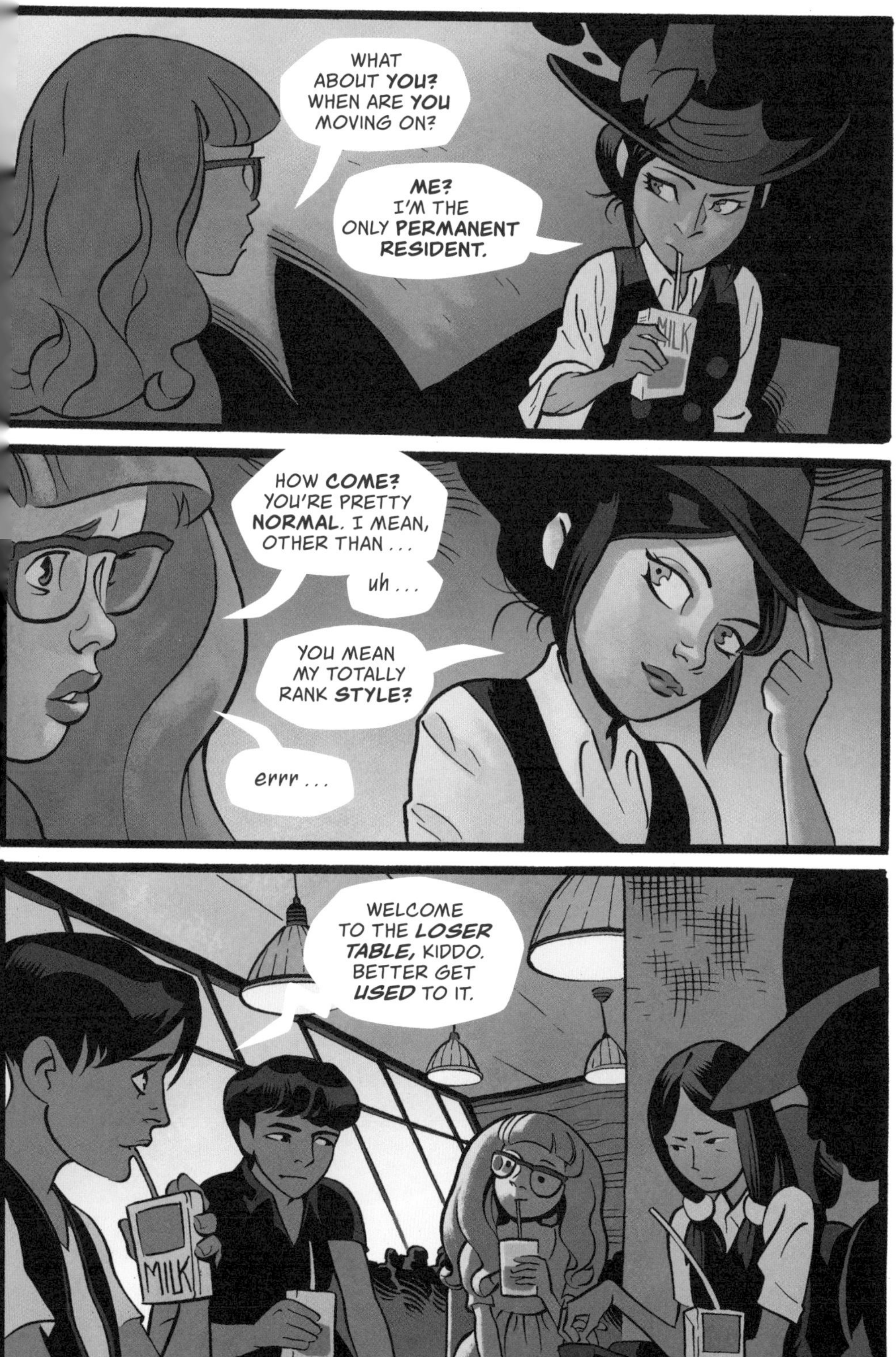
WHAT ABOUT **YOU?** WHEN ARE **YOU** MOVING ON?
ME? I'M THE ONLY **PERMANENT RESIDENT.**
MILK
HOW **COME?** YOU'RE PRETTY **NORMAL.** I MEAN, OTHER THAN . . .
uh . . .
YOU MEAN MY TOTALLY RANK **STYLE?**
errr . . .
WELCOME TO THE ***LOSER TABLE,*** KIDDO. BETTER GET ***USED*** TO IT.
MILK

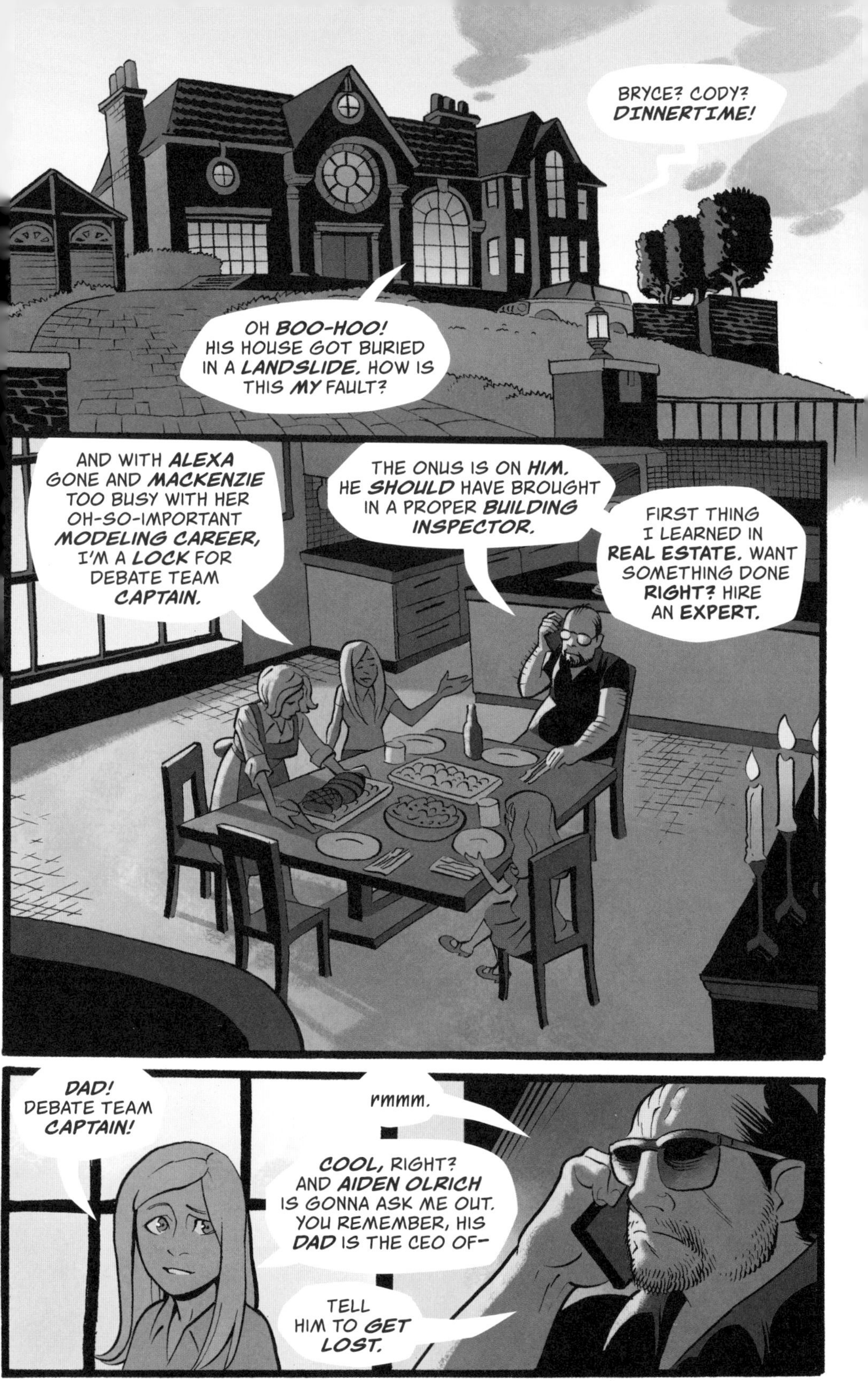
BRYCE? CODY? DINNERTIME!
OH BOO-HOO! HIS HOUSE GOT BURIED IN A LANDSLIDE. HOW IS THIS MY FAULT?
AND WITH ALEXA GONE AND MACKENZIE TOO BUSY WITH HER OH-SO-IMPORTANT MODELING CAREER, I'M A LOCK FOR DEBATE TEAM CAPTAIN.
THE ONUS IS ON HIM. HE SHOULD HAVE BROUGHT IN A PROPER BUILDING INSPECTOR.
FIRST THING I LEARNED IN REAL ESTATE. WANT SOMETHING DONE RIGHT? HIRE AN EXPERT.
DAD! DEBATE TEAM CAPTAIN!
rmmm.
COOL, RIGHT? AND AIDEN OLRICH IS GONNA ASK ME OUT. YOU REMEMBER, HIS DAD IS THE CEO OF-
TELL HIM TO GET LOST.

16

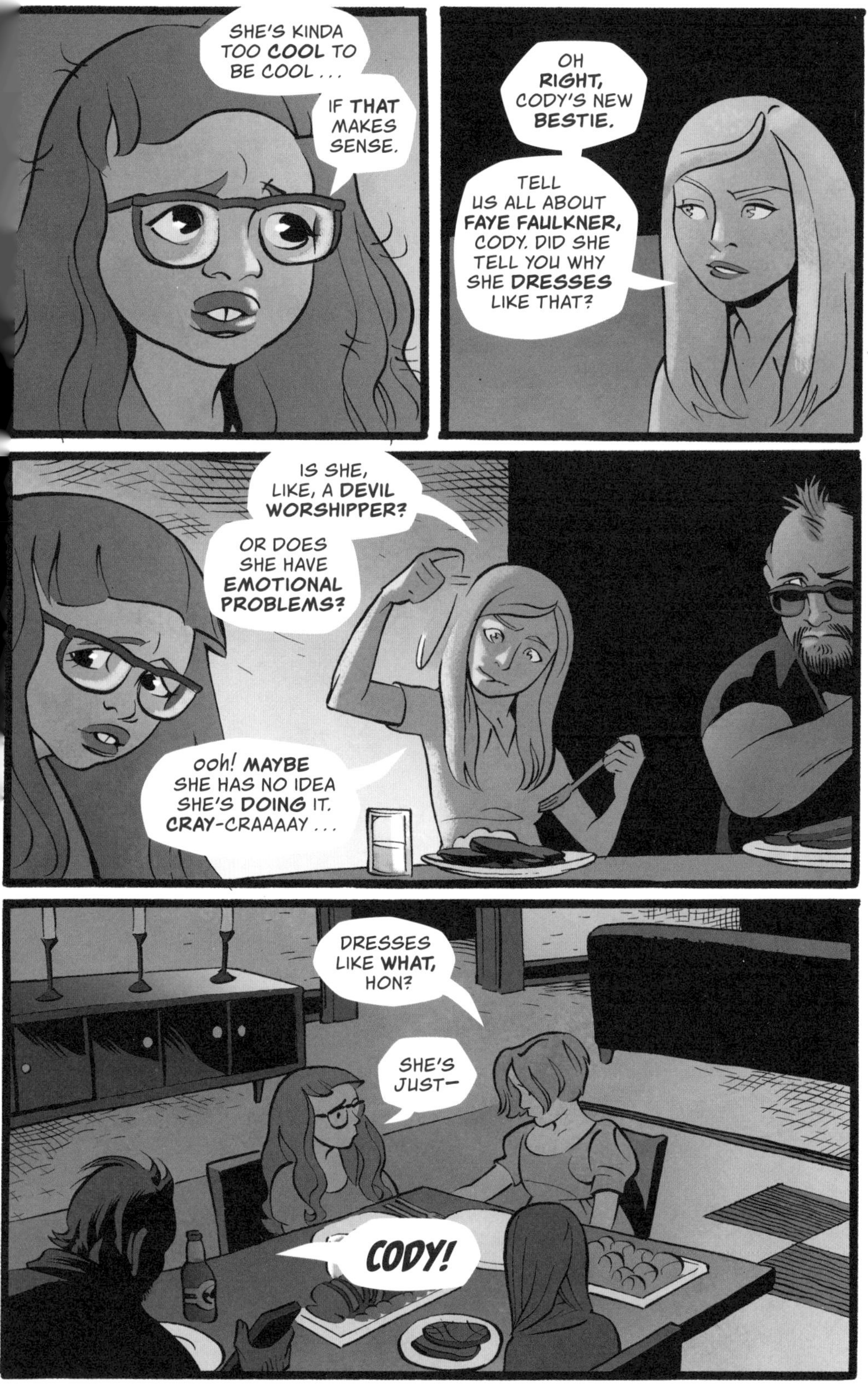
SHE'S KINDA TOO **COOL** TO BE COOL . . .
IF **THAT** MAKES SENSE.
OH **RIGHT,** CODY'S NEW **BESTIE.**
TELL US ALL ABOUT **FAYE FAULKNER,** CODY. DID SHE TELL YOU WHY SHE **DRESSES** LIKE THAT?
IS SHE, LIKE, A **DEVIL WORSHIPPER?**
OR DOES SHE HAVE **EMOTIONAL PROBLEMS?**
ooh! **MAYBE** SHE HAS NO IDEA SHE'S **DOING** IT. **CRAY**-CRAAAAY . . .
DRESSES LIKE **WHAT,** HON?
SHE'S JUST—
CODY!

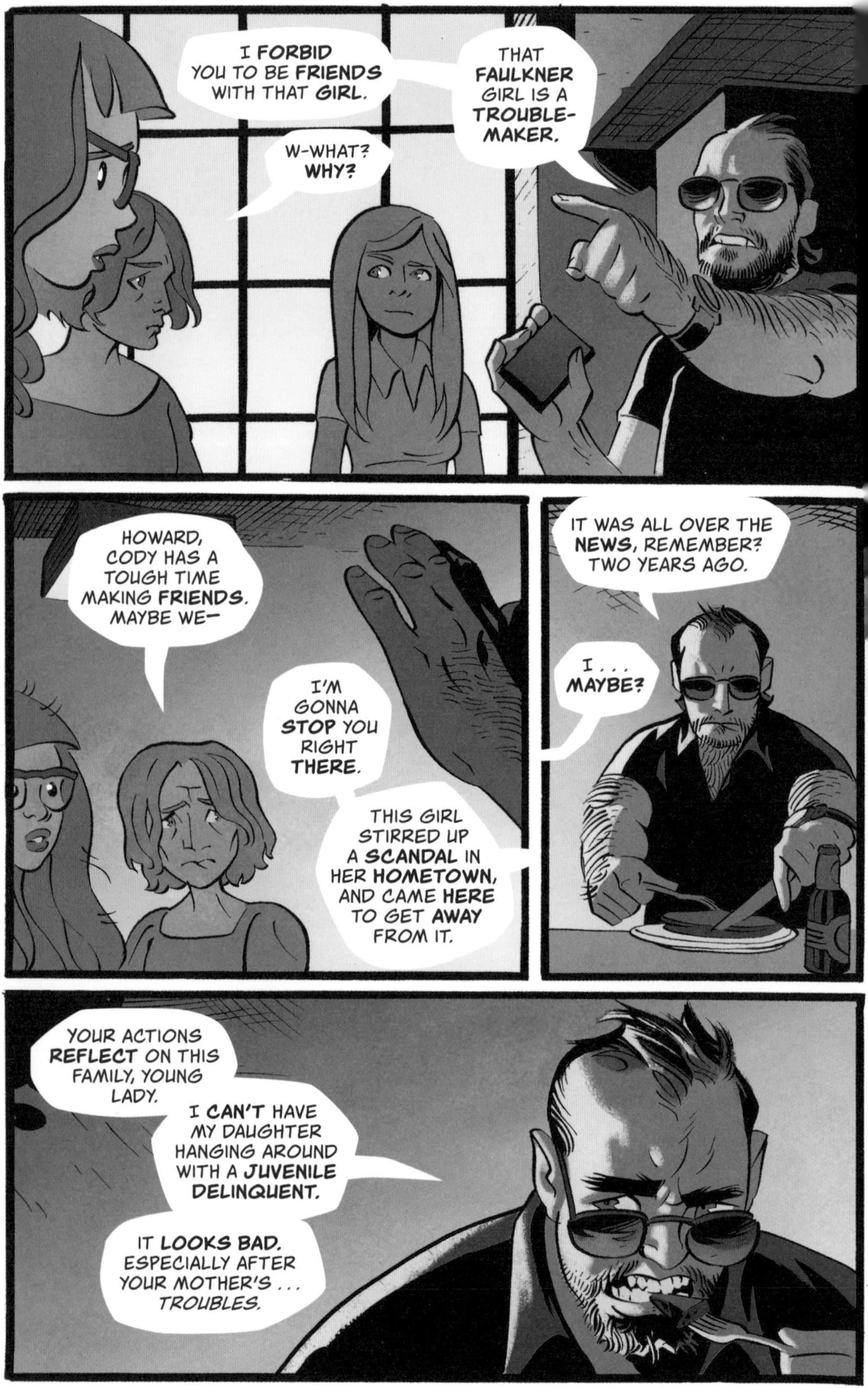
I FORBID YOU TO BE FRIENDS WITH THAT GIRL.
THAT FAULKNER GIRL IS A TROUBLE-MAKER.
W-WHAT? WHY?
HOWARD, CODY HAS A TOUGH TIME MAKING FRIENDS. MAYBE WE—
I'M GONNA STOP YOU RIGHT THERE.
THIS GIRL STIRRED UP A SCANDAL IN HER HOMETOWN, AND CAME HERE TO GET AWAY FROM IT.
IT WAS ALL OVER THE NEWS, REMEMBER? TWO YEARS AGO.
I . . . MAYBE?
YOUR ACTIONS REFLECT ON THIS FAMILY, YOUNG LADY.
I CAN'T HAVE MY DAUGHTER HANGING AROUND WITH A JUVENILE DELINQUENT.
IT LOOKS BAD. ESPECIALLY AFTER YOUR MOTHER'S . . . TROUBLES.

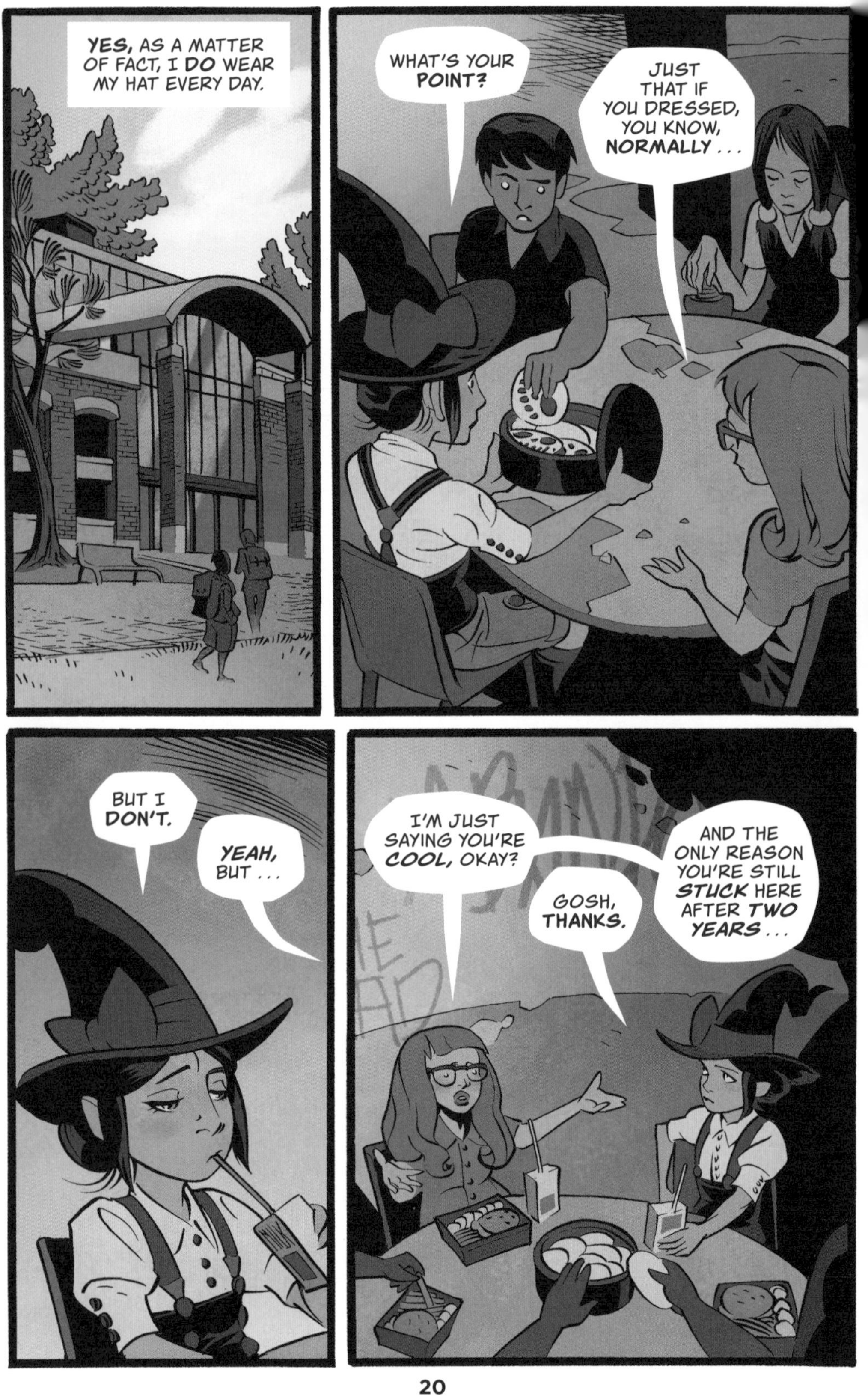
YES, AS A MATTER OF FACT, I DO WEAR MY HAT EVERY DAY.
WHAT'S YOUR POINT?
JUST THAT IF YOU DRESSED, YOU KNOW, NORMALLY . . .
BUT I DON'T.
YEAH, BUT . . .
I'M JUST SAYING YOU'RE COOL, OKAY?
AND THE ONLY REASON YOU'RE STILL STUCK HERE AFTER TWO YEARS . . .
GOSH, THANKS.

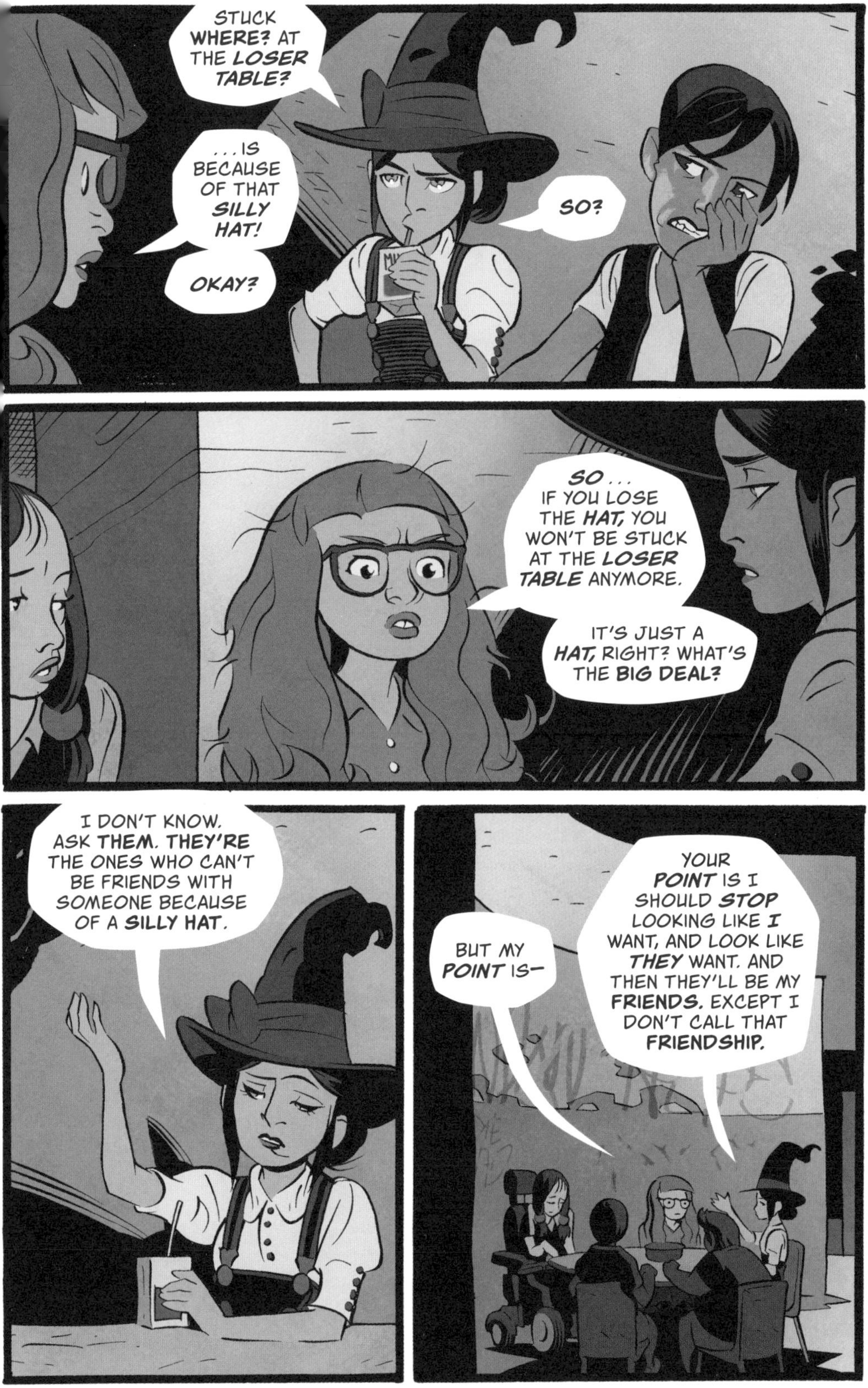

STUCK WHERE? AT THE LOSER TABLE?
. . . IS BECAUSE OF THAT SILLY HAT!
OKAY?
SO?
SO . . . IF YOU LOSE THE HAT, YOU WON'T BE STUCK AT THE LOSER TABLE ANYMORE.
IT'S JUST A HAT, RIGHT? WHAT'S THE BIG DEAL?
I DON'T KNOW. ASK THEM. THEY'RE THE ONES WHO CAN'T BE FRIENDS WITH SOMEONE BECAUSE OF A SILLY HAT.
BUT MY POINT IS—
YOUR POINT IS I SHOULD STOP LOOKING LIKE I WANT, AND LOOK LIKE THEY WANT. AND THEN THEY'LL BE MY FRIENDS. EXCEPT I DON'T CALL THAT FRIENDSHIP.

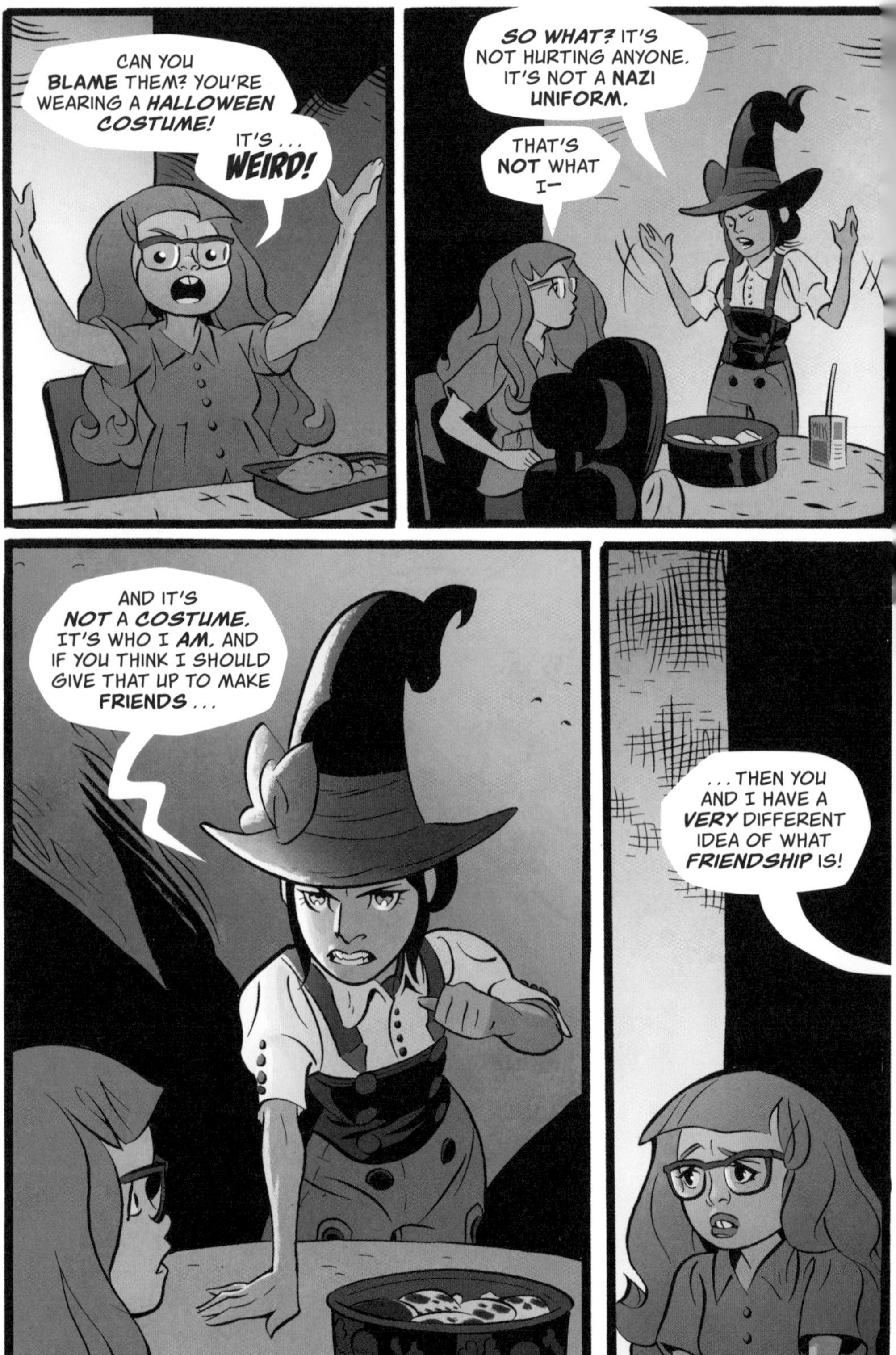
CAN YOU BLAME THEM? YOU'RE WEARING A HALLOWEEN COSTUME!
IT'S . . . WEIRD!
SO WHAT? IT'S NOT HURTING ANYONE. IT'S NOT A NAZI UNIFORM.
THAT'S NOT WHAT I—
MILK
AND IT'S NOT A COSTUME. IT'S WHO I AM. AND IF YOU THINK I SHOULD GIVE THAT UP TO MAKE FRIENDS . . .
. . . THEN YOU AND I HAVE A VERY DIFFERENT IDEA OF WHAT FRIENDSHIP IS!

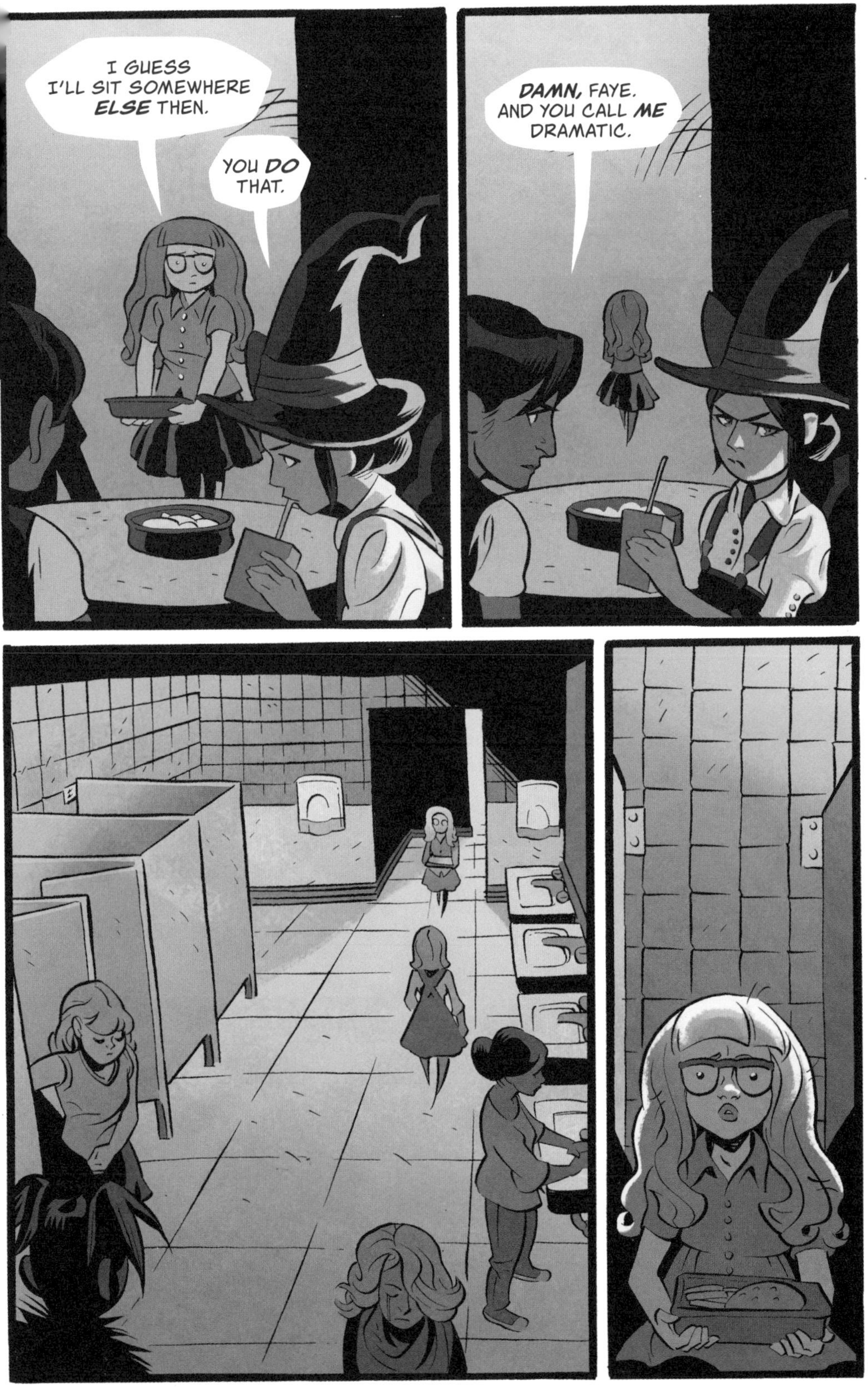
I GUESS I'LL SIT SOMEWHERE ELSE THEN.
YOU DO THAT.
DAMN, FAYE. AND YOU CALL ME DRAMATIC.

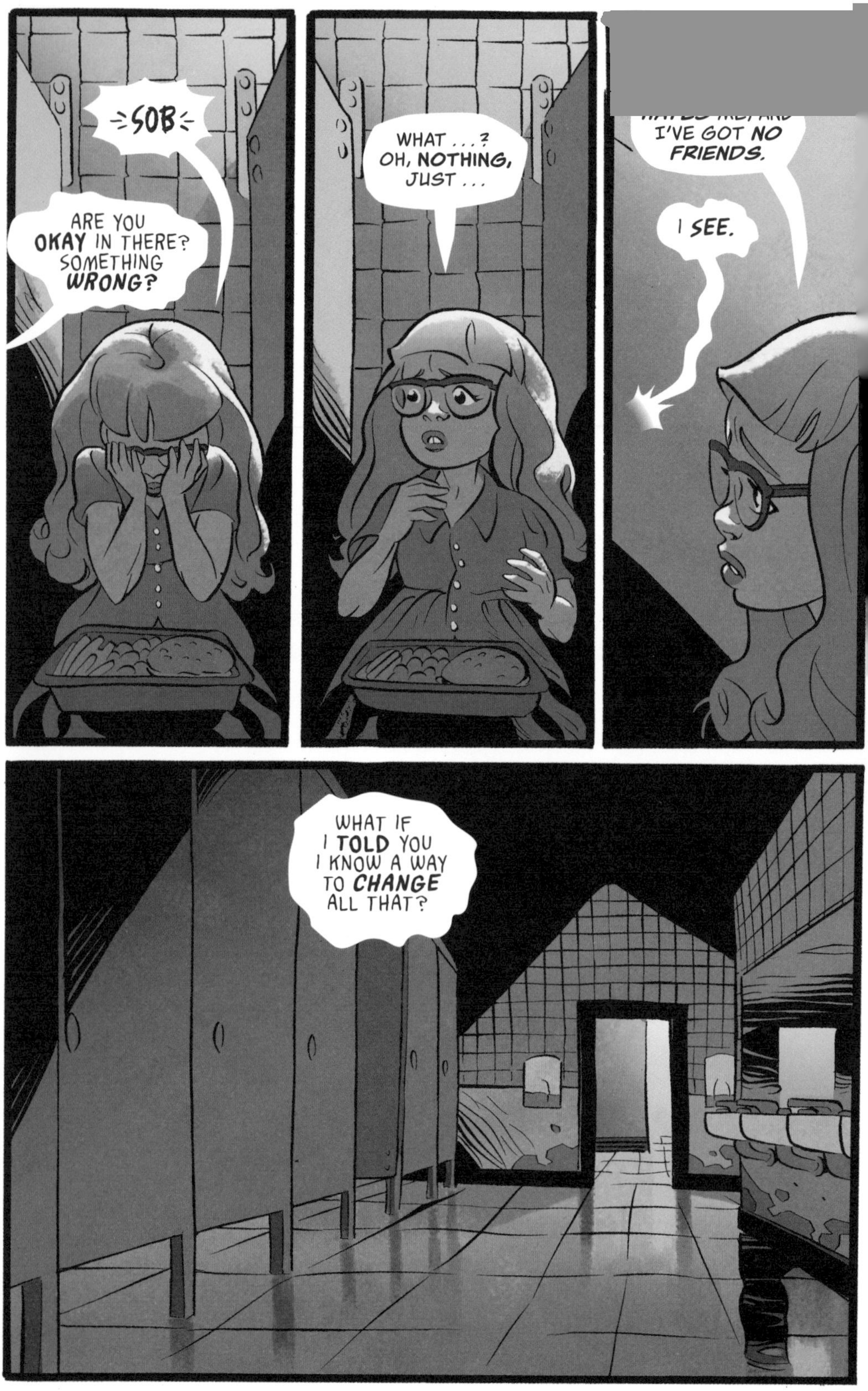
SOB
ARE YOU OKAY IN THERE? SOMETHING WRONG?
WHAT . . . ? OH, NOTHING, JUST . . .
I'VE GOT NO FRIENDS.
I SEE.
WHAT IF I TOLD YOU I KNOW A WAY TO CHANGE ALL THAT?

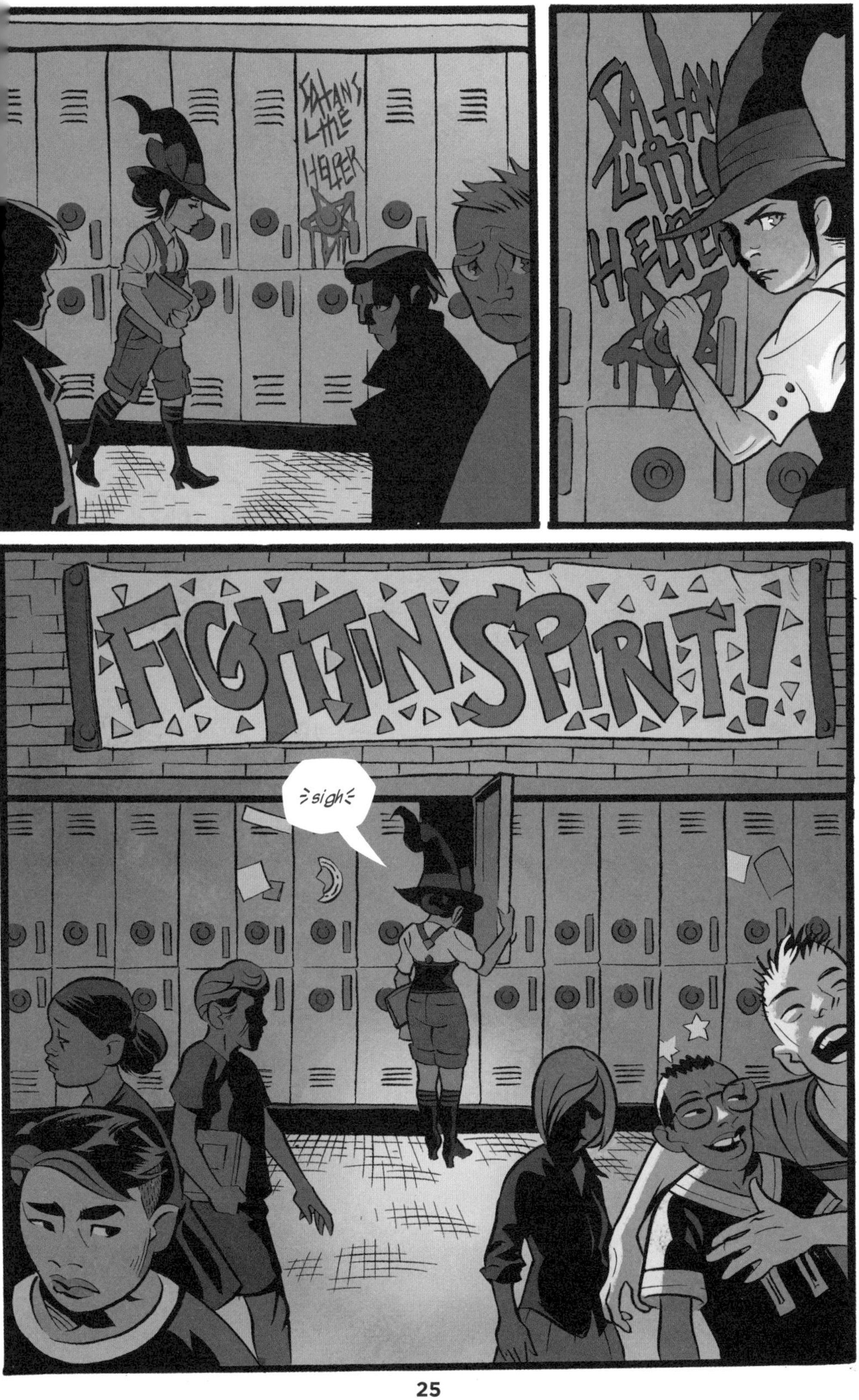
SATANS LITTLE HELPER
FIGHTIN SPIRIT!
sigh

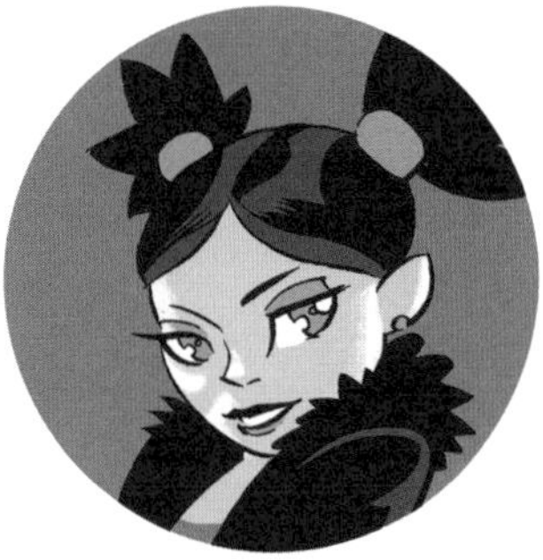

the shy_shelbi program

Step 2: Sounds like a "you" problem

People often think that because they have an issue, it's everyone's issue. Don't let them weigh you down with their emotional baggage. Step 2, detachment . . . more

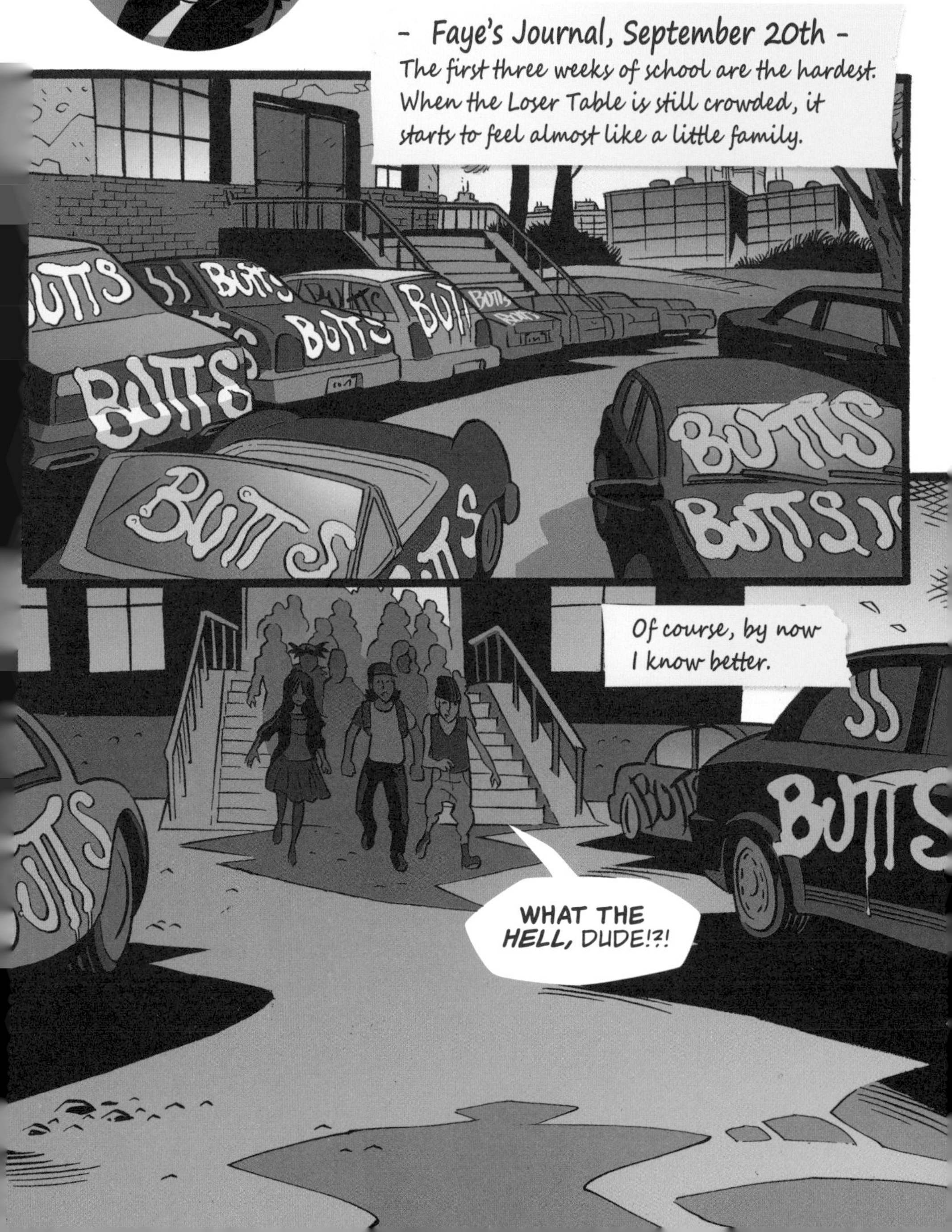
- Faye's Journal, September 20th -
The first three weeks of school are the hardest. When the Loser Table is still crowded, it starts to feel almost like a little family.
Of course, by now I know better.
WHAT THE HELL, DUDE!?!

ONE MORE **WEEK**, JIYOUNG. STAY **STRONG**.

YOU **TOO**, FAYE.

One by one, they all move on, saying we'll stay friends, never really meaning it.

HEY, **FAYE**?

It's fine, though. I've learned not to get attached. Being alone is one thing I know how to handle.

oh, **CODY**. WHAT DO YOU **WANT**?

uh . . .

I, uh . . .

MY BIG SISTER THINKS YOU DID THE . . . **"BUTTS"** THING.

I **THINK** THEY'RE GONNA . . .

YEAH. THEY'RE ALREADY **HERE**.

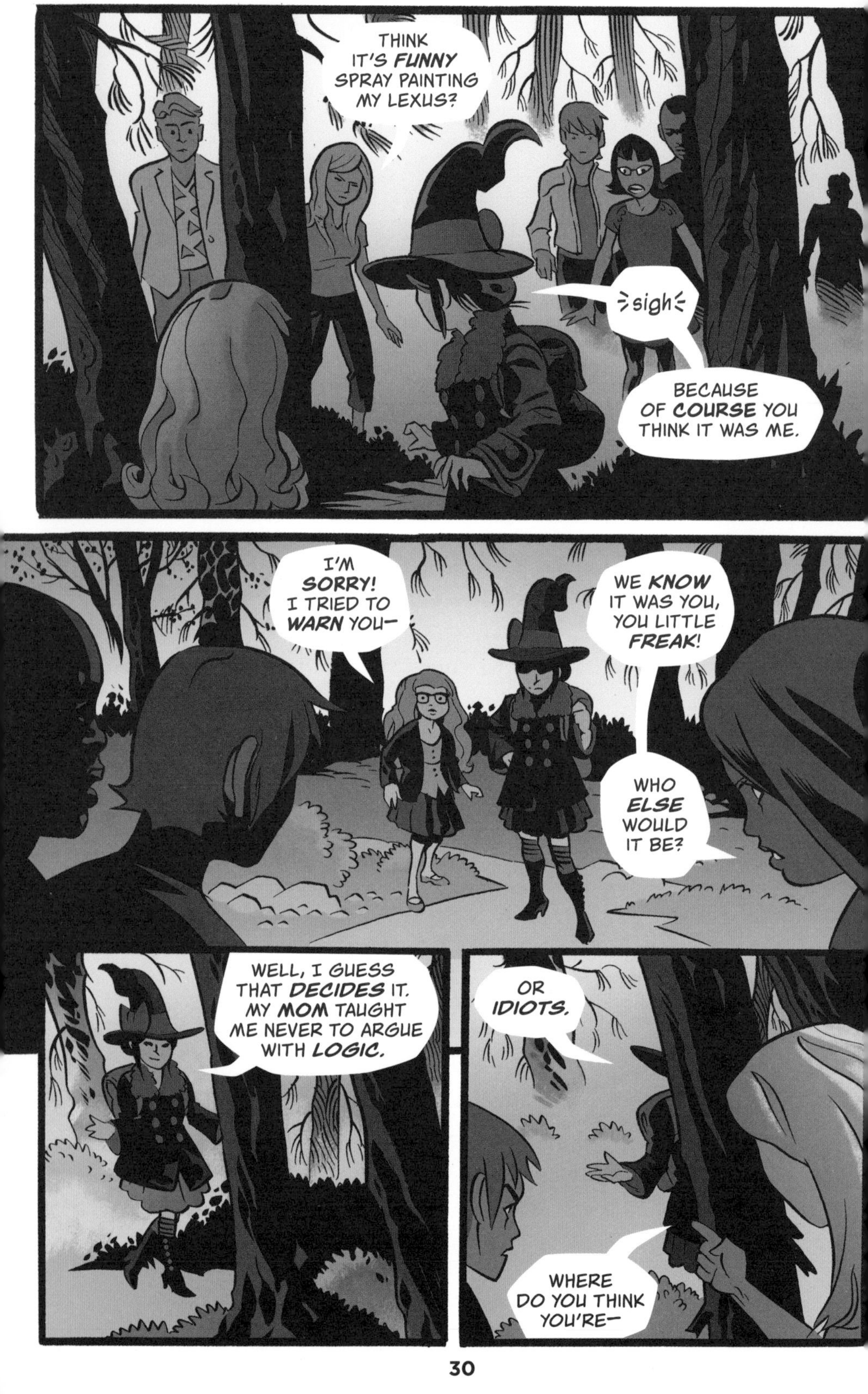
THINK IT'S FUNNY SPRAY PAINTING MY LEXUS?
sigh
BECAUSE OF COURSE YOU THINK IT WAS ME.
I'M SORRY! I TRIED TO WARN YOU—
WE KNOW IT WAS YOU, YOU LITTLE FREAK!
WHO ELSE WOULD IT BE?
WELL, I GUESS THAT DECIDES IT. MY MOM TAUGHT ME NEVER TO ARGUE WITH LOGIC.
OR IDIOTS.
WHERE DO YOU THINK YOU'RE—

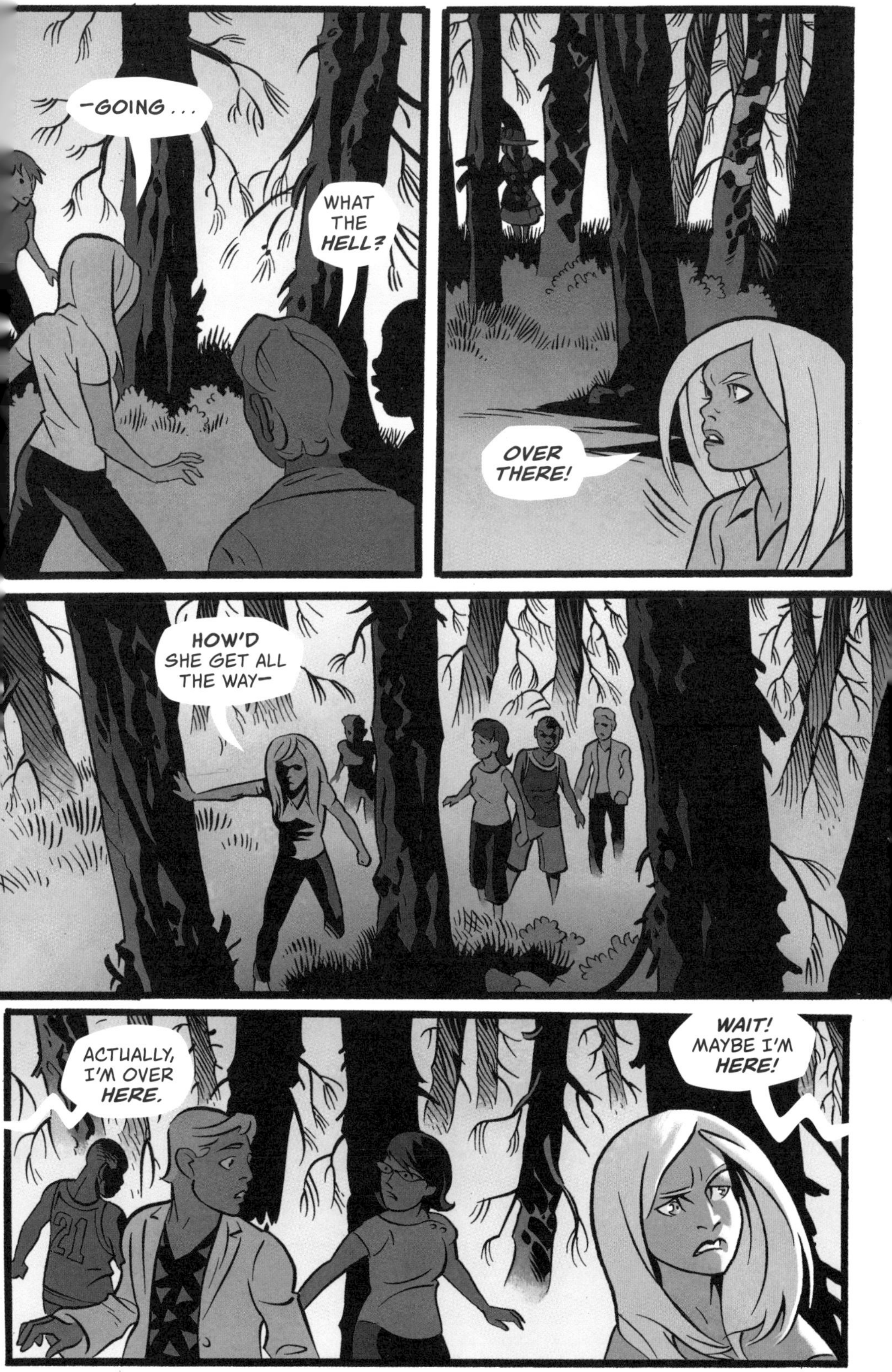

—GOING . . .
WHAT THE HELL?
OVER THERE!
HOW'D SHE GET ALL THE WAY—
ACTUALLY, I'M OVER HERE.
WAIT! MAYBE I'M HERE!

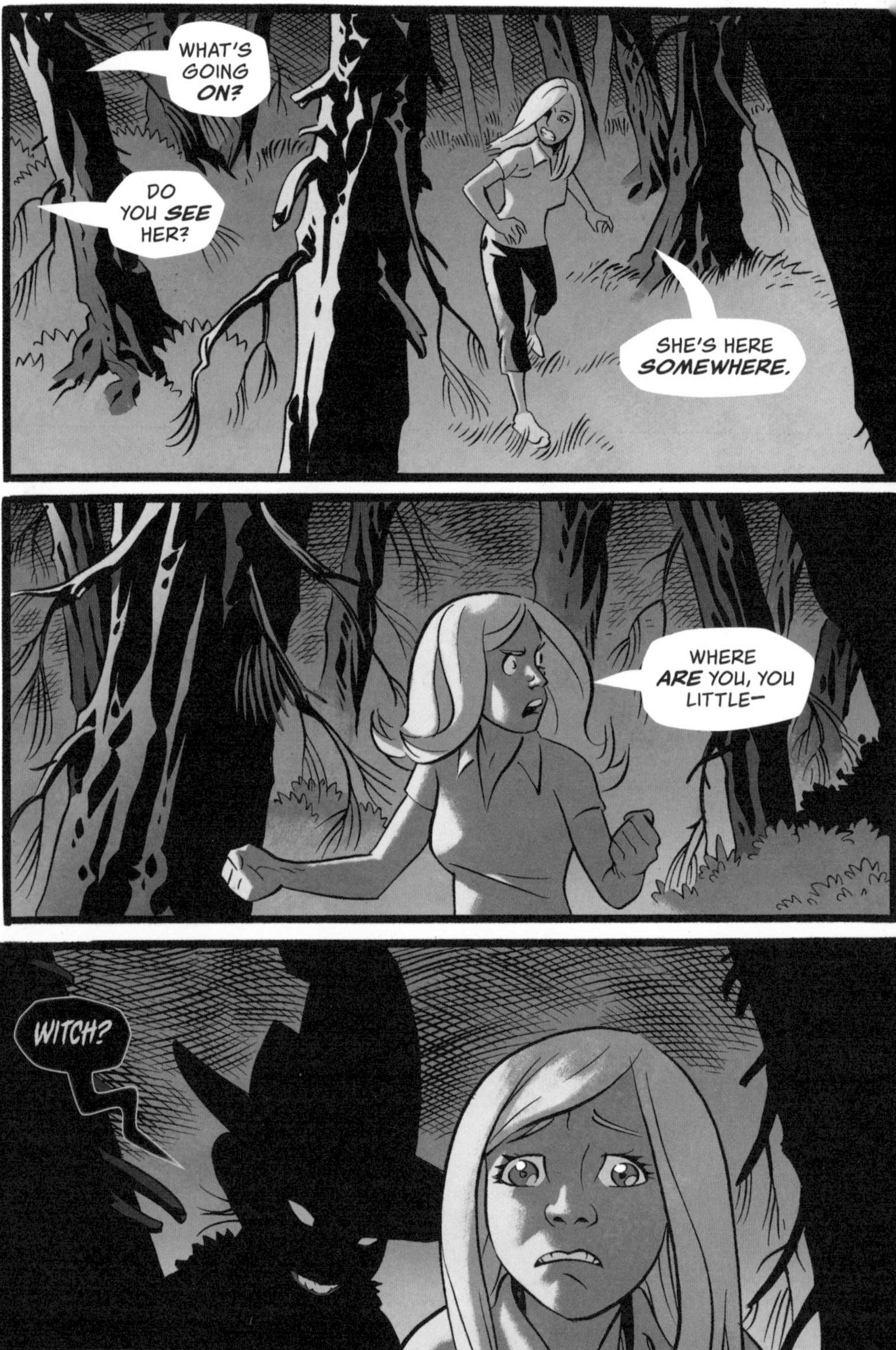
WHAT'S GOING ON?
DO YOU SEE HER?
SHE'S HERE SOMEWHERE.
WHERE ARE YOU, YOU LITTLE—
WITCH?

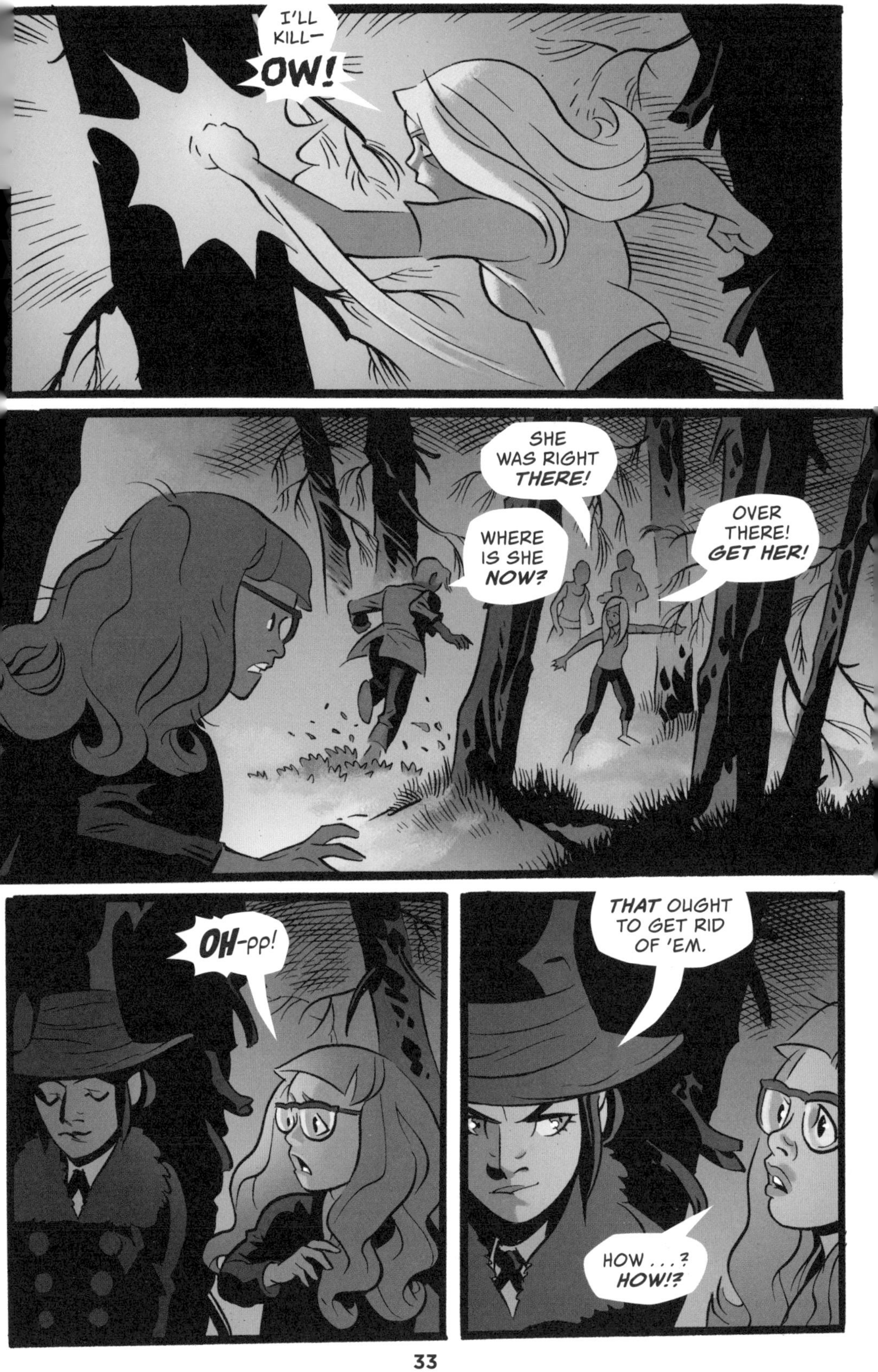
I'LL KILL—
OW!
SHE WAS RIGHT THERE!
WHERE IS SHE NOW?
OVER THERE! GET HER!
OH-pp!
THAT OUGHT TO GET RID OF 'EM.
HOW . . . ? HOW!?

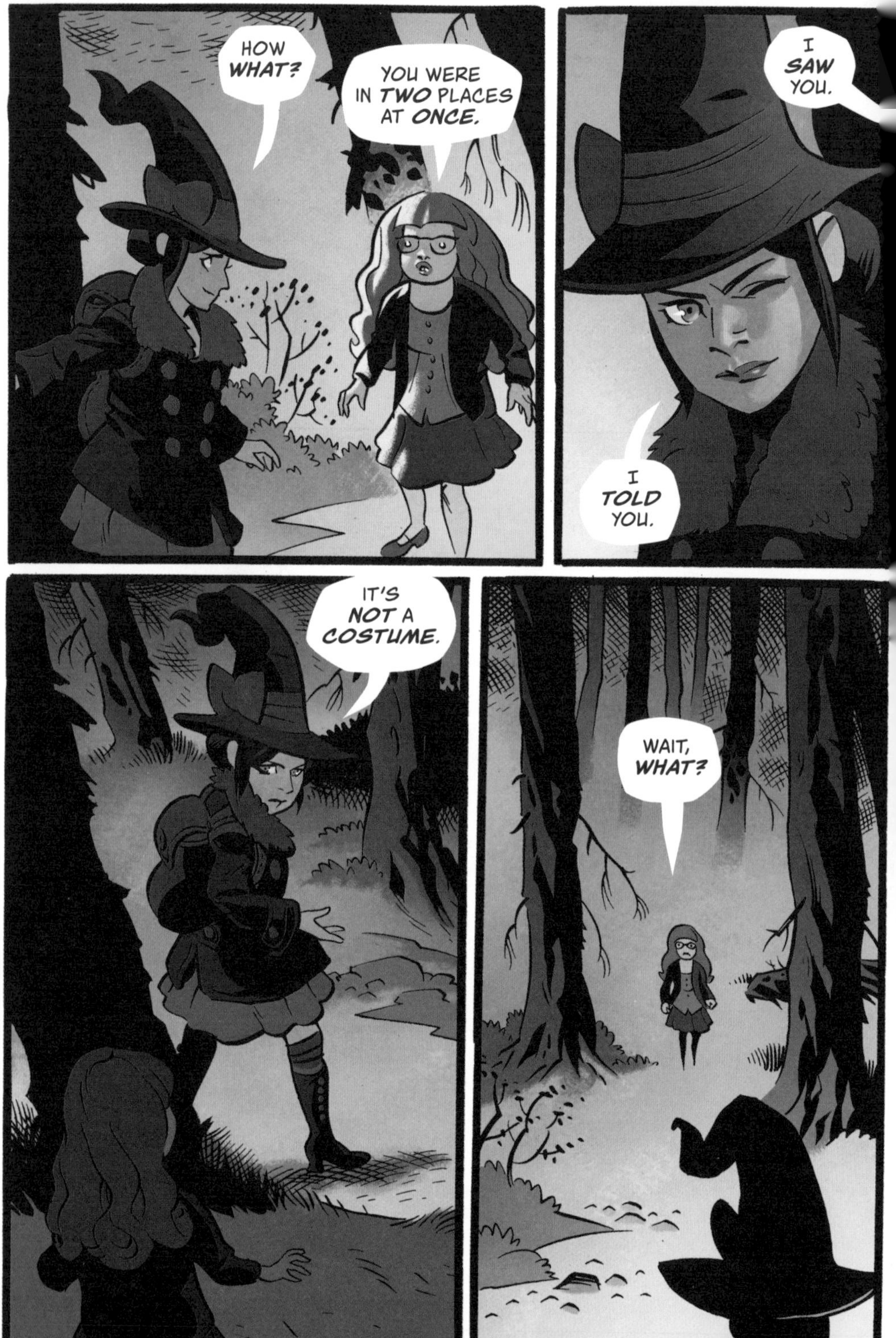
HOW WHAT?
YOU WERE IN TWO PLACES AT ONCE.
I SAW YOU.
I TOLD YOU.
IT'S NOT A COSTUME.
WAIT, WHAT?

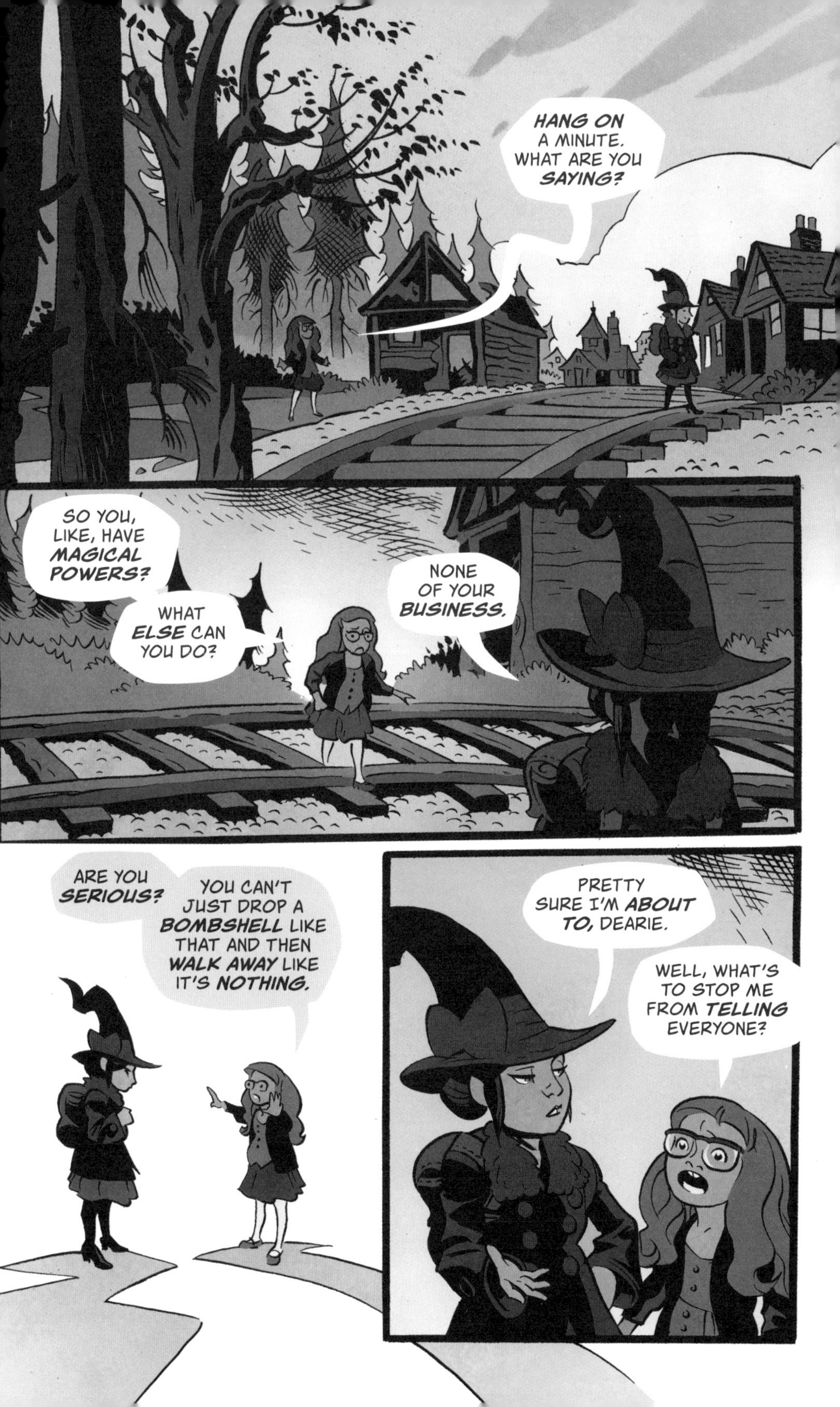
HANG ON A MINUTE. WHAT ARE YOU SAYING?
SO YOU, LIKE, HAVE MAGICAL POWERS?
WHAT ELSE CAN YOU DO?
NONE OF YOUR BUSINESS.
ARE YOU SERIOUS?
YOU CAN'T JUST DROP A BOMBSHELL LIKE THAT AND THEN WALK AWAY LIKE IT'S NOTHING.
PRETTY SURE I'M ABOUT TO, DEARIE.
WELL, WHAT'S TO STOP ME FROM TELLING EVERYONE?

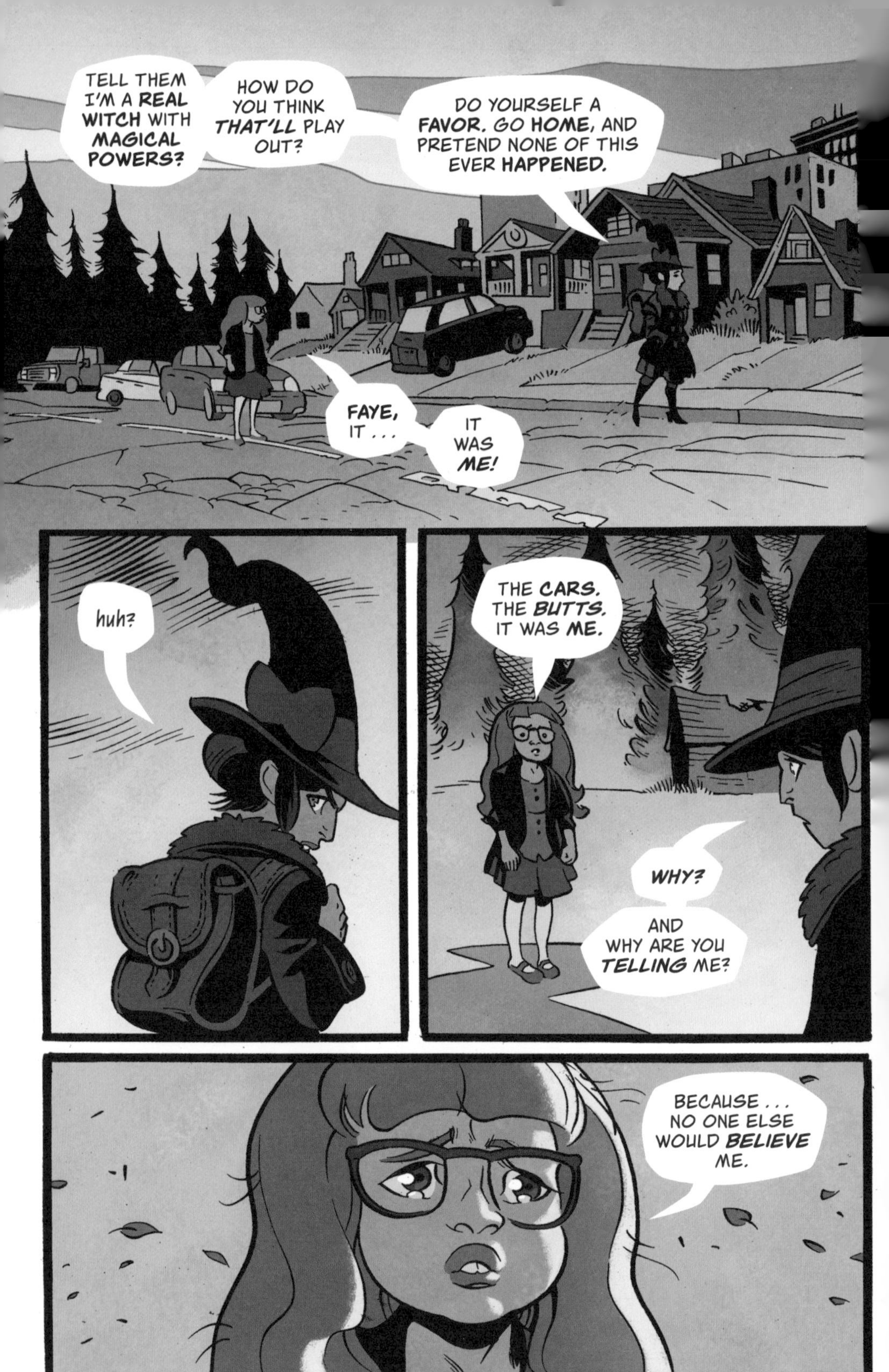
TELL THEM I'M A REAL WITCH WITH MAGICAL POWERS?
HOW DO YOU THINK THAT'LL PLAY OUT?
DO YOURSELF A FAVOR. GO HOME, AND PRETEND NONE OF THIS EVER HAPPENED.
FAYE, IT . . .
IT WAS ME!
huh?
THE CARS. THE BUTTS. IT WAS ME.
WHY?
AND WHY ARE YOU TELLING ME?
BECAUSE . . . NO ONE ELSE WOULD BELIEVE ME.

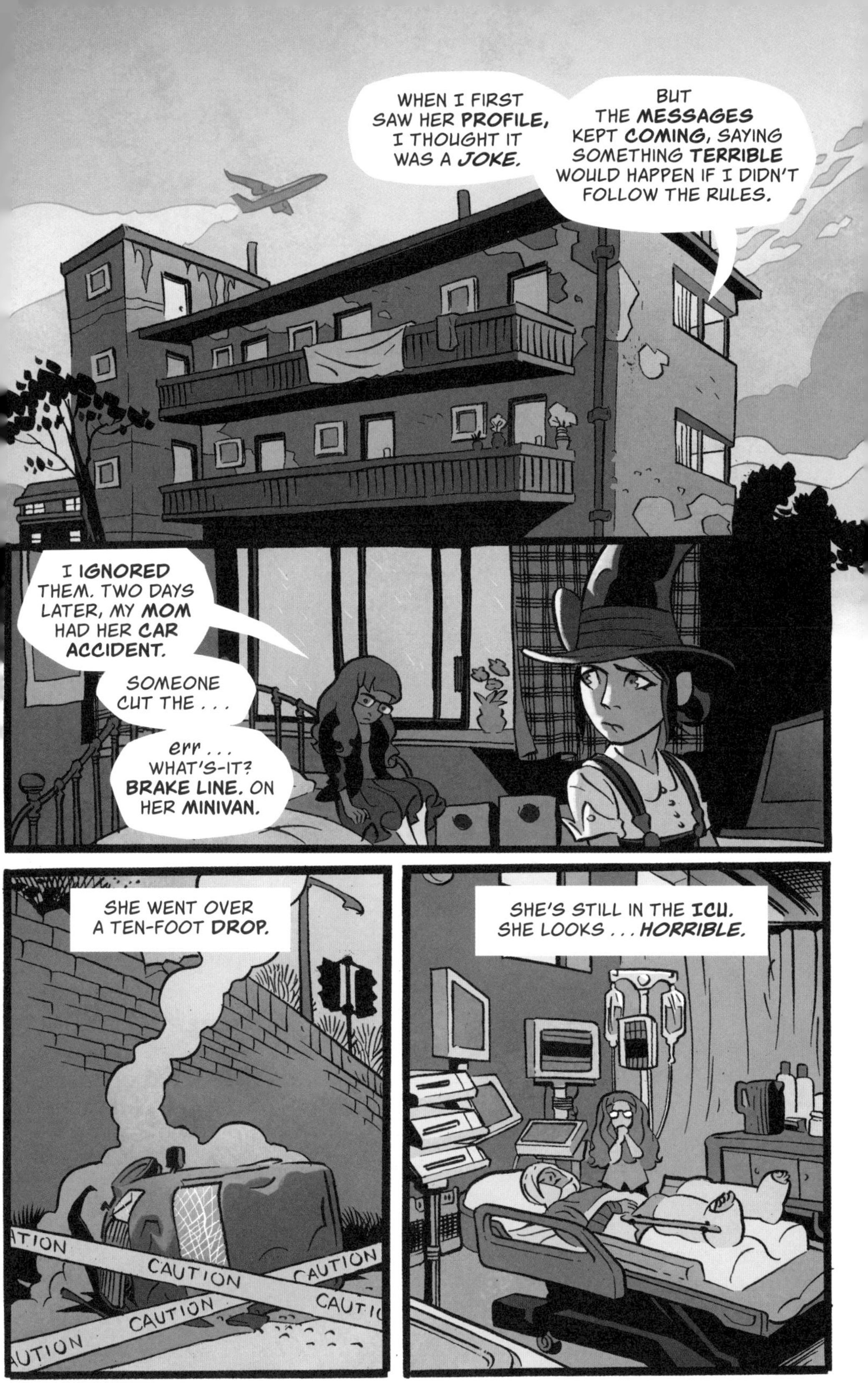
WHEN I FIRST SAW HER PROFILE, I THOUGHT IT WAS A JOKE.
BUT THE MESSAGES KEPT COMING, SAYING SOMETHING TERRIBLE WOULD HAPPEN IF I DIDN'T FOLLOW THE RULES.
I IGNORED THEM. TWO DAYS LATER, MY MOM HAD HER CAR ACCIDENT.
SOMEONE CUT THE . . .
err . . . WHAT'S-IT? BRAKE LINE. ON HER MINIVAN.
SHE WENT OVER A TEN-FOOT DROP.
CAUTION
CAUTION
CAUTION
SHE'S STILL IN THE ICU. SHE LOOKS . . . HORRIBLE.

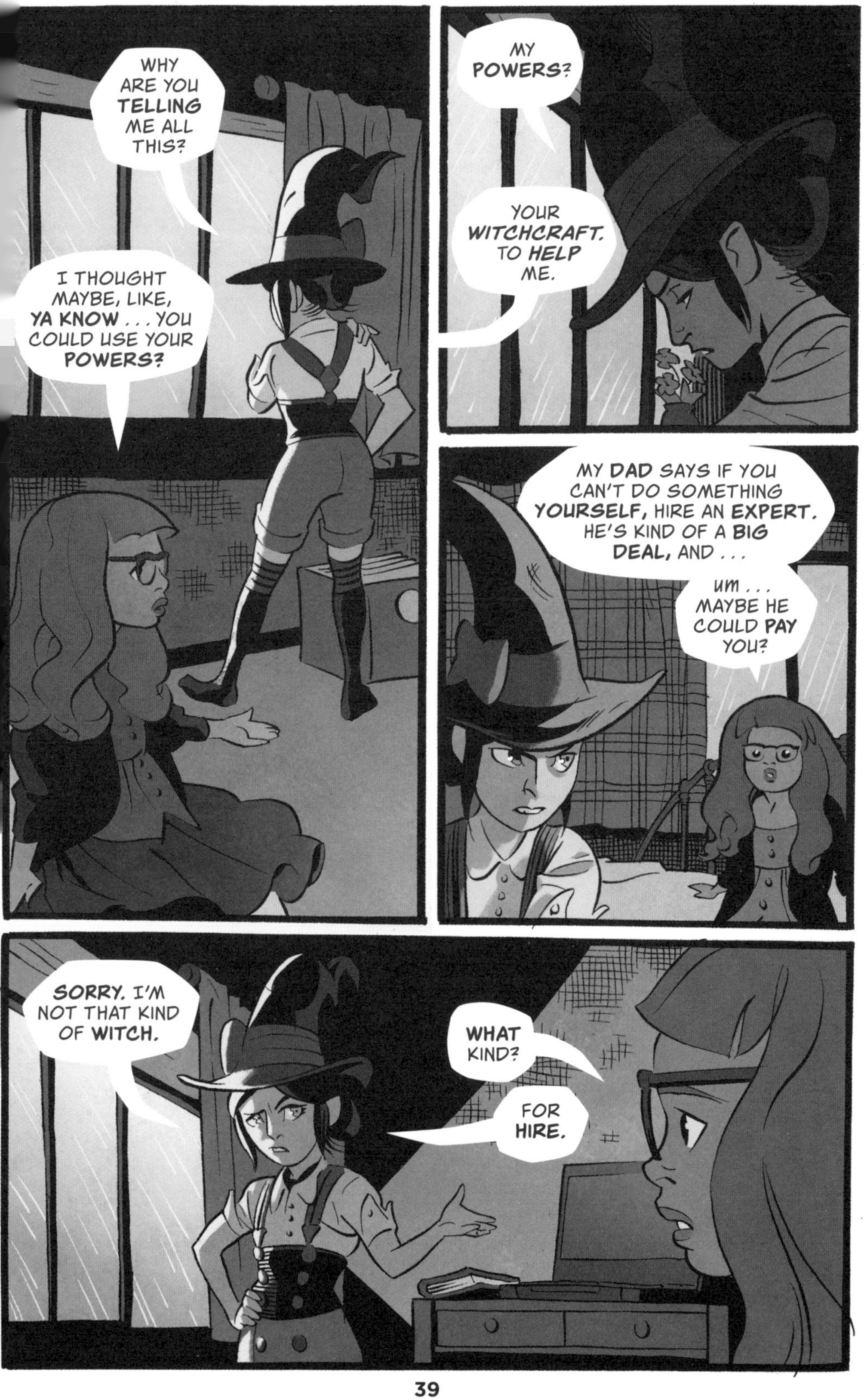
WHY ARE YOU TELLING ME ALL THIS?
I THOUGHT MAYBE, LIKE, YA KNOW . . . YOU COULD USE YOUR POWERS?
MY POWERS?
YOUR WITCHCRAFT. TO HELP ME.
MY DAD SAYS IF YOU CAN'T DO SOMETHING YOURSELF, HIRE AN EXPERT. HE'S KIND OF A BIG DEAL, AND . . .
um . . . MAYBE HE COULD PAY YOU?
SORRY. I'M NOT THAT KIND OF WITCH.
WHAT KIND?
FOR HIRE.

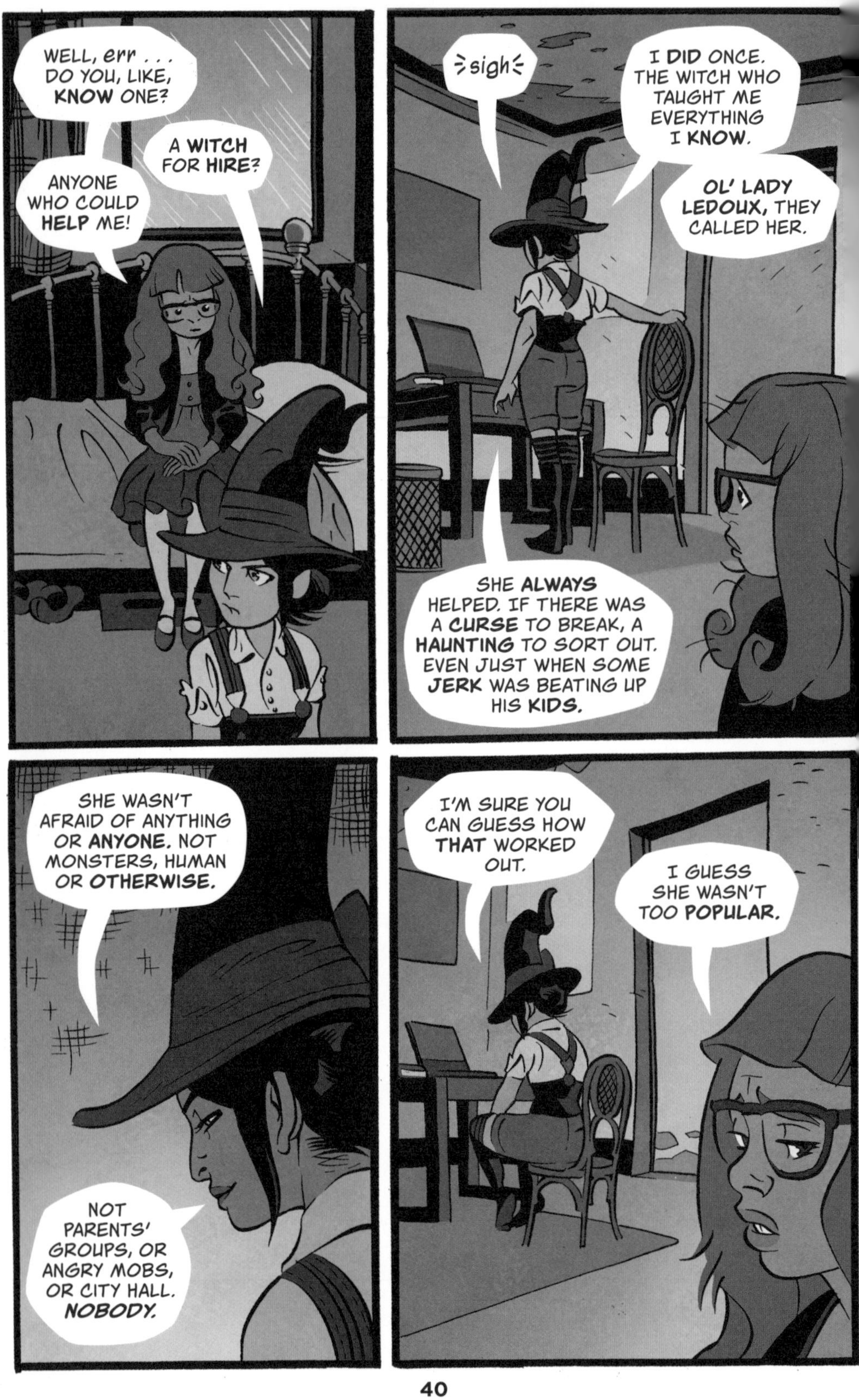
WELL, err . . . DO YOU, LIKE, KNOW ONE?
A WITCH FOR HIRE?
ANYONE WHO COULD HELP ME!
sigh
I DID ONCE. THE WITCH WHO TAUGHT ME EVERYTHING I KNOW.
OL' LADY LEDOUX, THEY CALLED HER.
SHE ALWAYS HELPED. IF THERE WAS A CURSE TO BREAK, A HAUNTING TO SORT OUT. EVEN JUST WHEN SOME JERK WAS BEATING UP HIS KIDS.
SHE WASN'T AFRAID OF ANYTHING OR ANYONE. NOT MONSTERS, HUMAN OR OTHERWISE.
NOT PARENTS' GROUPS, OR ANGRY MOBS, OR CITY HALL. NOBODY.
I'M SURE YOU CAN GUESS HOW THAT WORKED OUT.
I GUESS SHE WASN'T TOO POPULAR.

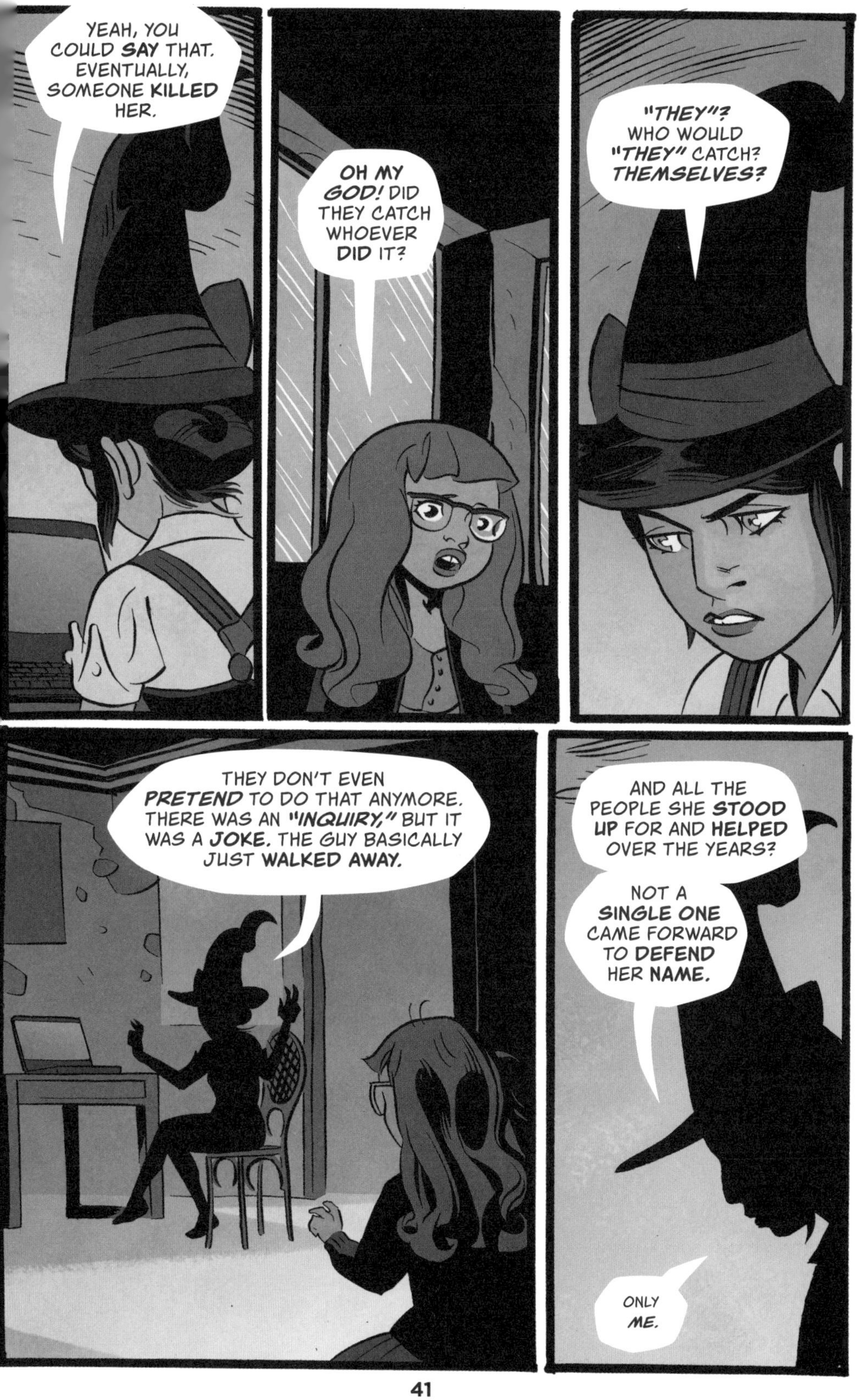
YEAH, YOU COULD SAY THAT. EVENTUALLY, SOMEONE KILLED HER.
OH MY GOD! DID THEY CATCH WHOEVER DID IT?
"THEY"? WHO WOULD "THEY" CATCH? THEMSELVES?
THEY DON'T EVEN PRETEND TO DO THAT ANYMORE. THERE WAS AN "INQUIRY," BUT IT WAS A JOKE. THE GUY BASICALLY JUST WALKED AWAY.
AND ALL THE PEOPLE SHE STOOD UP FOR AND HELPED OVER THE YEARS?
NOT A SINGLE ONE CAME FORWARD TO DEFEND HER NAME.
ONLY ME.

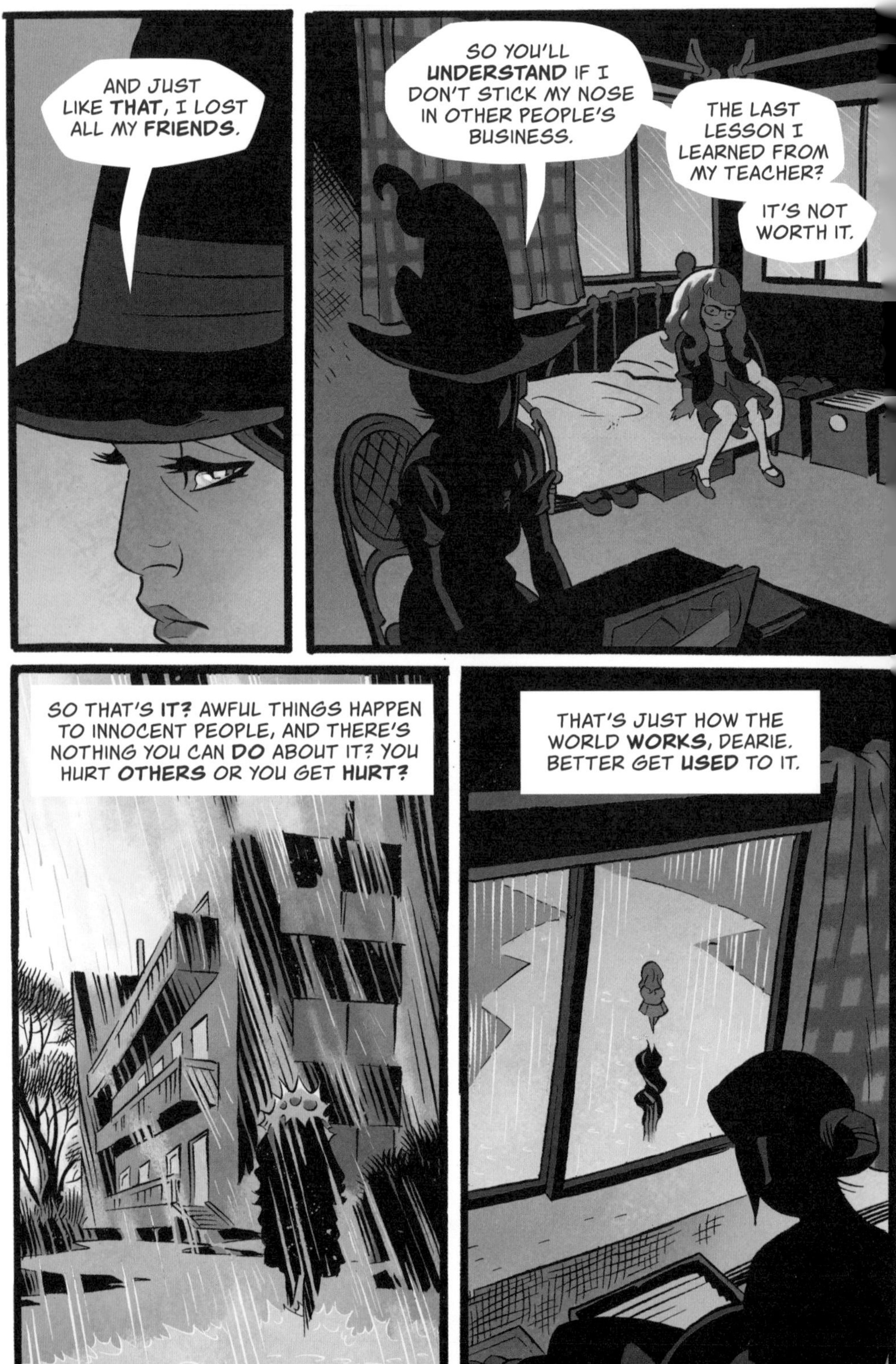
AND JUST LIKE THAT, I LOST ALL MY FRIENDS.
SO YOU'LL UNDERSTAND IF I DON'T STICK MY NOSE IN OTHER PEOPLE'S BUSINESS.
THE LAST LESSON I LEARNED FROM MY TEACHER?
IT'S NOT WORTH IT.
SO THAT'S IT? AWFUL THINGS HAPPEN TO INNOCENT PEOPLE, AND THERE'S NOTHING YOU CAN DO ABOUT IT? YOU HURT OTHERS OR YOU GET HURT?
THAT'S JUST HOW THE WORLD WORKS, DEARIE. BETTER GET USED TO IT.

MONKEY'S PAW CURSES OVER THE INTERNET. GUESS IT WAS INEVITABLE.

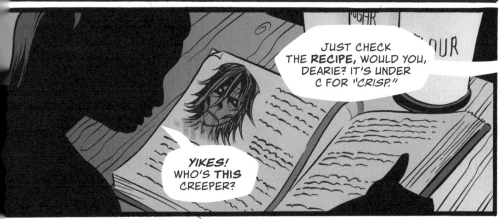

JUST CHECK THE RECIPE, WOULD YOU, DEARIE? IT'S UNDER C FOR "CRISP."

YIKES! WHO'S THIS CREEPER?

OH, HIM. THAT'S WHAT I CALL A "CURSE CREATURE." THAT ONE WAS A REAL CHARMER.

WAIT, THIS IS A REAL THING?

NOT **EXACTLY**. CURSE CREATURES EXIST SOMEWHERE BETWEEN THE **REAL** WORLD AND THE REALM OF **IDEAS**, I GUESS YOU COULD SAY.

WHAT DOES **THAT** MEAN? **DOES** IT EXIST OR **DOESN'T** IT?

EXACTLY.

ARE YOU **MAKING FUN** OF ME?

THINGS AIN'T ALWAYS **ONE** THING OR THE **OTHER**. THEY CAN BE IN **BETWEEN**.

CURSES CAN BE LIKE THAT, NEITHER **REAL** NOR **UNREAL**. YOU CAN'T NEVER **PROVE** THEY MAKE THINGS HAPPEN.

BUT YOU CAN'T **DENY** 'EM NEITHER, 'CAUSE THINGS KEEP **HAPPENIN'** WHETHER YOU BELIEVE IT OR **NOT**.

REMEMBER THE **MONKEY'S PAW** CURSE?

A MONKEY PUTS ITS HAND IN A **HOLE** TO GET THE **TREAT** INSIDE. BUT WHEN IT CLOSES ITS **FIST**, IT CAN'T PULL IT **OUT**.

NOW IT'S **TRAPPED**, 'CAUSE IT CAN'T BRING ITSELF TO **LET GO** OF THE TREAT.

SO, THE **CURSE** IS **THREE WISHES** THAT ALWAYS GO **WRONG**.

BUT THE VICTIM CAN'T NEVER **ABANDON** THE WISHES, 'CAUSE THEY CAN'T RESIST HOPING THE **NEXT ONE** WILL GIVE 'EM THEIR HEART'S **DESIRE**.

THAT WAS **THIS** HANDSOME FELLA'S LITTLE GAME. TILL **I** CAME ALONG.

YOU **STOPPED** HIM? **HOW?**

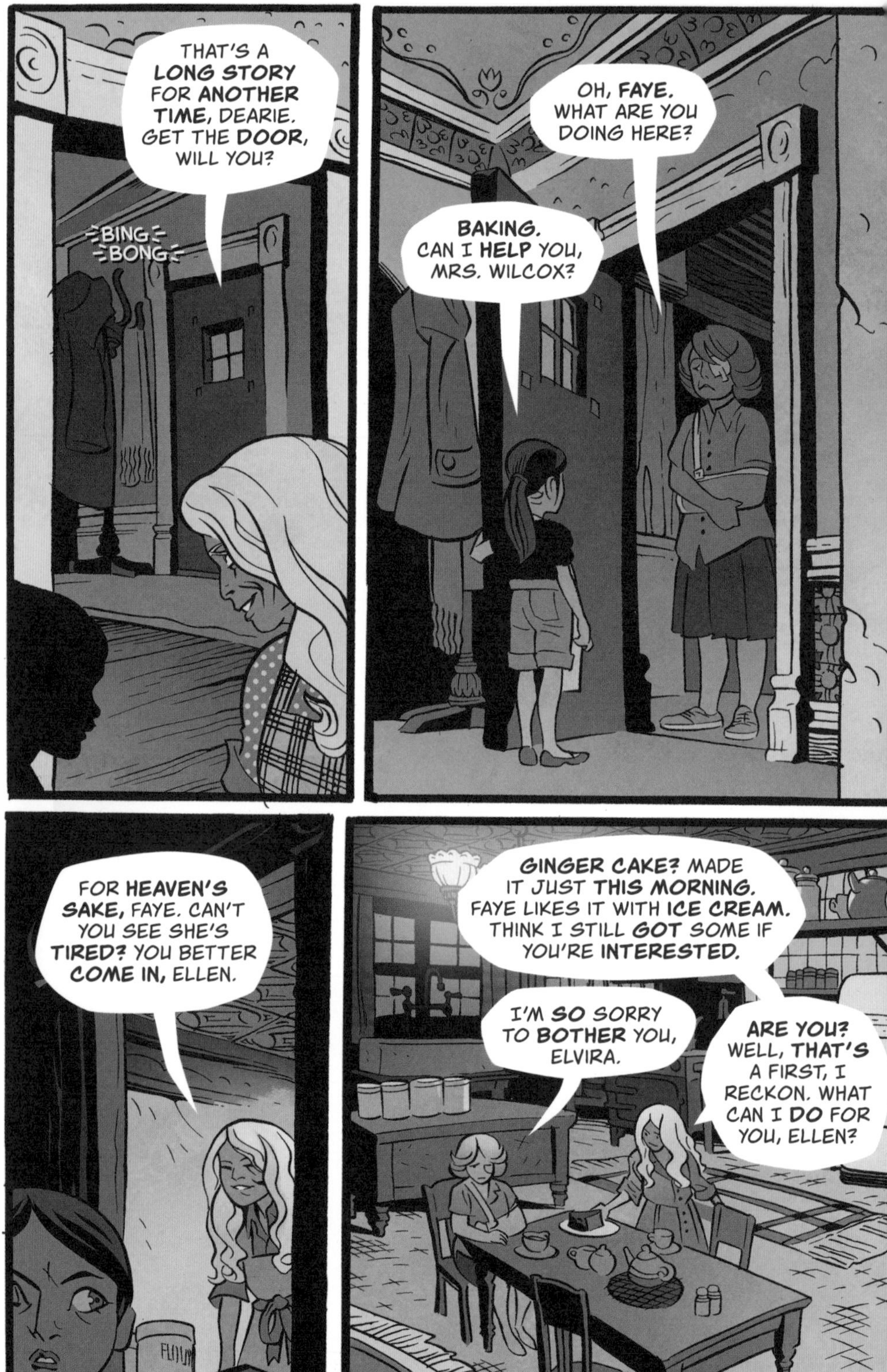
THAT'S A LONG STORY FOR ANOTHER TIME, DEARIE. GET THE DOOR, WILL YOU?
BING BONG
OH, FAYE. WHAT ARE YOU DOING HERE?
BAKING. CAN I HELP YOU, MRS. WILCOX?
FOR HEAVEN'S SAKE, FAYE. CAN'T YOU SEE SHE'S TIRED? YOU BETTER COME IN, ELLEN.
GINGER CAKE? MADE IT JUST THIS MORNING. FAYE LIKES IT WITH ICE CREAM. THINK I STILL GOT SOME IF YOU'RE INTERESTED.
I'M SO SORRY TO BOTHER YOU, ELVIRA.
ARE YOU? WELL, THAT'S A FIRST, I RECKON. WHAT CAN I DO FOR YOU, ELLEN?

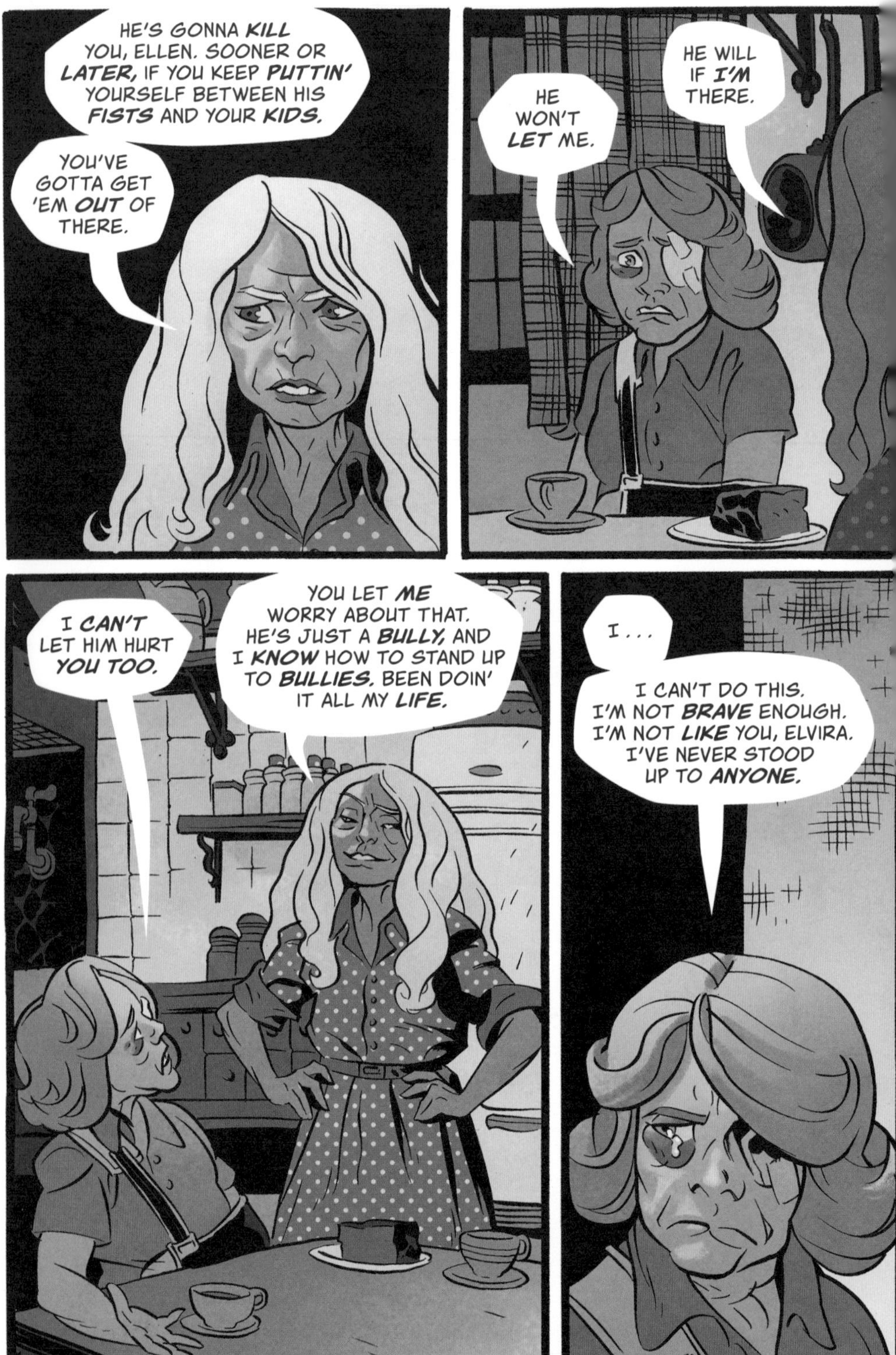
HE'S GONNA KILL YOU, ELLEN. SOONER OR LATER, IF YOU KEEP PUTTIN' YOURSELF BETWEEN HIS FISTS AND YOUR KIDS.
YOU'VE GOTTA GET 'EM OUT OF THERE.
HE WON'T LET ME.
HE WILL IF I'M THERE.
I CAN'T LET HIM HURT YOU TOO.
YOU LET ME WORRY ABOUT THAT. HE'S JUST A BULLY, AND I KNOW HOW TO STAND UP TO BULLIES. BEEN DOIN' IT ALL MY LIFE.
I . . .
I CAN'T DO THIS. I'M NOT BRAVE ENOUGH. I'M NOT LIKE YOU, ELVIRA. I'VE NEVER STOOD UP TO ANYONE.

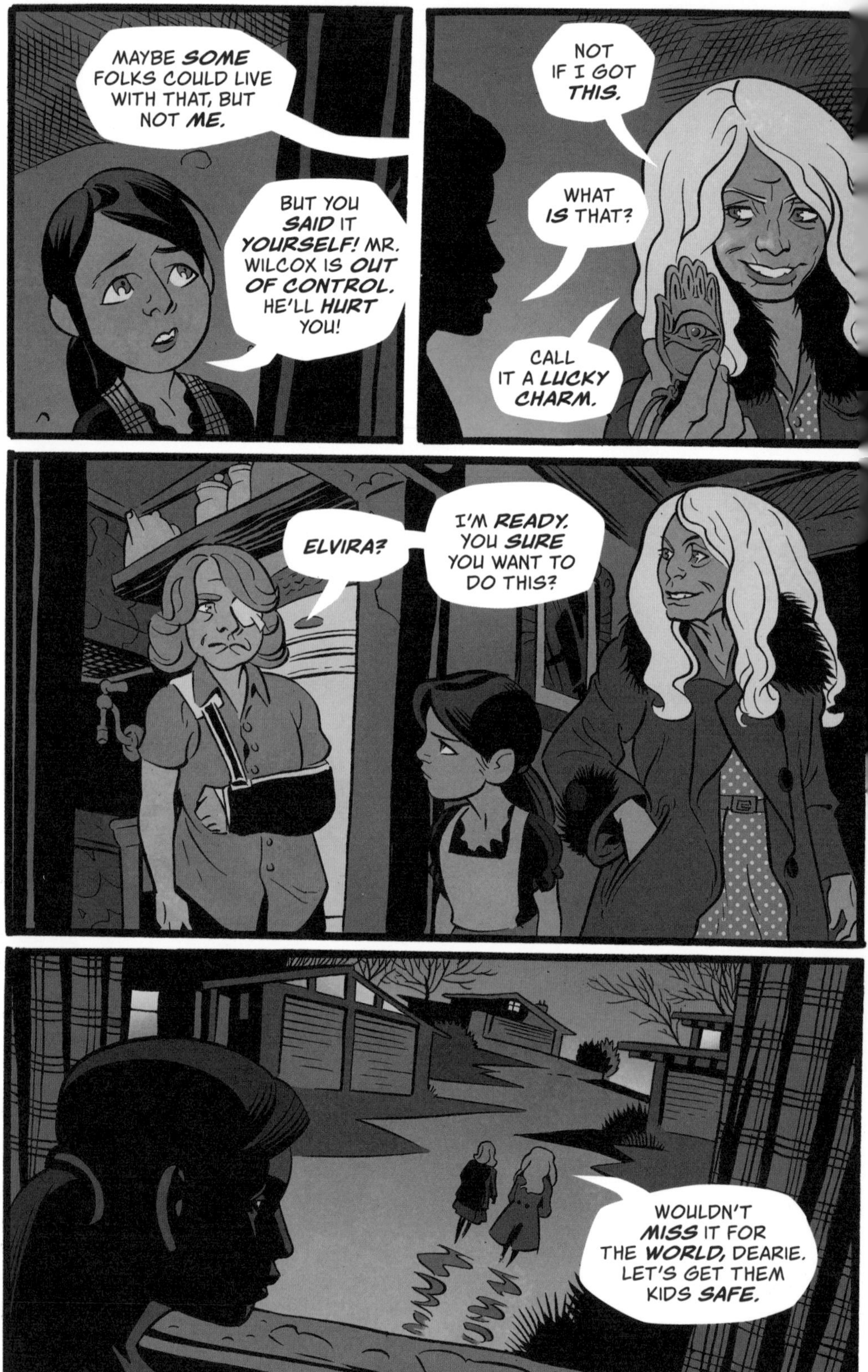
MAYBE SOME FOLKS COULD LIVE WITH THAT, BUT NOT ME.
BUT YOU SAID IT YOURSELF! MR. WILCOX IS OUT OF CONTROL. HE'LL HURT YOU!
NOT IF I GOT THIS.
WHAT IS THAT?
CALL IT A LUCKY CHARM.
ELVIRA?
I'M READY. YOU SURE YOU WANT TO DO THIS?
WOULDN'T MISS IT FOR THE WORLD, DEARIE. LET'S GET THEM KIDS SAFE.

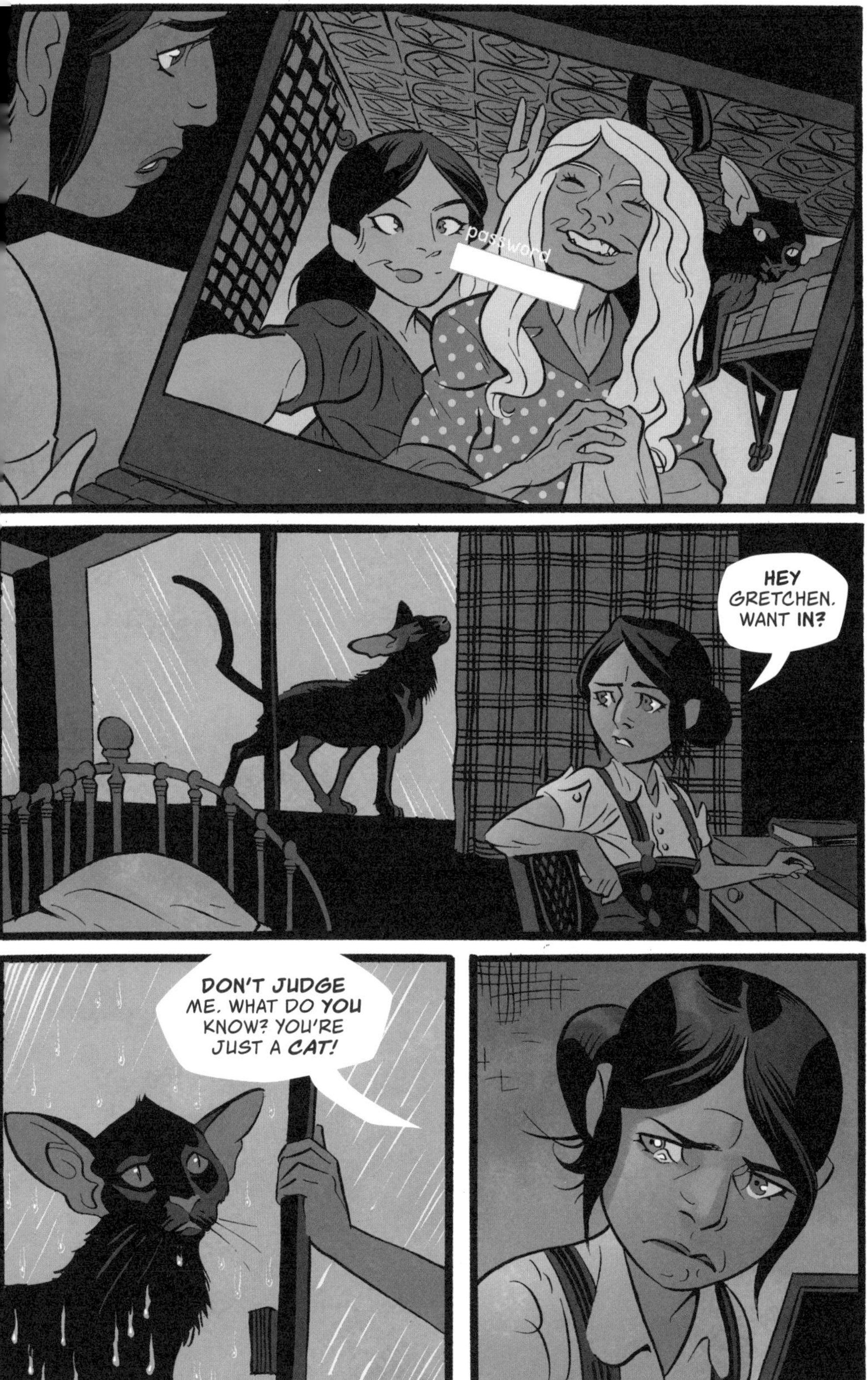
password
HEY GRETCHEN. WANT IN?
DON'T JUDGE ME. WHAT DO YOU KNOW? YOU'RE JUST A CAT!

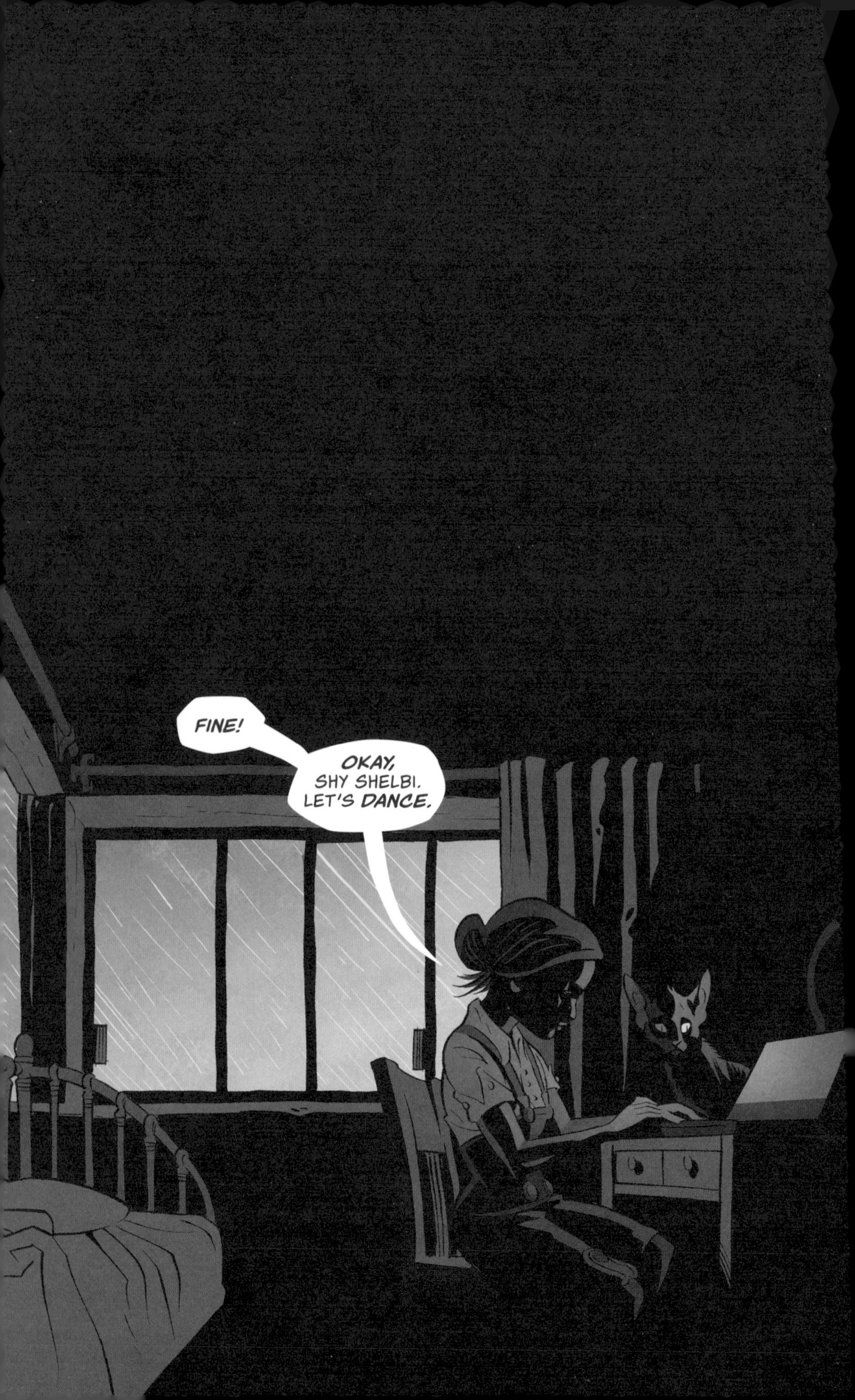
FINE!
OKAY, SHY SHELBI. LET'S DANCE.

the shy_shelbi program

Step 3: Don't @ Me

No one will thank you for living your best life. They'll act like your #selfactualization is somehow hurting them. Before you take on other people's interpretation of reality, ask yourself, how right could it be if it just makes their life suck? Step 3, defending your reality . . . more

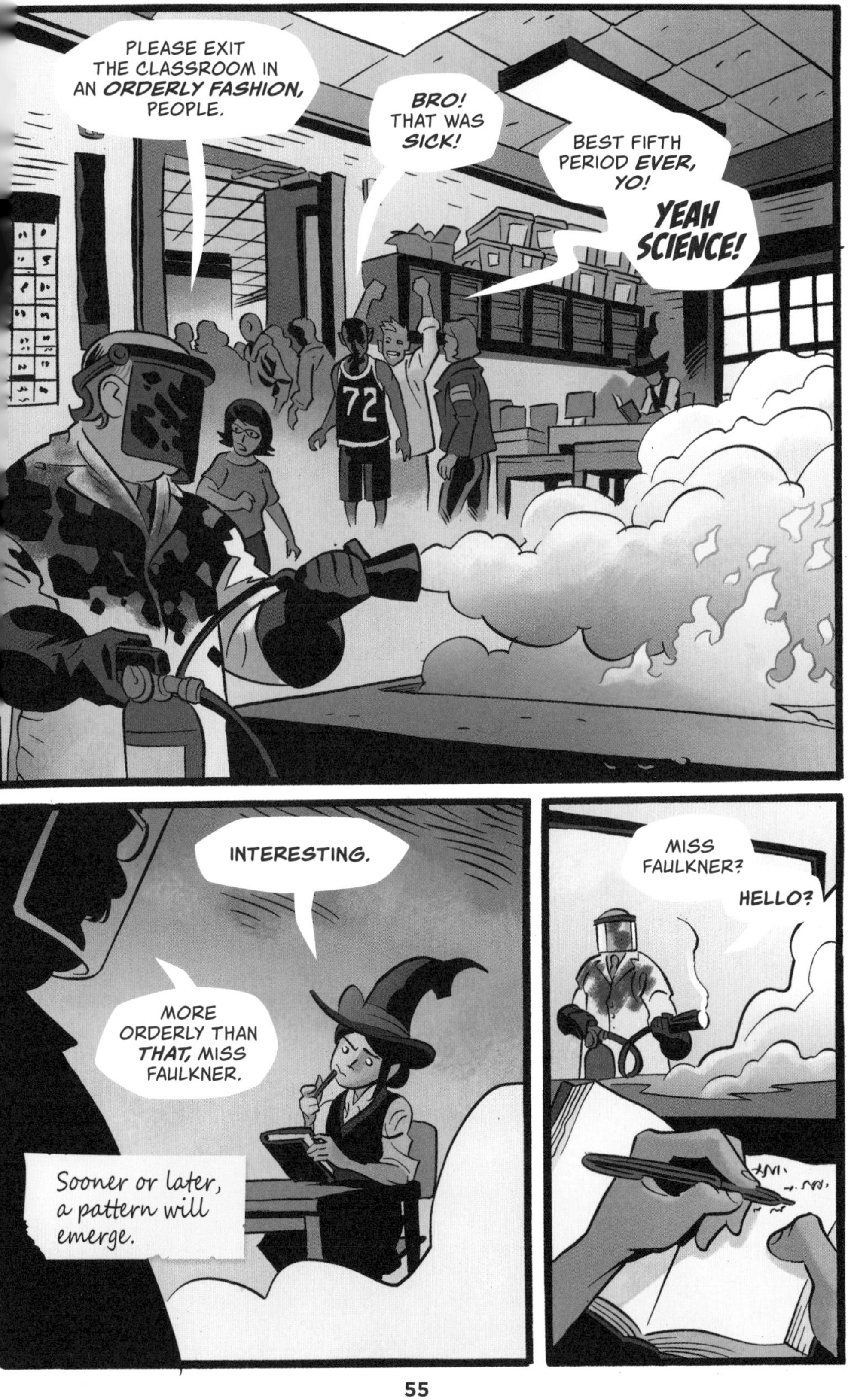
PLEASE EXIT THE CLASSROOM IN AN ORDERLY FASHION, PEOPLE.
BRO! THAT WAS SICK!
BEST FIFTH PERIOD EVER, YO!
YEAH SCIENCE!
INTERESTING.
MORE ORDERLY THAN THAT, MISS FAULKNER.
Sooner or later, a pattern will emerge.
MISS FAULKNER?
HELLO?

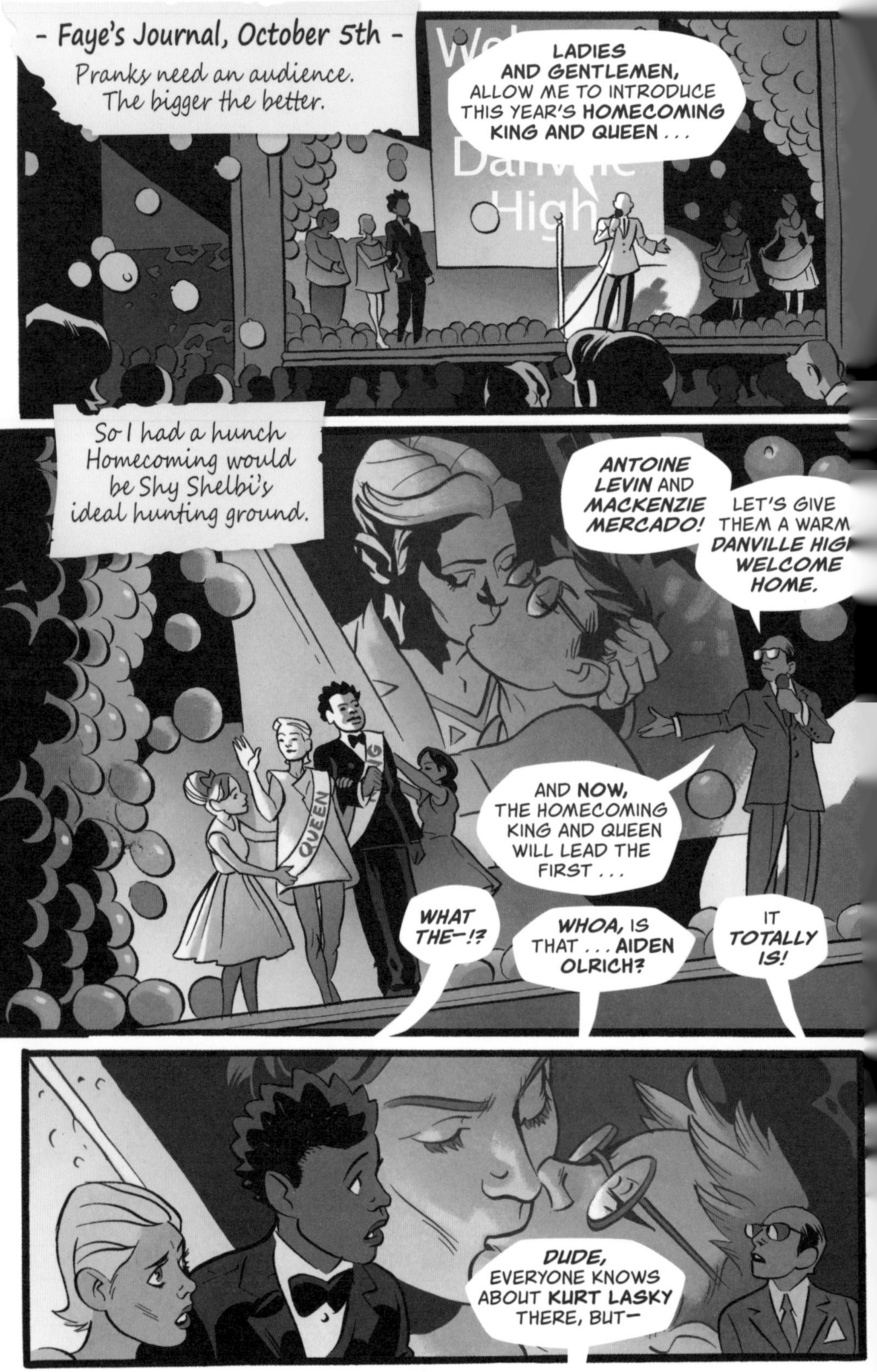
- Faye's Journal, October 5th -
Pranks need an audience. The bigger the better.
LADIES AND GENTLEMEN, ALLOW ME TO INTRODUCE THIS YEAR'S HOMECOMING KING AND QUEEN . . .
So I had a hunch Homecoming would be Shy Shelbi's ideal hunting ground.
ANTOINE LEVIN AND MACKENZIE MERCADO!
LET'S GIVE THEM A WARM DANVILLE HIGH WELCOME HOME.
QUEEN
AND NOW, THE HOMECOMING KING AND QUEEN WILL LEAD THE FIRST . . .
WHAT THE—!?
WHOA, IS THAT . . . AIDEN OLRICH?
IT TOTALLY IS!
DUDE, EVERYONE KNOWS ABOUT KURT LASKY THERE, BUT—

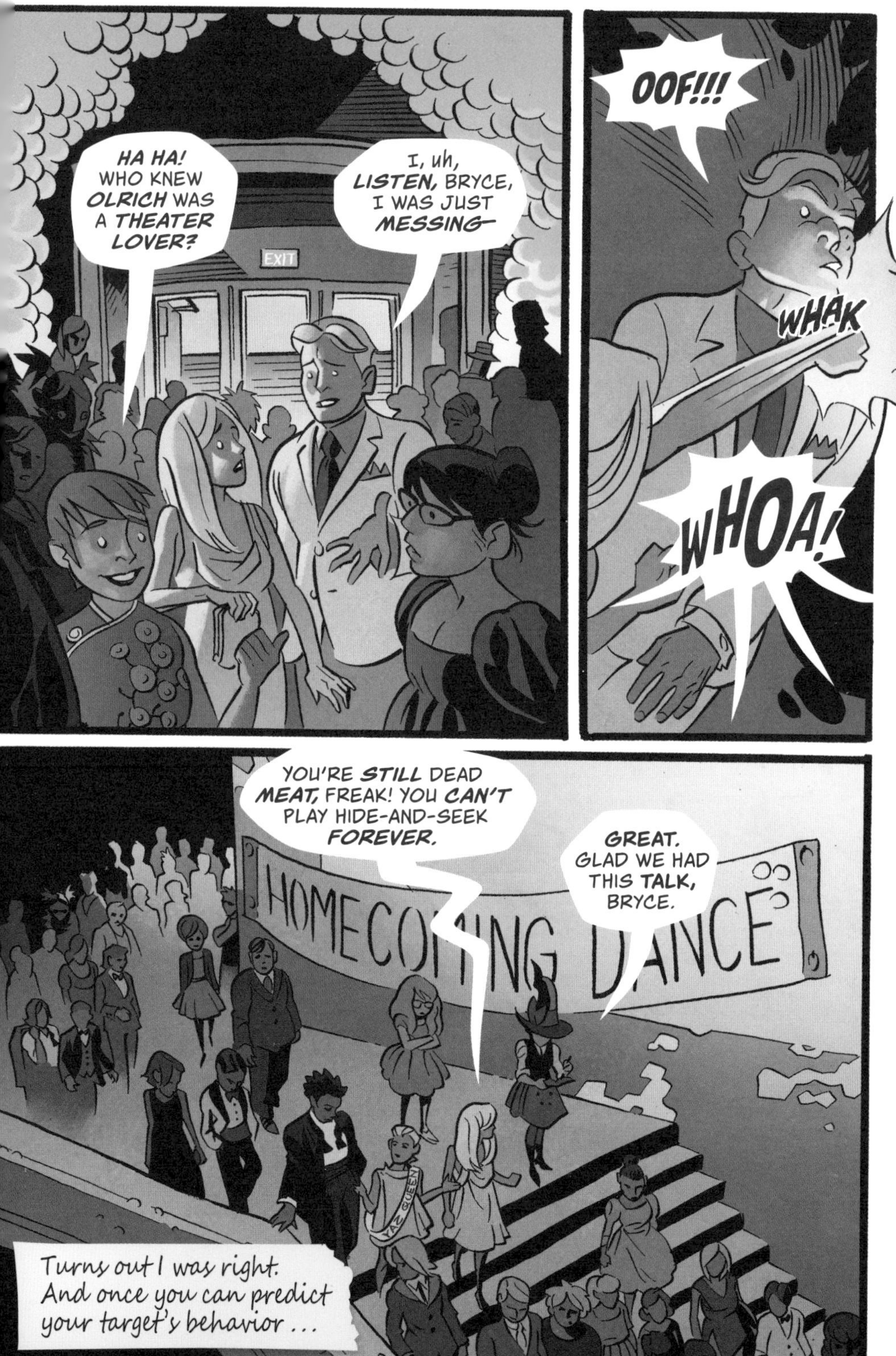
HA HA! WHO KNEW OLRICH WAS A THEATER LOVER?
I, uh, LISTEN, BRYCE, I WAS JUST MESSING—
OOF!!!
WHAK
WHOA!
YOU'RE STILL DEAD MEAT, FREAK! YOU CAN'T PLAY HIDE-AND-SEEK FOREVER.
GREAT. GLAD WE HAD THIS TALK, BRYCE.
HOMECOMING DANCE
Turns out I was right. And once you can predict your target's behavior . . .

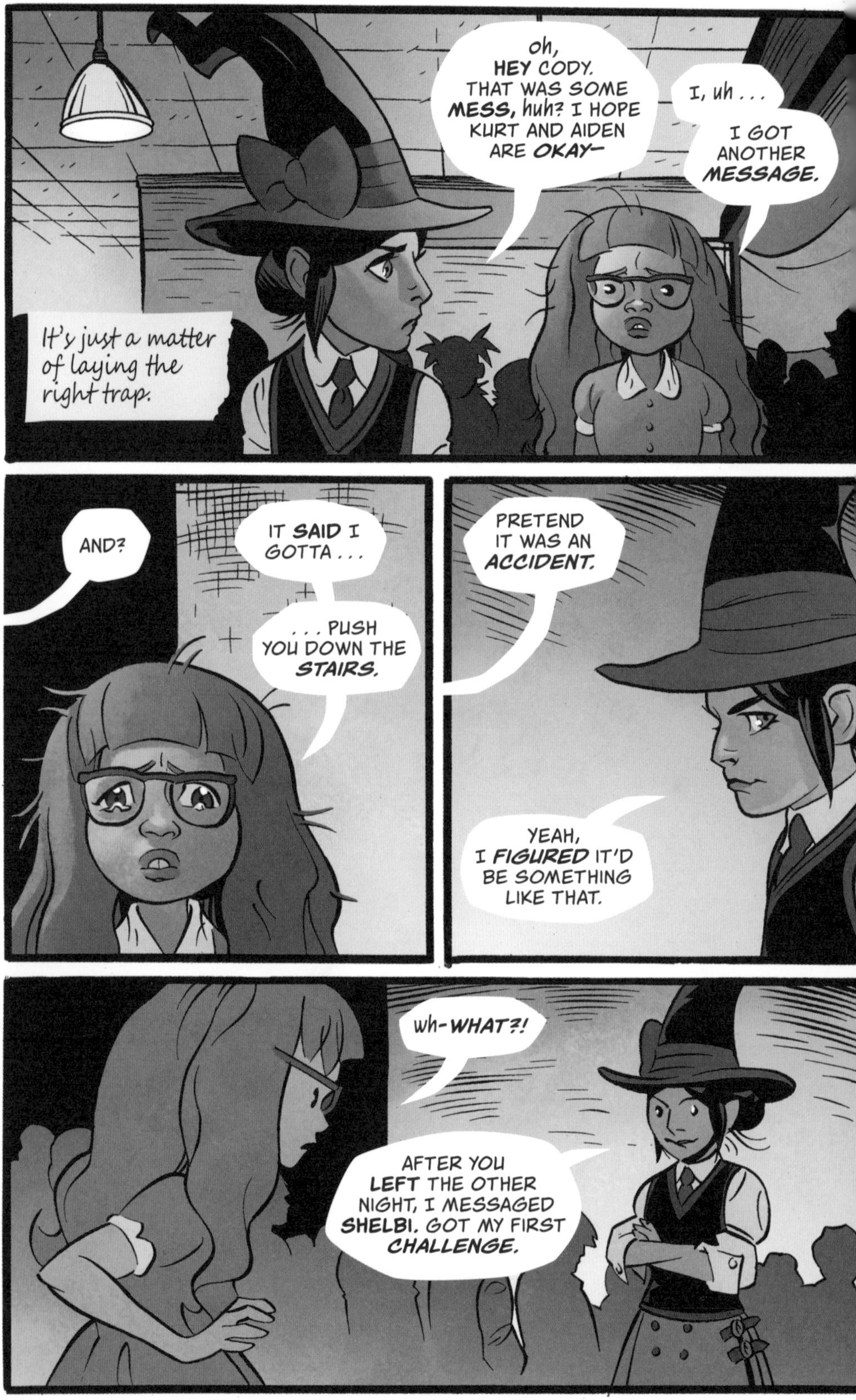
It's just a matter of laying the right trap.
oh, HEY CODY. THAT WAS SOME MESS, huh? I HOPE KURT AND AIDEN ARE OKAY—
I, uh . . .
I GOT ANOTHER MESSAGE.
AND?
IT SAID I GOTTA . . .
. . . PUSH YOU DOWN THE STAIRS.
PRETEND IT WAS AN ACCIDENT.
YEAH, I FIGURED IT'D BE SOMETHING LIKE THAT.
wh-WHAT?!
AFTER YOU LEFT THE OTHER NIGHT, I MESSAGED SHELBI. GOT MY FIRST CHALLENGE.

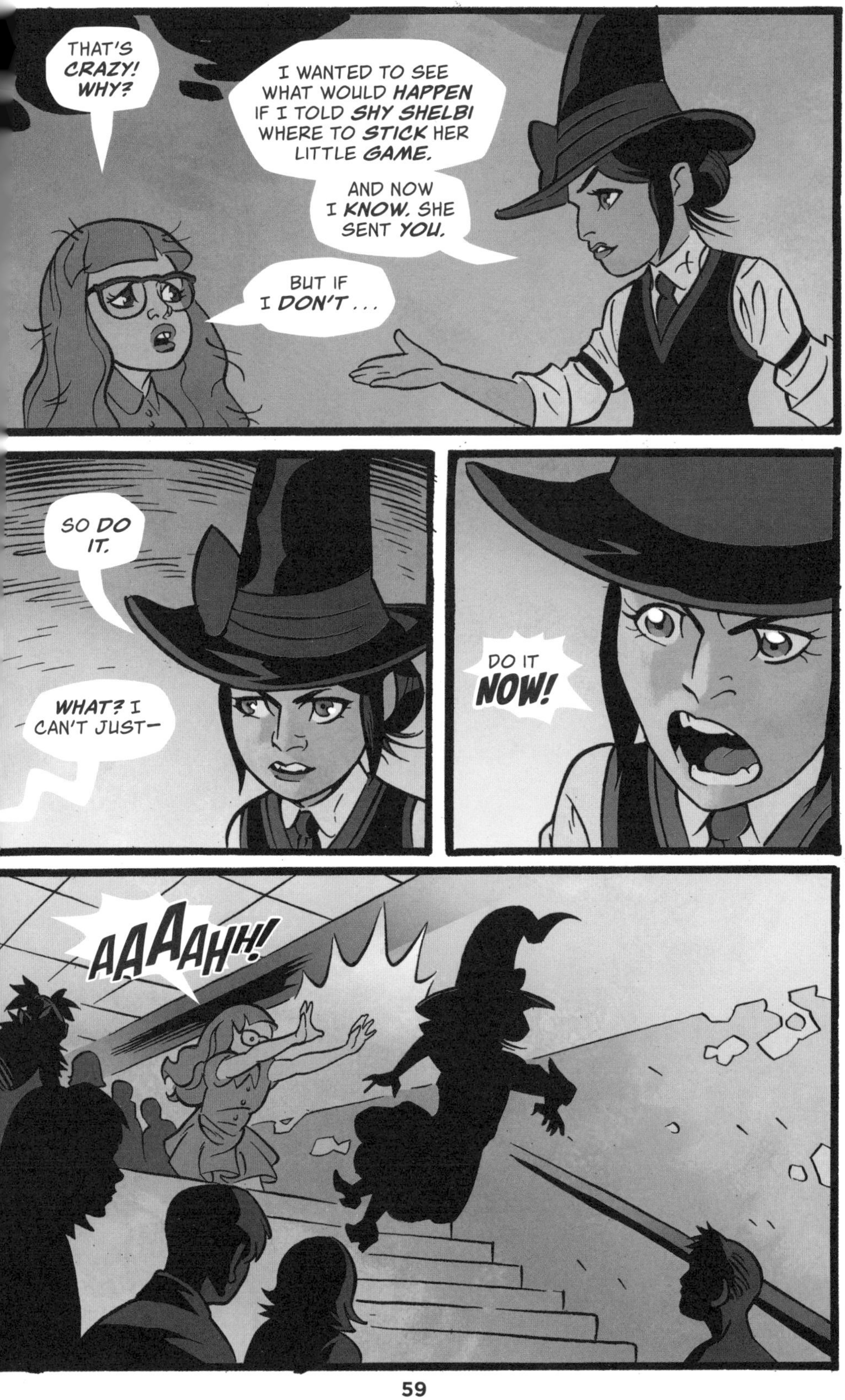
THAT'S CRAZY! WHY?
I WANTED TO SEE WHAT WOULD HAPPEN IF I TOLD SHY SHELBI WHERE TO STICK HER LITTLE GAME.
AND NOW I KNOW. SHE SENT YOU.
BUT IF I DON'T . . .
SO DO IT.
WHAT? I CAN'T JUST—
DO IT NOW!
AAAAHH!

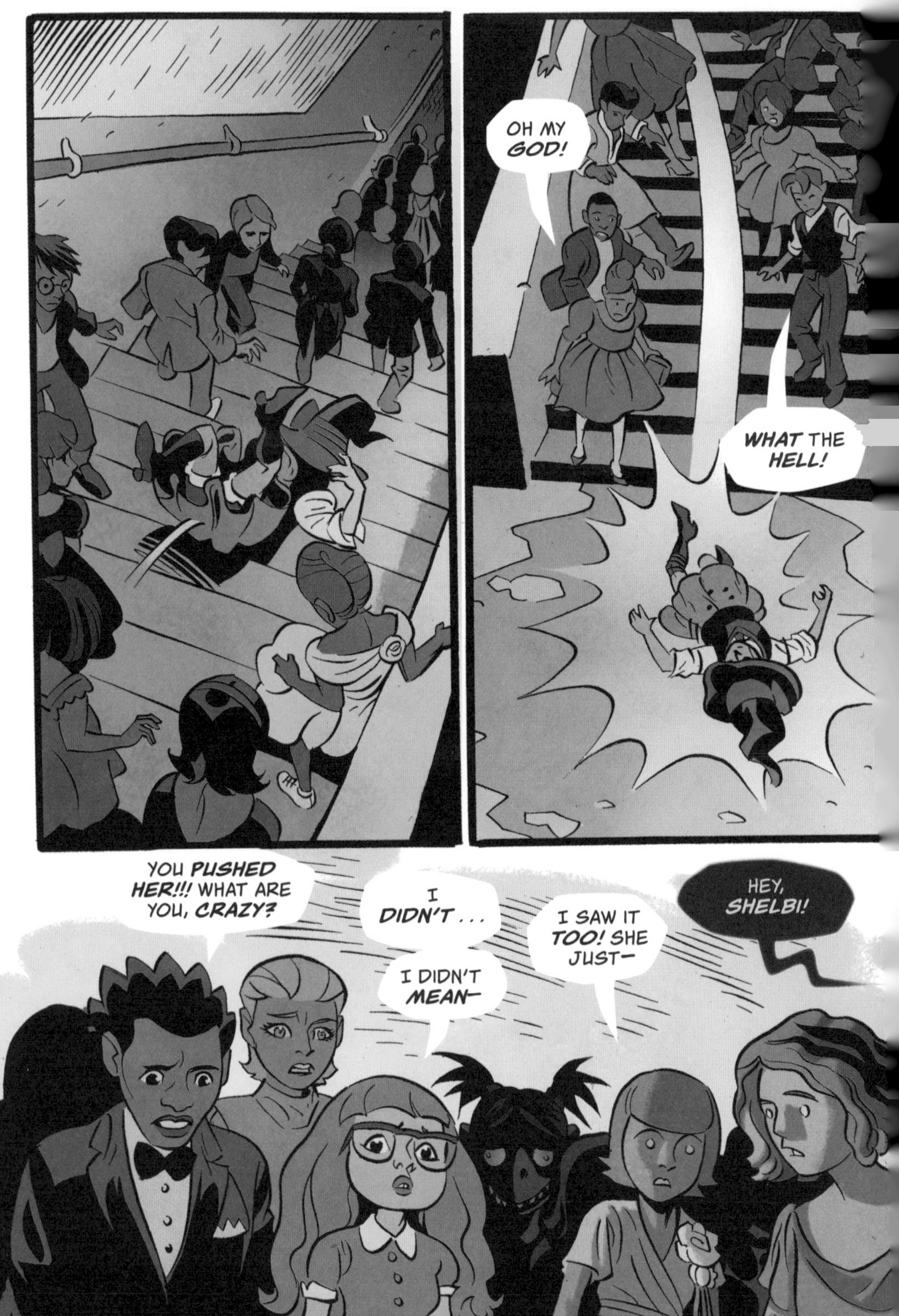

OH MY GOD!
WHAT THE HELL!
YOU PUSHED HER!!! WHAT ARE YOU, CRAZY?
I DIDN'T . . .
I DIDN'T MEAN—
I SAW IT TOO! SHE JUST—
HEY, SHELBI!

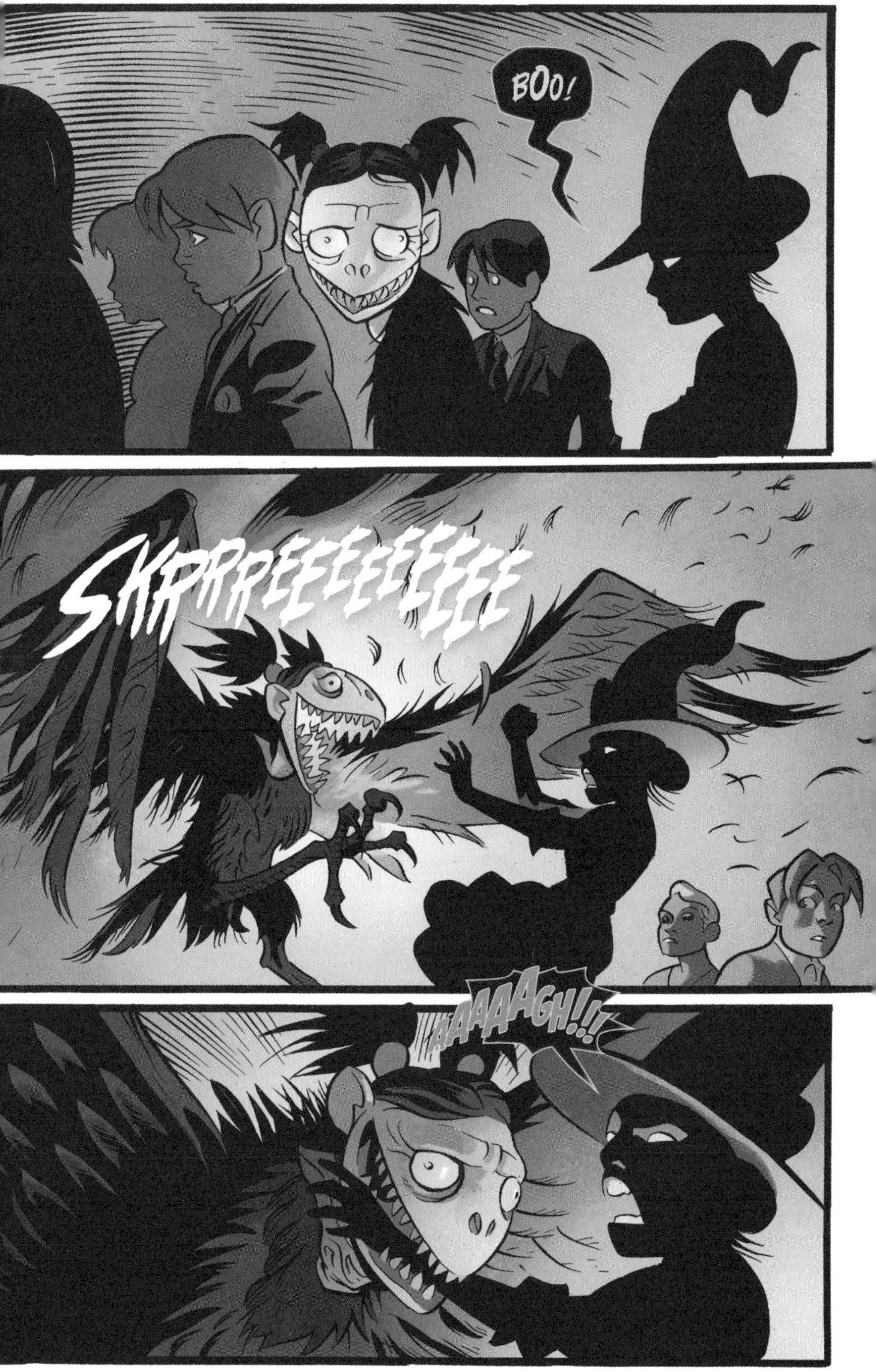
BOO!
SKRRREEEEEEEEEE
AAAAAGH!!!

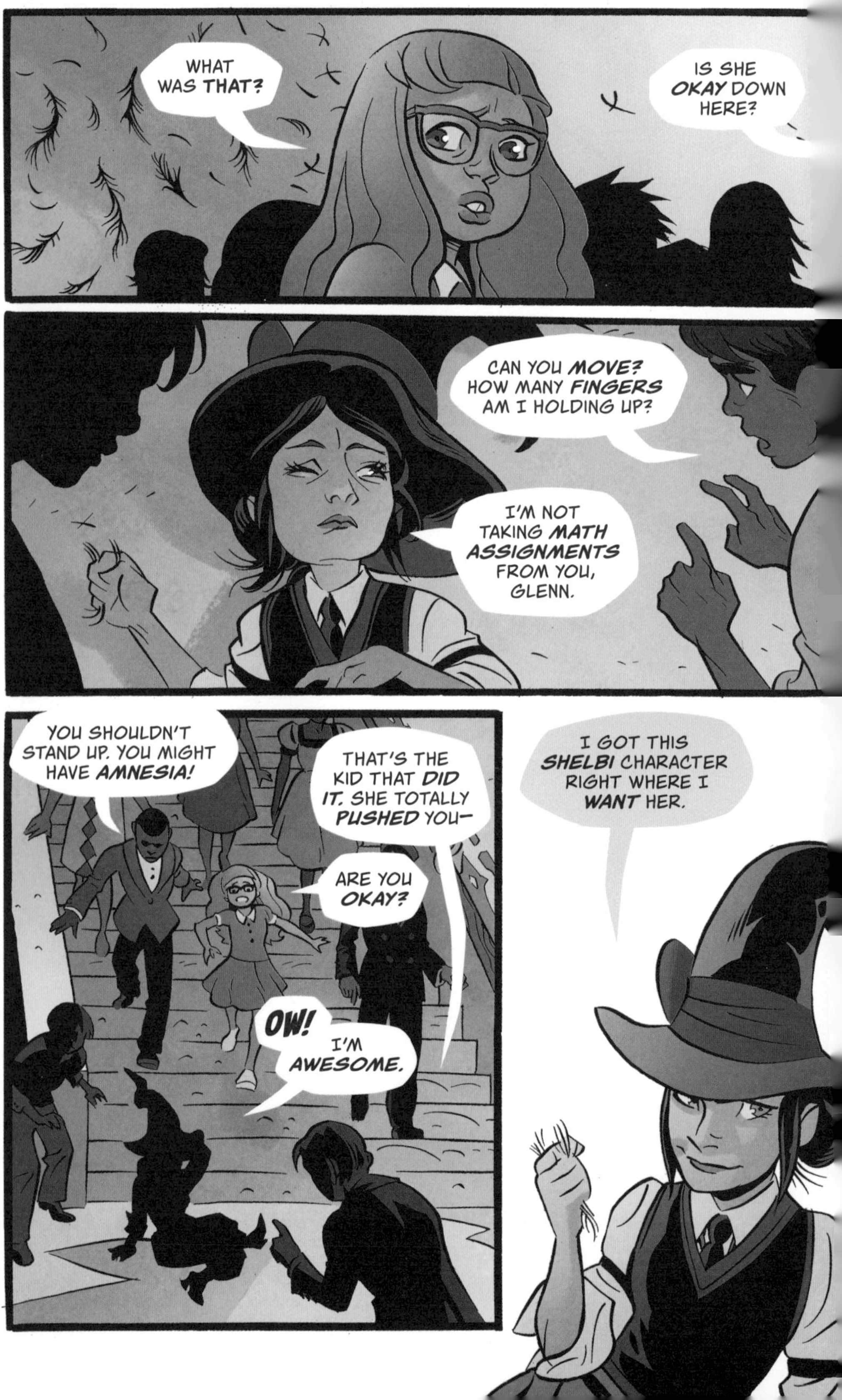
WHAT WAS THAT?
IS SHE OKAY DOWN HERE?
CAN YOU MOVE? HOW MANY FINGERS AM I HOLDING UP?
I'M NOT TAKING MATH ASSIGNMENTS FROM YOU, GLENN.
YOU SHOULDN'T STAND UP. YOU MIGHT HAVE AMNESIA!
THAT'S THE KID THAT DID IT. SHE TOTALLY PUSHED YOU—
ARE YOU OKAY?
OW! I'M AWESOME.
I GOT THIS SHELBI CHARACTER RIGHT WHERE I WANT HER.

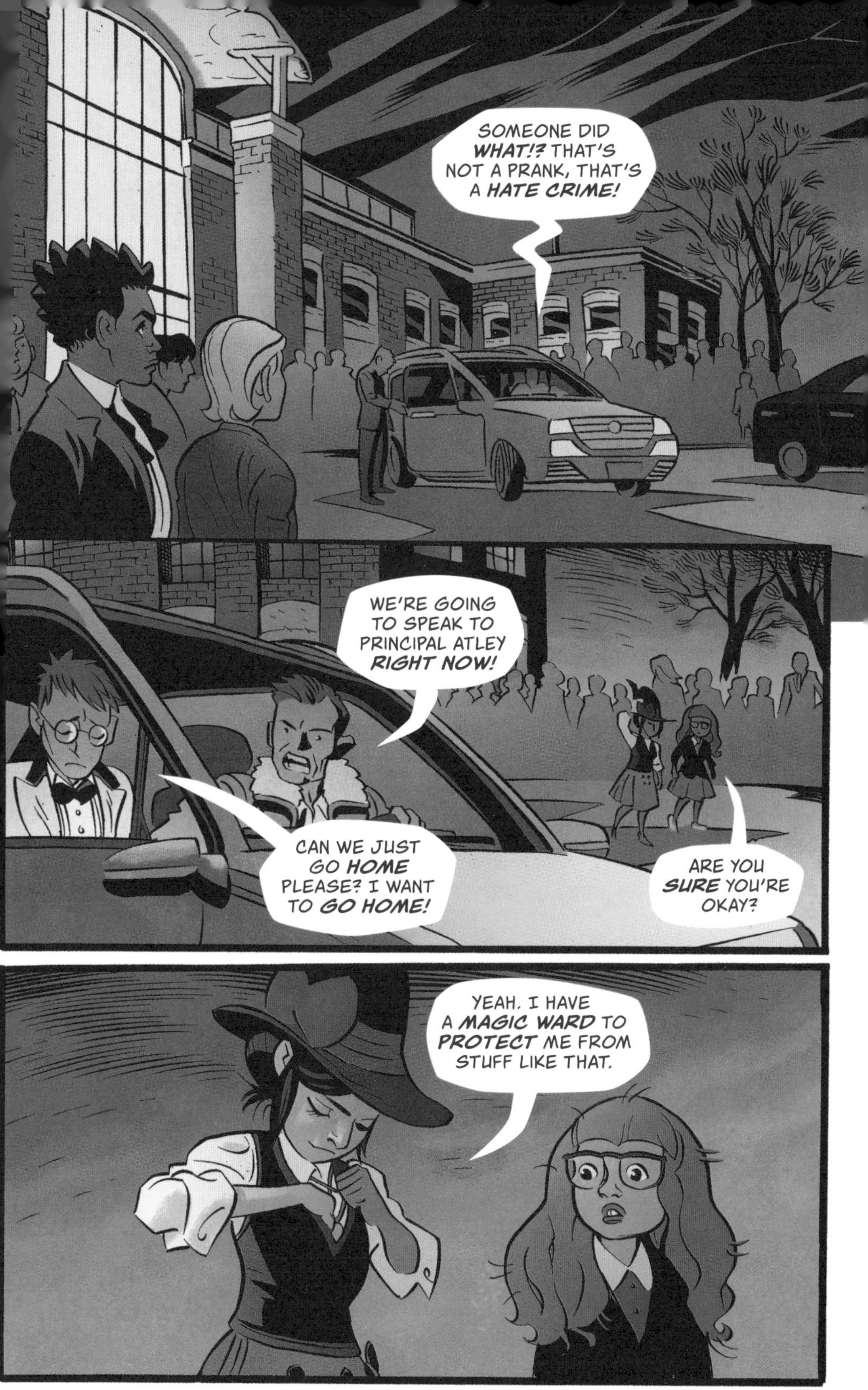
SOMEONE DID WHAT!? THAT'S NOT A PRANK, THAT'S A HATE CRIME!
WE'RE GOING TO SPEAK TO PRINCIPAL ATLEY RIGHT NOW!
CAN WE JUST GO HOME PLEASE? I WANT TO GO HOME!
ARE YOU SURE YOU'RE OKAY?
YEAH. I HAVE A MAGIC WARD TO PROTECT ME FROM STUFF LIKE THAT.

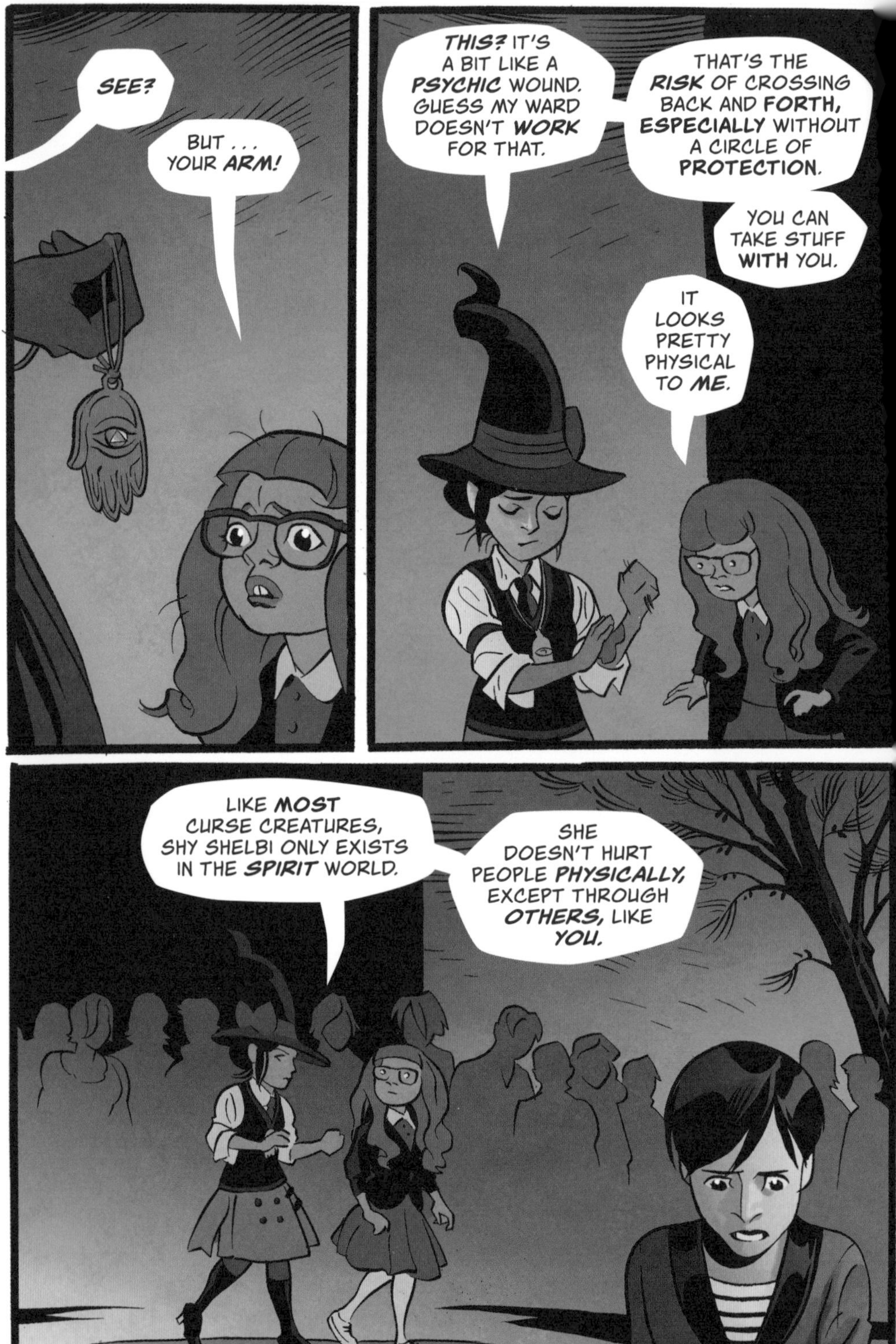
SEE?
BUT . . . YOUR ARM!
THIS? IT'S A BIT LIKE A PSYCHIC WOUND. GUESS MY WARD DOESN'T WORK FOR THAT.
THAT'S THE RISK OF CROSSING BACK AND FORTH, ESPECIALLY WITHOUT A CIRCLE OF PROTECTION.
YOU CAN TAKE STUFF WITH YOU.
IT LOOKS PRETTY PHYSICAL TO ME.
LIKE MOST CURSE CREATURES, SHY SHELBI ONLY EXISTS IN THE SPIRIT WORLD.
SHE DOESN'T HURT PEOPLE PHYSICALLY, EXCEPT THROUGH OTHERS, LIKE YOU.

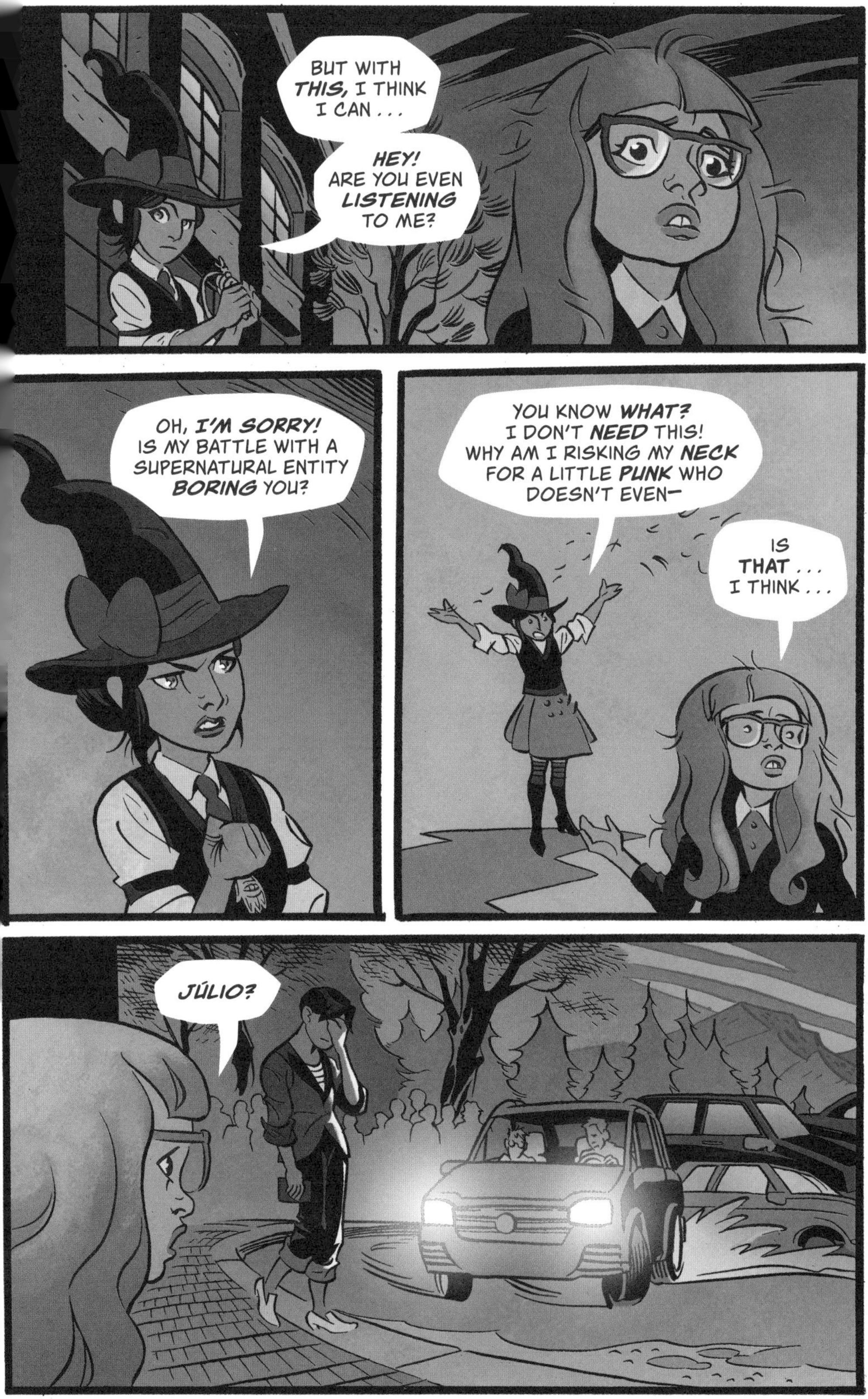
BUT WITH THIS, I THINK I CAN . . .
HEY! ARE YOU EVEN LISTENING TO ME?
OH, I'M SORRY! IS MY BATTLE WITH A SUPERNATURAL ENTITY BORING YOU?
YOU KNOW WHAT? I DON'T NEED THIS! WHY AM I RISKING MY NECK FOR A LITTLE PUNK WHO DOESN'T EVEN—
IS THAT . . . I THINK . . .
JÚLIO?

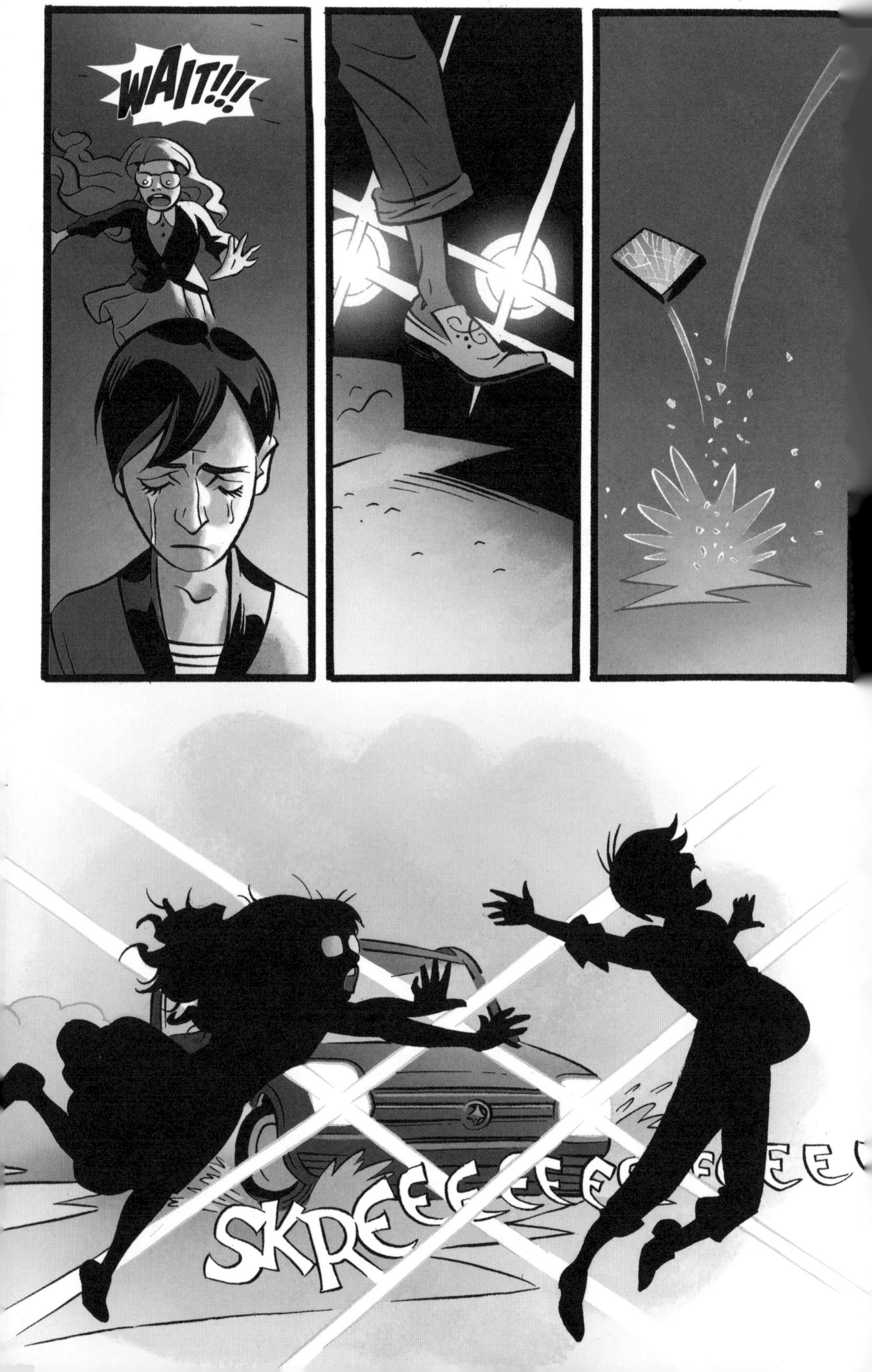
WAIT!!!
SKREEEEEEEEEEE

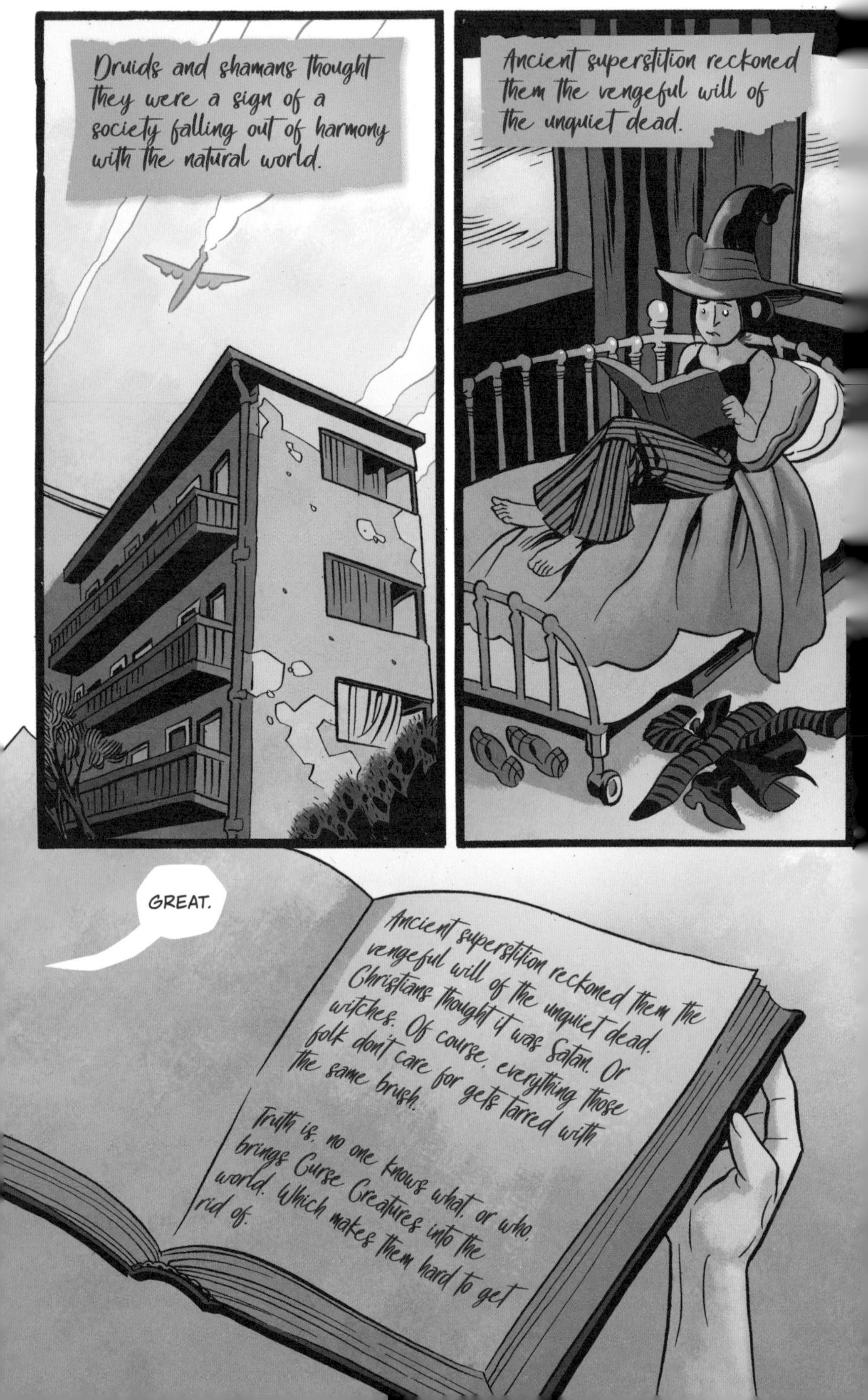
Druids and shamans thought they were a sign of a society falling out of harmony with the natural world.
Ancient superstition reckoned them the vengeful will of the unquiet dead.
GREAT.
Ancient superstition reckoned them the vengeful will of the unquiet dead. Christians thought it was Satan. Or witches. Of course, everything those folk don't care for gets tarred with the same brush.
Truth is, no one knows what, or who, brings Curse Creatures into the world. Which makes them hard to get rid of.

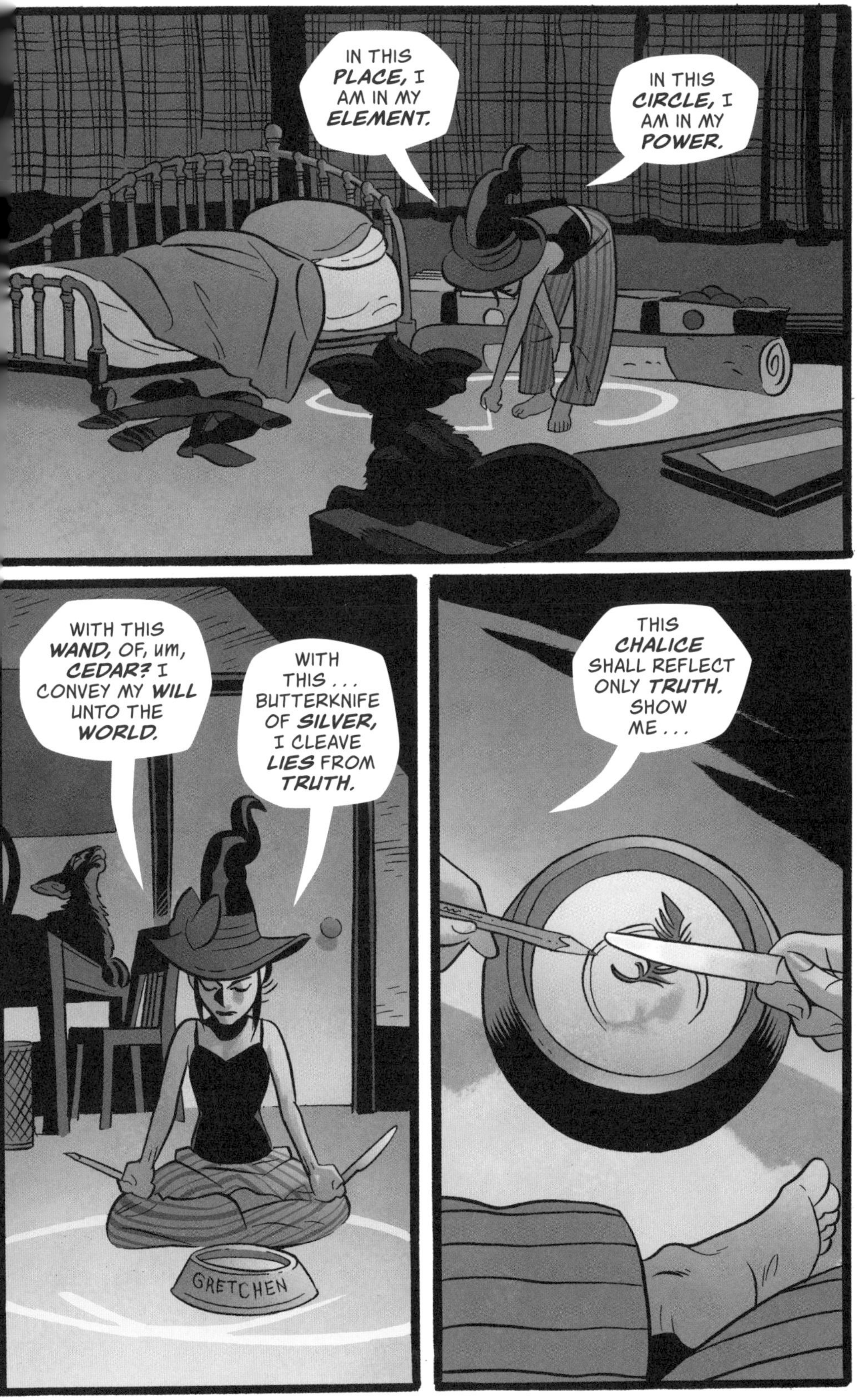
IN THIS PLACE, I AM IN MY ELEMENT.
IN THIS CIRCLE, I AM IN MY POWER.
WITH THIS WAND, OF, um, CEDAR? I CONVEY MY WILL UNTO THE WORLD.
WITH THIS . . . BUTTERKNIFE OF SILVER, I CLEAVE LIES FROM TRUTH.
GRETCHEN
THIS CHALICE SHALL REFLECT ONLY TRUTH. SHOW ME . . .

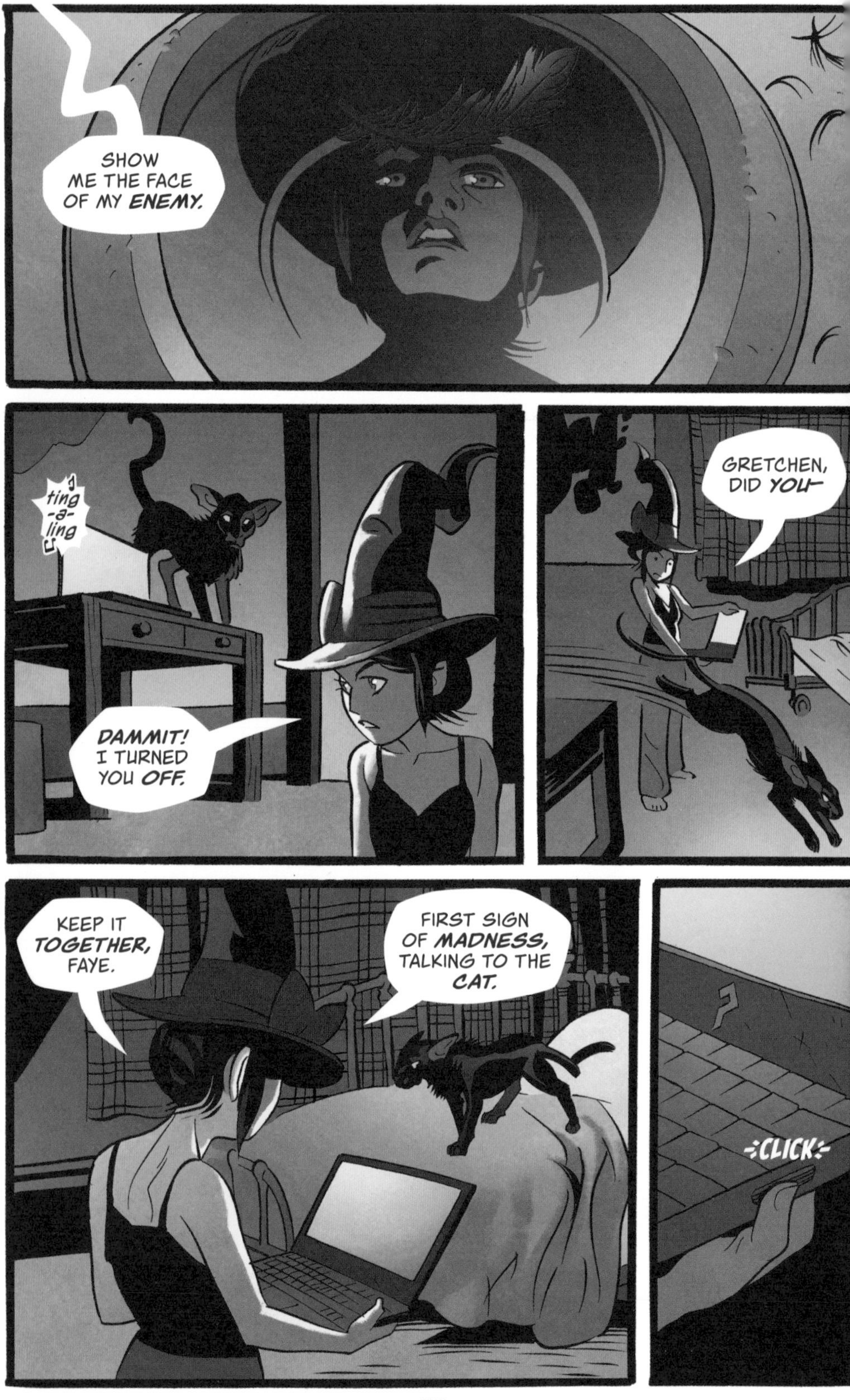
SHOW ME THE FACE OF MY ENEMY.
ting-a-ling
DAMMIT! I TURNED YOU OFF.
GRETCHEN, DID YOU—
KEEP IT TOGETHER, FAYE.
FIRST SIGN OF MADNESS, TALKING TO THE CAT.
CLICK

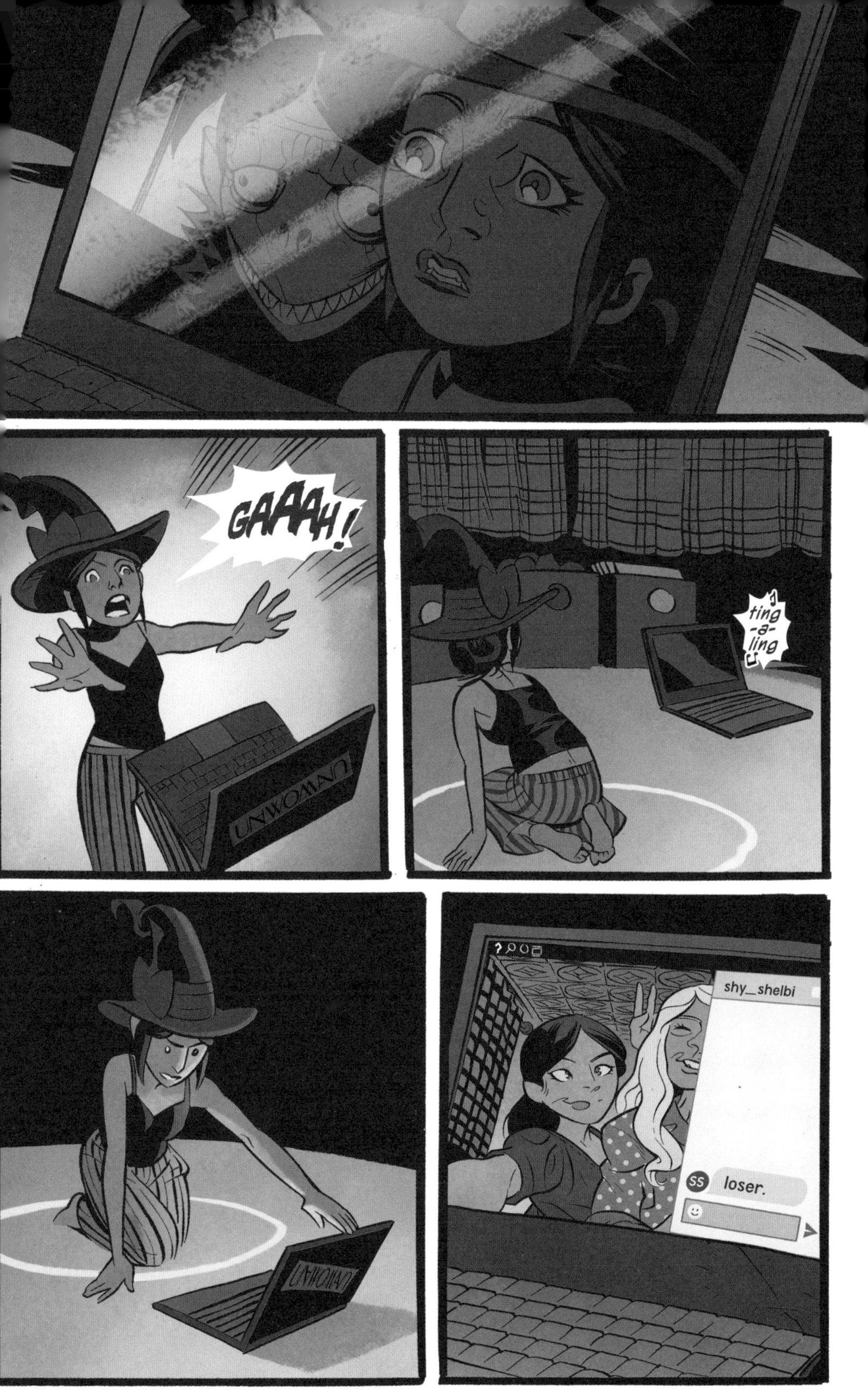
GAAAH!
UNWOMAN
ting-a-ling
UNWOMAN
shy__shelbi
SS loser.

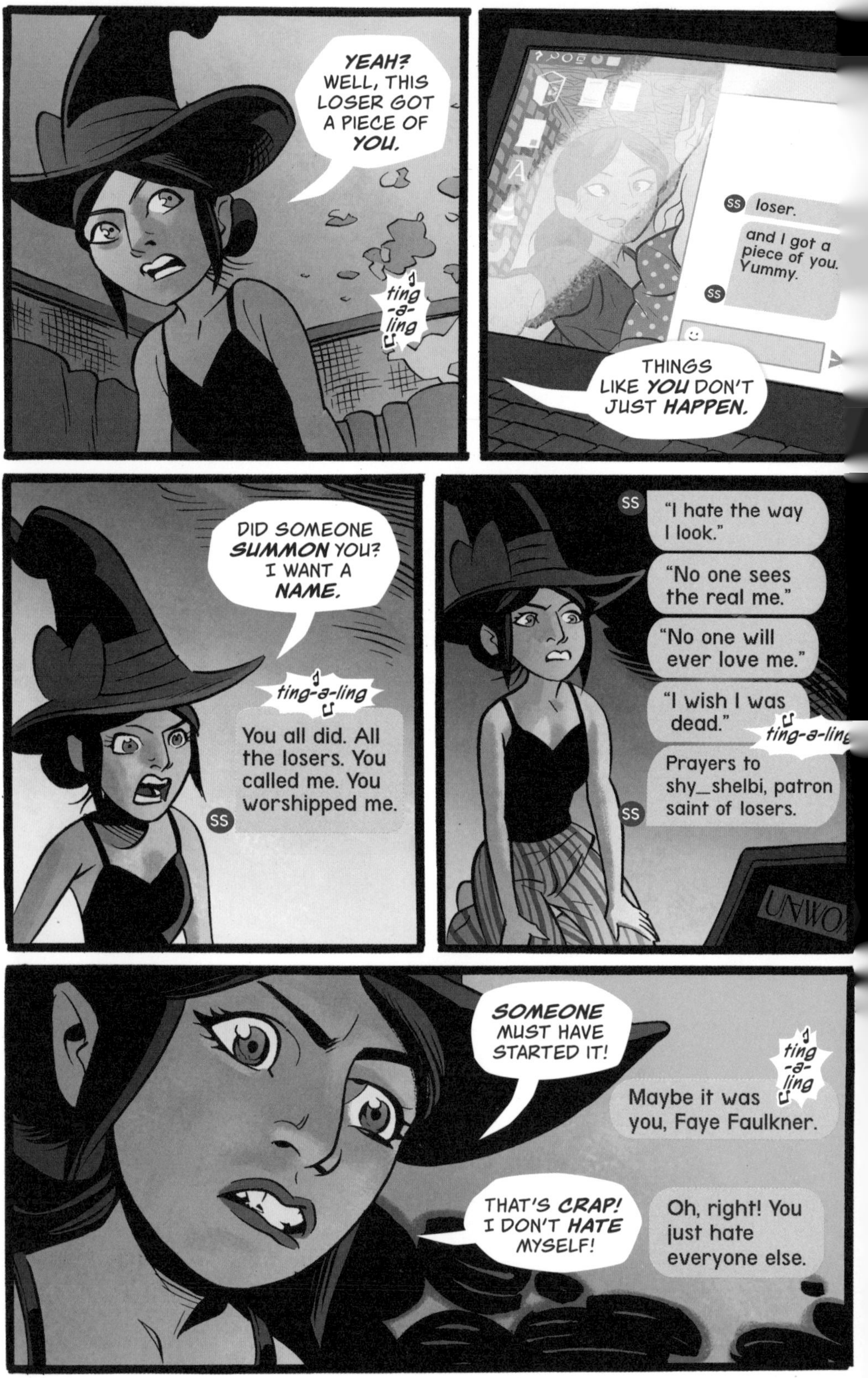
YEAH? WELL, THIS LOSER GOT A PIECE OF YOU.
ting-a-ling
loser.
and I got a piece of you. Yummy.
THINGS LIKE YOU DON'T JUST HAPPEN.
DID SOMEONE SUMMON YOU? I WANT A NAME.
ting-a-ling
You all did. All the losers. You called me. You worshipped me.
"I hate the way I look."
"No one sees the real me."
"No one will ever love me."
"I wish I was dead."
ting-a-ling
Prayers to shy_shelbi, patron saint of losers.
SOMEONE MUST HAVE STARTED IT!
ting-a-ling
Maybe it was you, Faye Faulkner.
THAT'S CRAP! I DON'T HATE MYSELF!
Oh, right! You just hate everyone else.

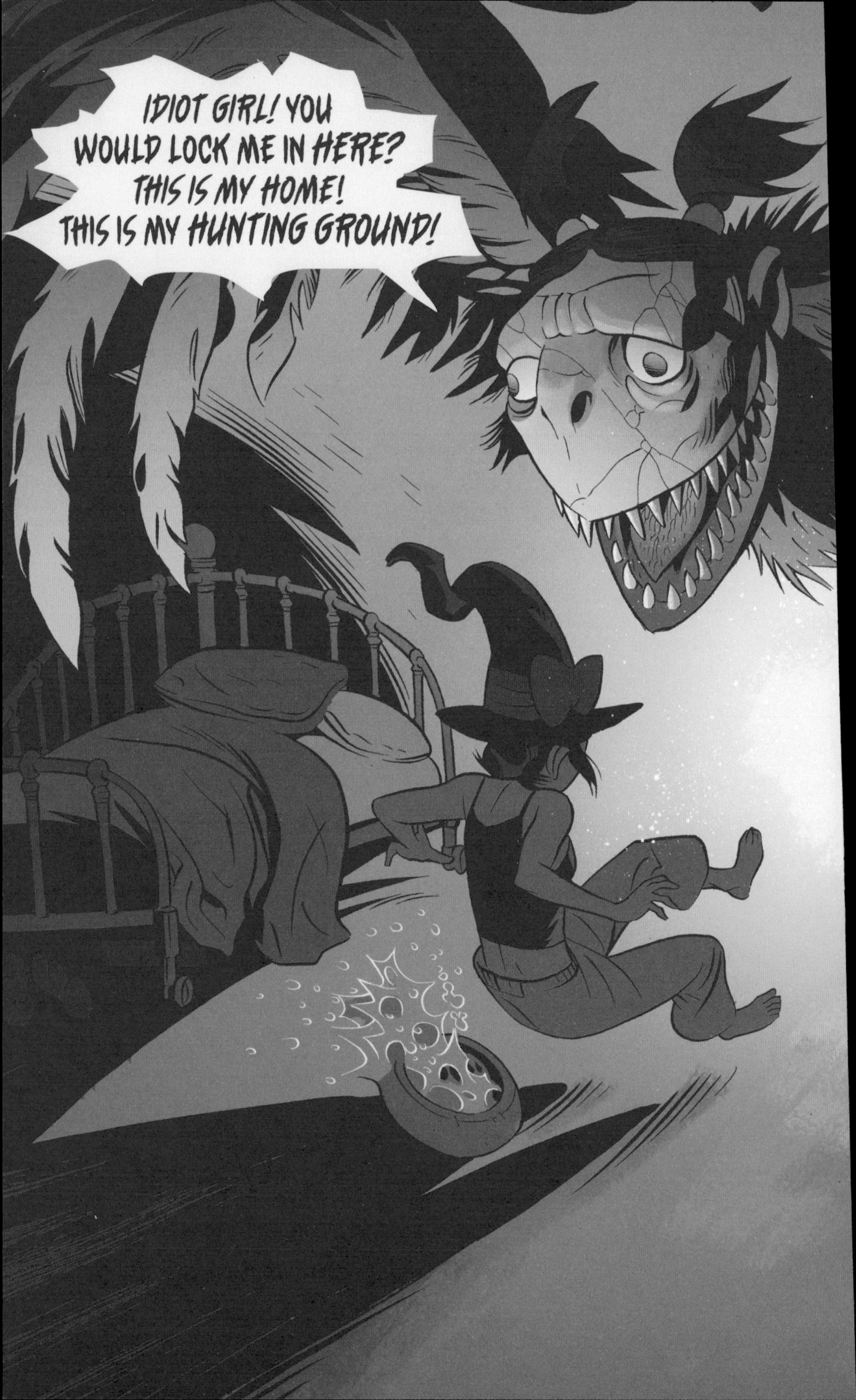
IDIOT GIRL! YOU WOULD LOCK ME IN HERE? THIS IS MY HOME! THIS IS MY HUNTING GROUND!

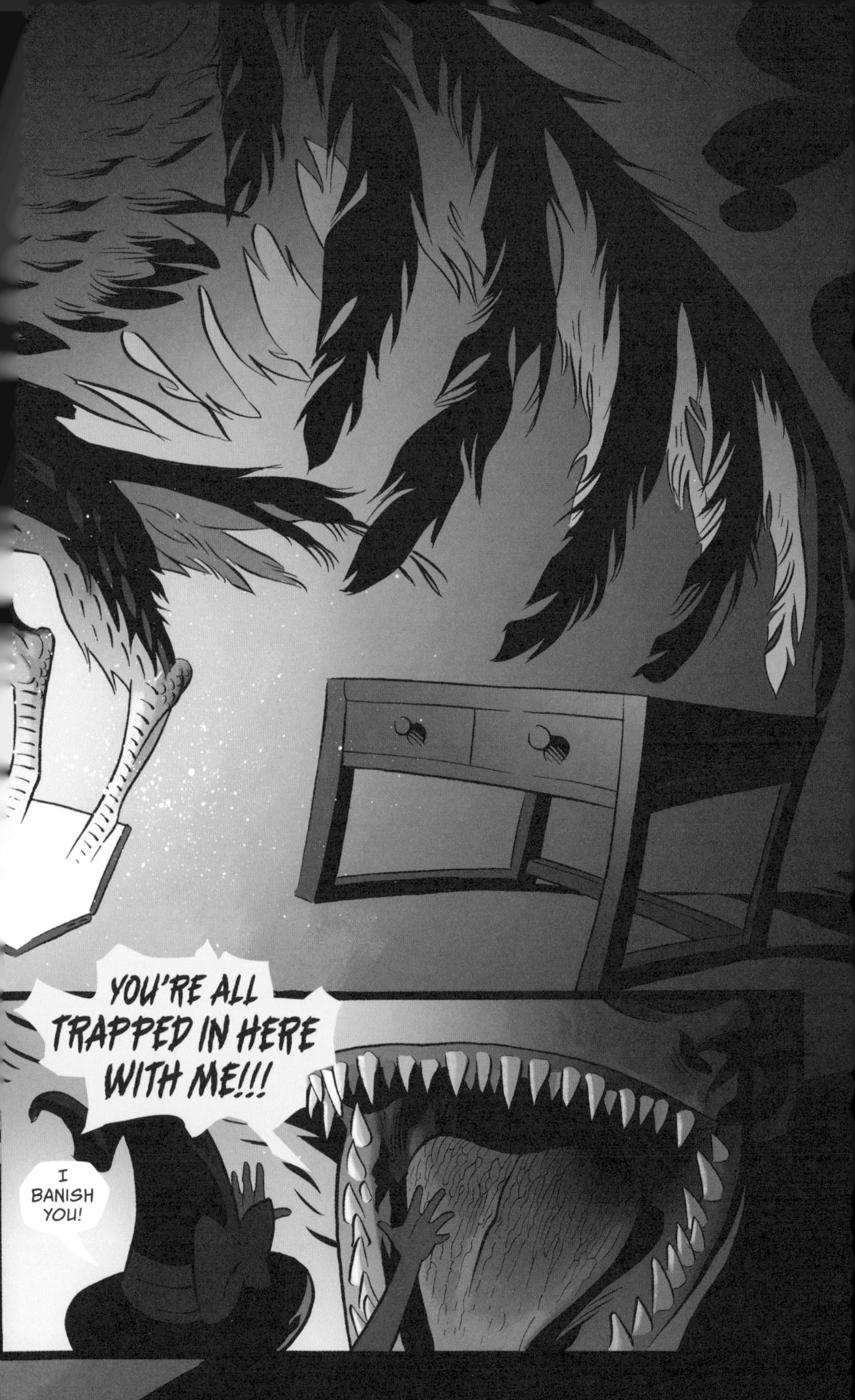
YOU'RE ALL TRAPPED IN HERE WITH ME!!!
I BANISH YOU!

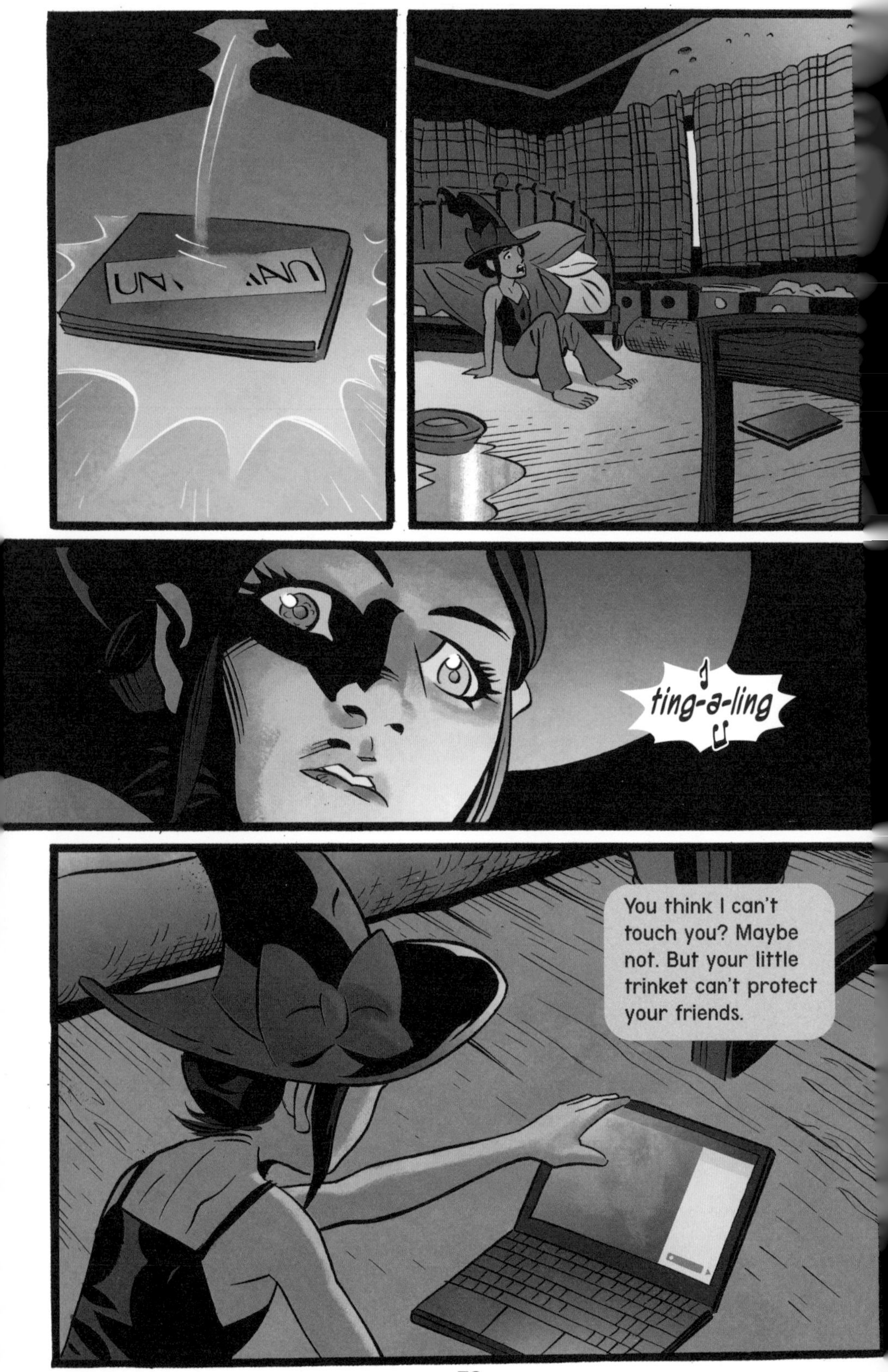
ting-a-ling
You think I can't touch you? Maybe not. But your little trinket can't protect your friends.

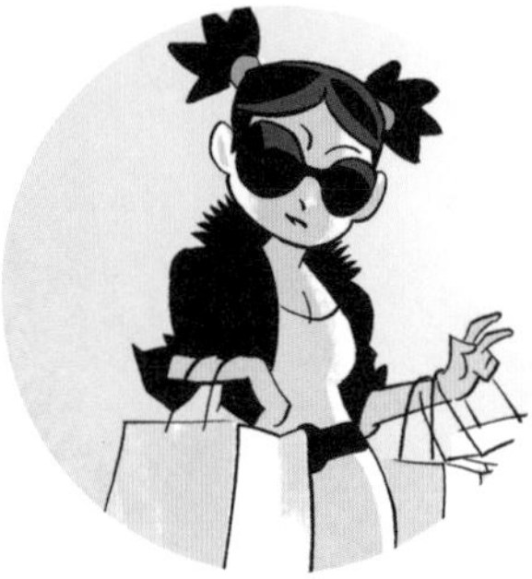

the shy_shelbi program

Step 4: Too Blessed to be Stressed

Successful people make losers uncomfortable. They will act there's something wrong with you when you leave them behind in their misery. But you get to decide what matters what's not worth losing sleep over. Step 4 is turning other people's jealousy to your benefit . . . more

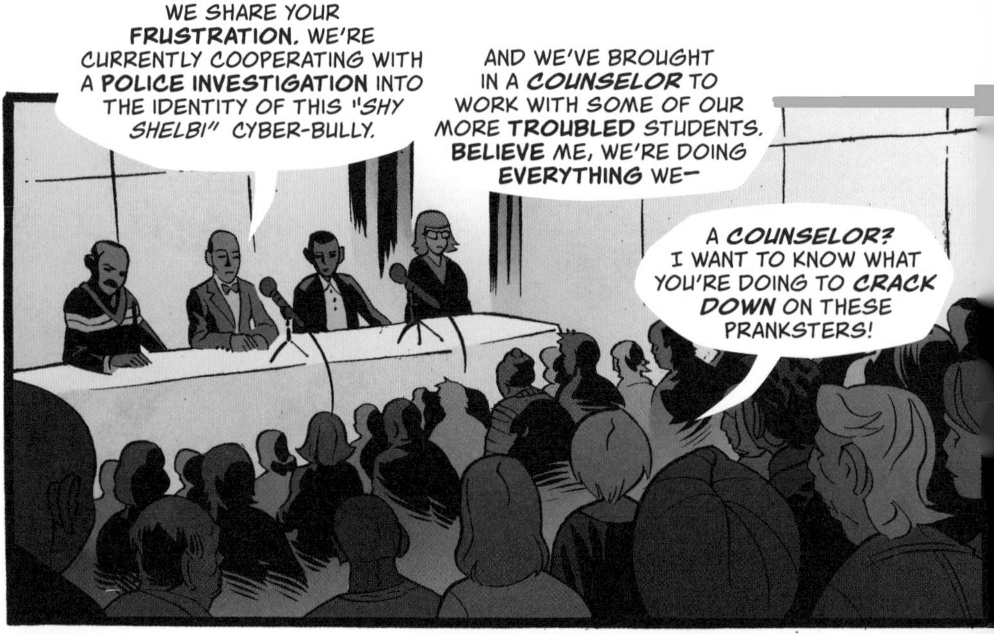
WE SHARE YOUR FRUSTRATION. WE'RE CURRENTLY COOPERATING WITH A POLICE INVESTIGATION INTO THE IDENTITY OF THIS "SHY SHELBI" CYBER-BULLY.
AND WE'VE BROUGHT IN A COUNSELOR TO WORK WITH SOME OF OUR MORE TROUBLED STUDENTS. BELIEVE ME, WE'RE DOING EVERYTHING WE—
A COUNSELOR? I WANT TO KNOW WHAT YOU'RE DOING TO CRACK DOWN ON THESE PRANKSTERS!

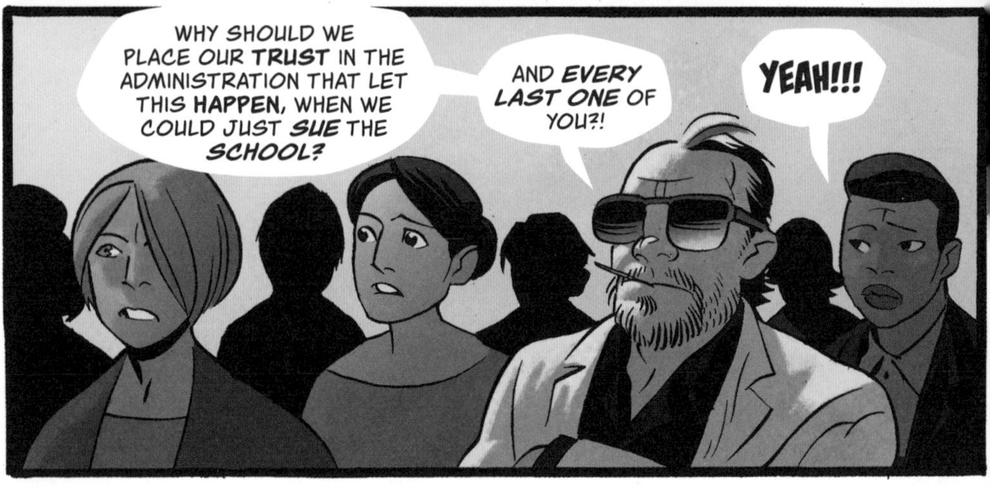
WHY SHOULD WE PLACE OUR TRUST IN THE ADMINISTRATION THAT LET THIS HAPPEN, WHEN WE COULD JUST SUE THE SCHOOL?
AND EVERY LAST ONE OF YOU?!
YEAH!!!

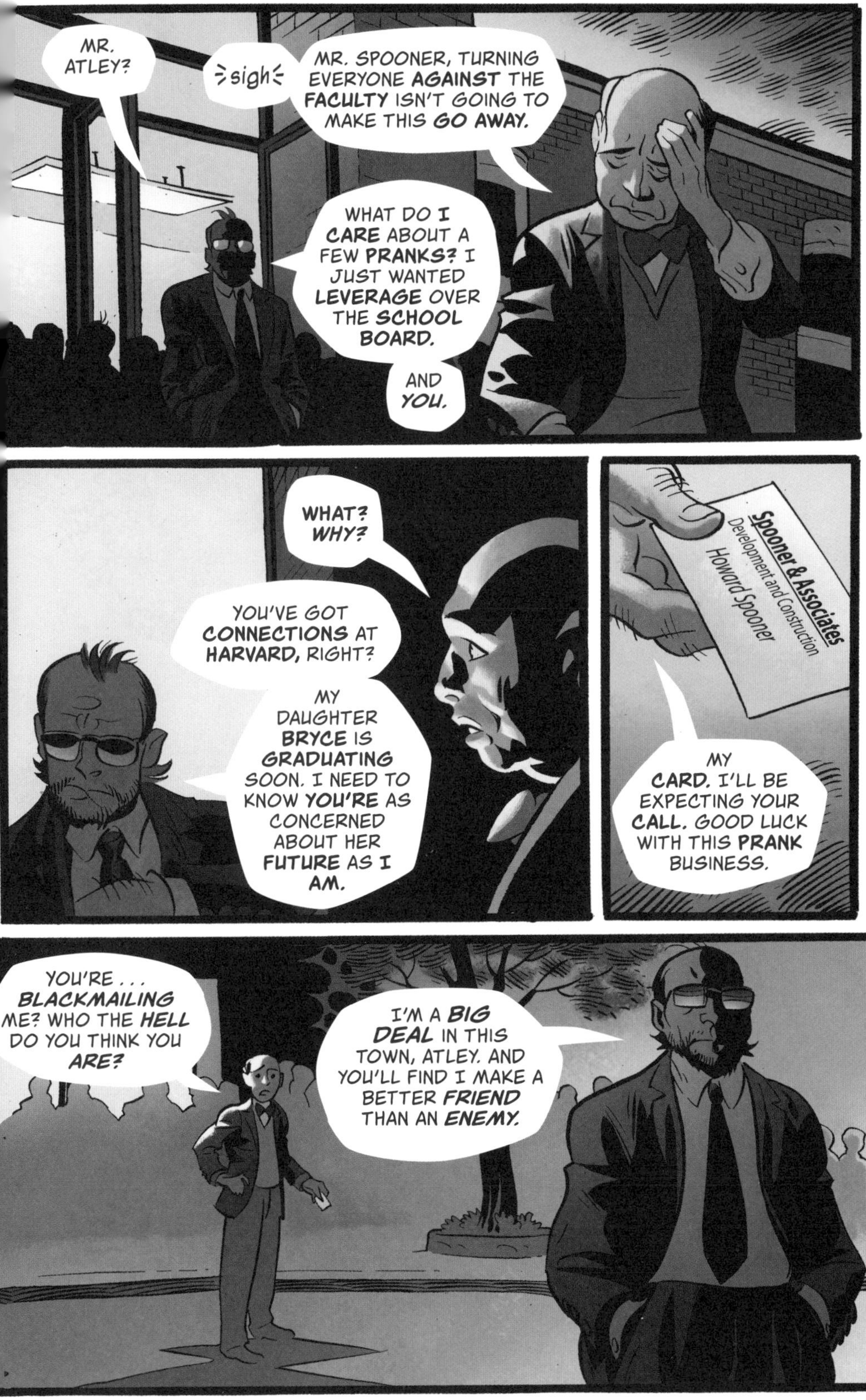
MR. ATLEY?
sigh
MR. SPOONER, TURNING EVERYONE AGAINST THE FACULTY ISN'T GOING TO MAKE THIS GO AWAY.
WHAT DO I CARE ABOUT A FEW PRANKS? I JUST WANTED LEVERAGE OVER THE SCHOOL BOARD.
AND YOU.
WHAT? WHY?
YOU'VE GOT CONNECTIONS AT HARVARD, RIGHT?
MY DAUGHTER BRYCE IS GRADUATING SOON. I NEED TO KNOW YOU'RE AS CONCERNED ABOUT HER FUTURE AS I AM.
Spooner & Associates
Development and Construction
Howard Spooner
MY CARD. I'LL BE EXPECTING YOUR CALL. GOOD LUCK WITH THIS PRANK BUSINESS.
YOU'RE . . . BLACKMAILING ME? WHO THE HELL DO YOU THINK YOU ARE?
I'M A BIG DEAL IN THIS TOWN, ATLEY. AND YOU'LL FIND I MAKE A BETTER FRIEND THAN AN ENEMY.

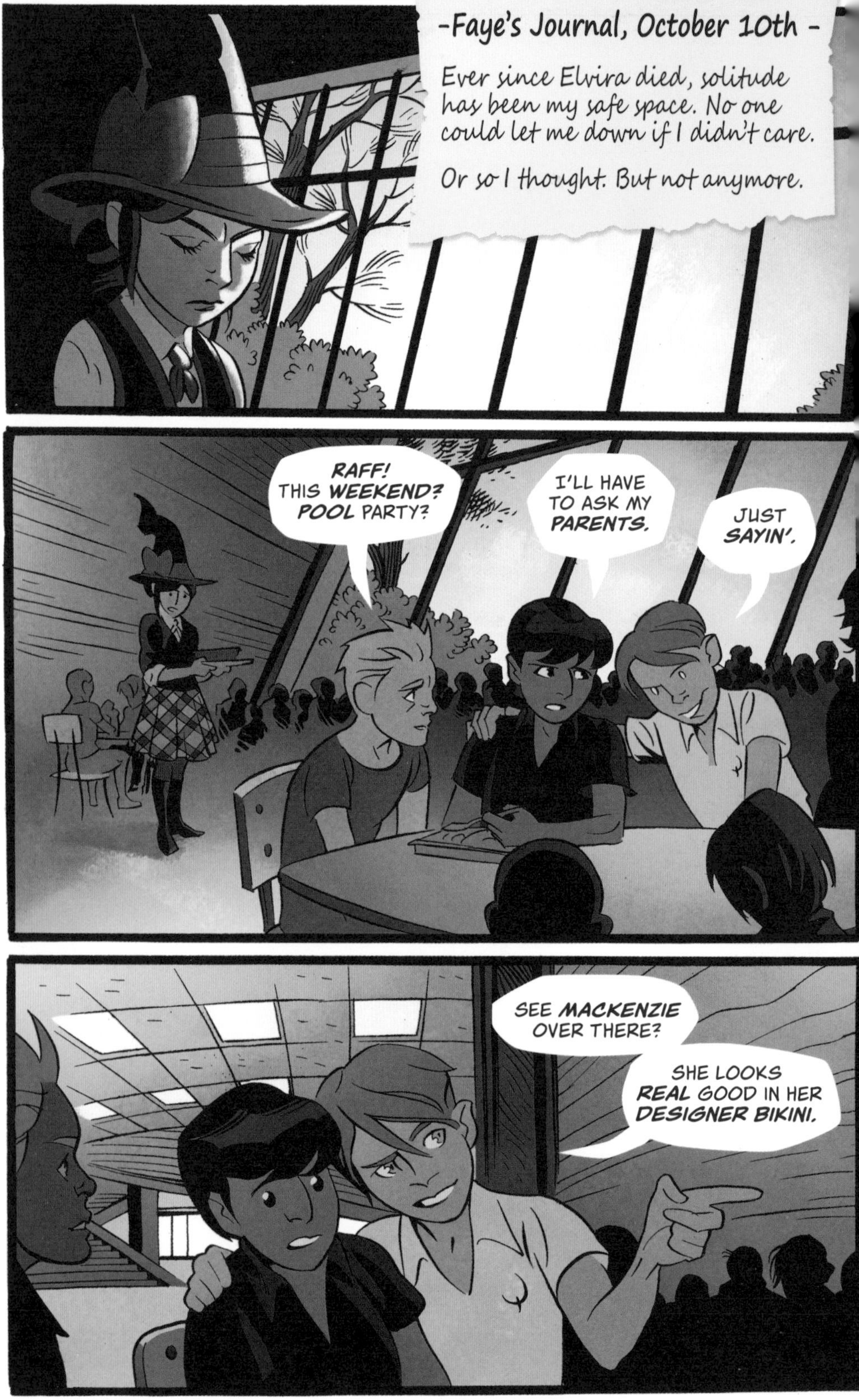
-Faye's Journal, October 10th -
Ever since Elvira died, solitude has been my safe space. No one could let me down if I didn't care.
Or so I thought. But not anymore.
RAFF! THIS WEEKEND? POOL PARTY?
I'LL HAVE TO ASK MY PARENTS.
JUST SAYIN'.
SEE MACKENZIE OVER THERE?
SHE LOOKS REAL GOOD IN HER DESIGNER BIKINI.

82

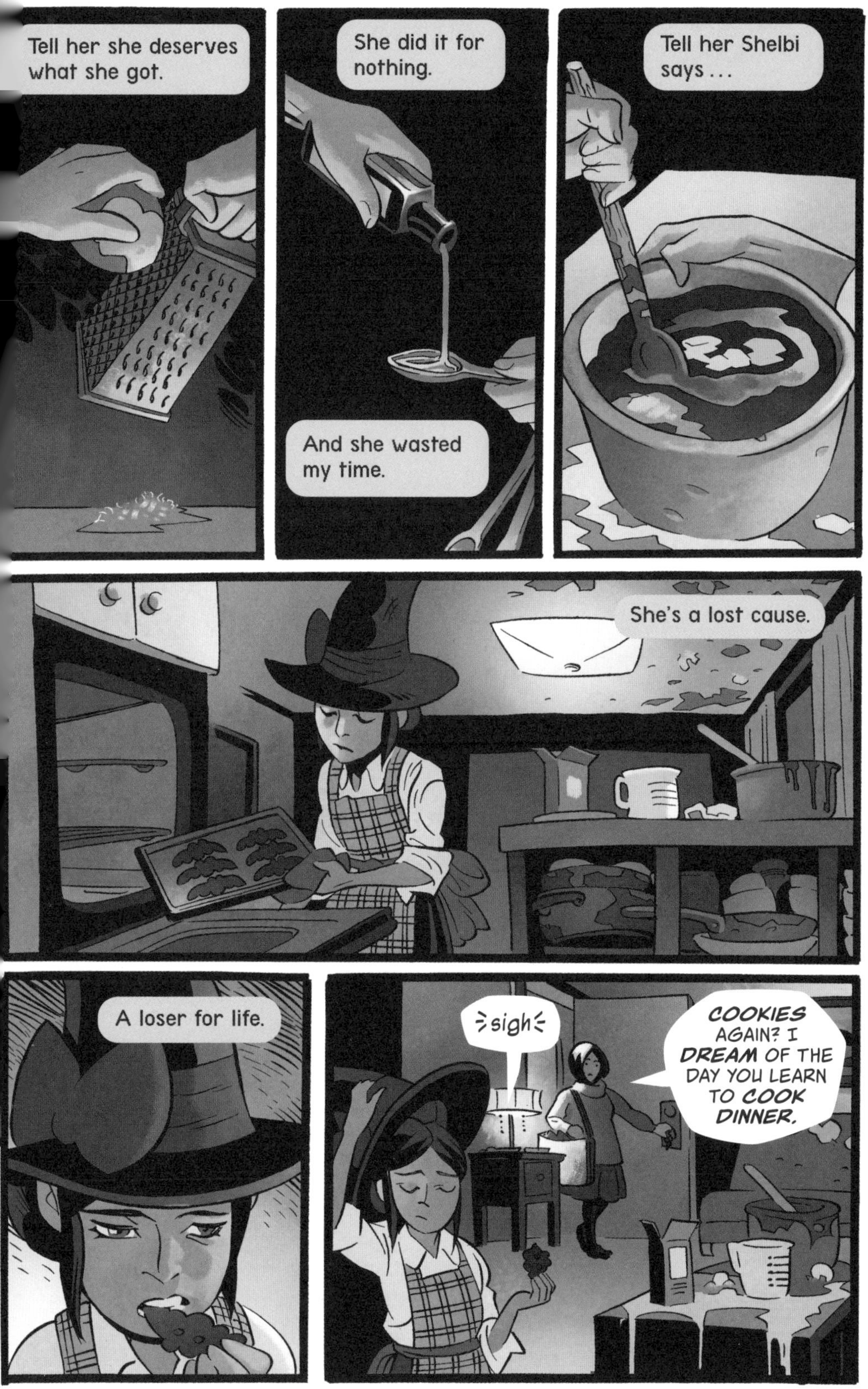
Tell her she deserves what she got.
She did it for nothing.
And she wasted my time.
Tell her Shelbi says . . .
She's a lost cause.
A loser for life.
sigh
COOKIES AGAIN? I DREAM OF THE DAY YOU LEARN TO COOK DINNER.

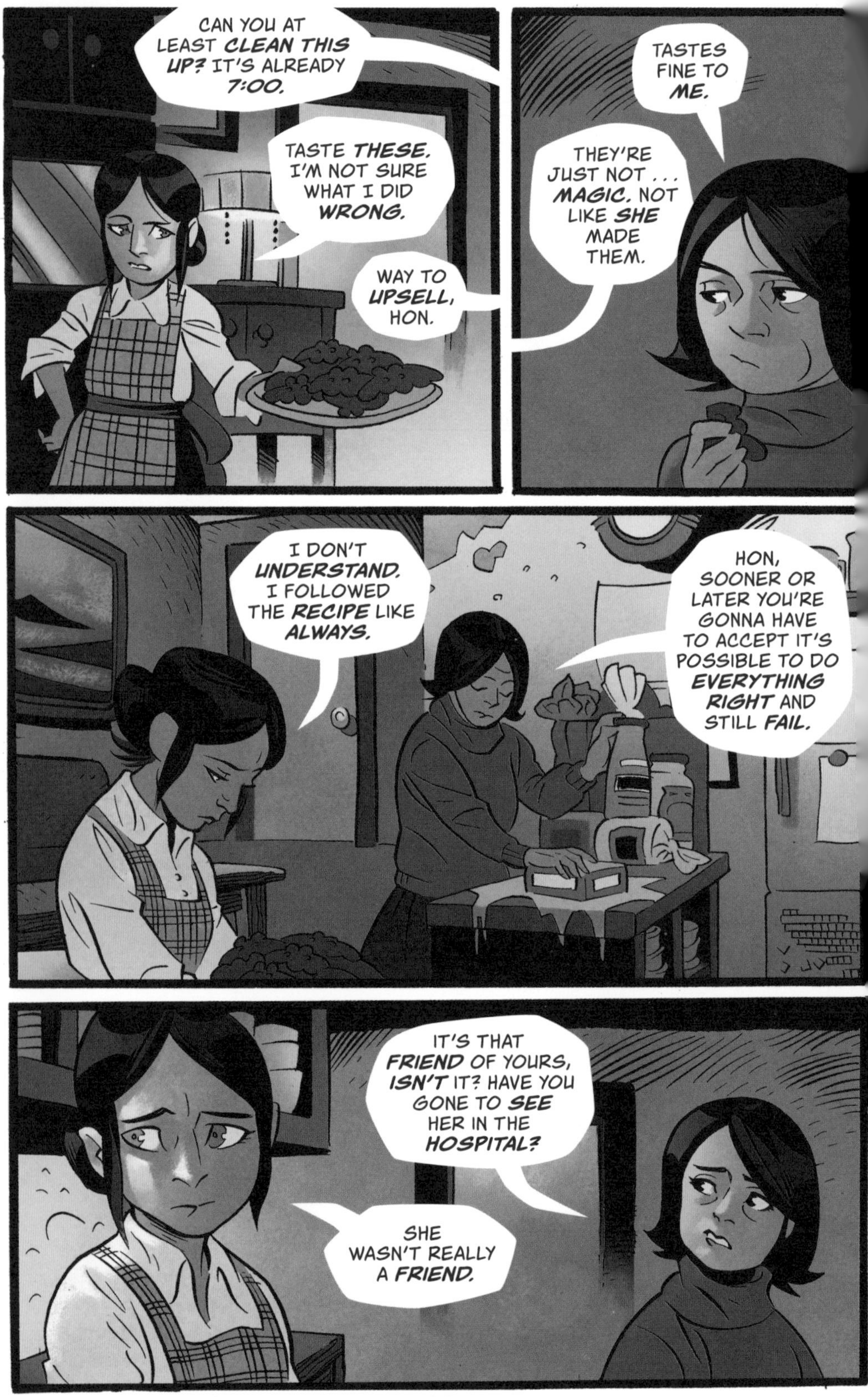
CAN YOU AT LEAST CLEAN THIS UP? IT'S ALREADY 7:00.
TASTE THESE. I'M NOT SURE WHAT I DID WRONG.
WAY TO UPSELL, HON.
TASTES FINE TO ME.
THEY'RE JUST NOT . . . MAGIC. NOT LIKE SHE MADE THEM.
I DON'T UNDERSTAND. I FOLLOWED THE RECIPE LIKE ALWAYS.
HON, SOONER OR LATER YOU'RE GONNA HAVE TO ACCEPT IT'S POSSIBLE TO DO EVERYTHING RIGHT AND STILL FAIL.
IT'S THAT FRIEND OF YOURS, ISN'T IT? HAVE YOU GONE TO SEE HER IN THE HOSPITAL?
SHE WASN'T REALLY A FRIEND.

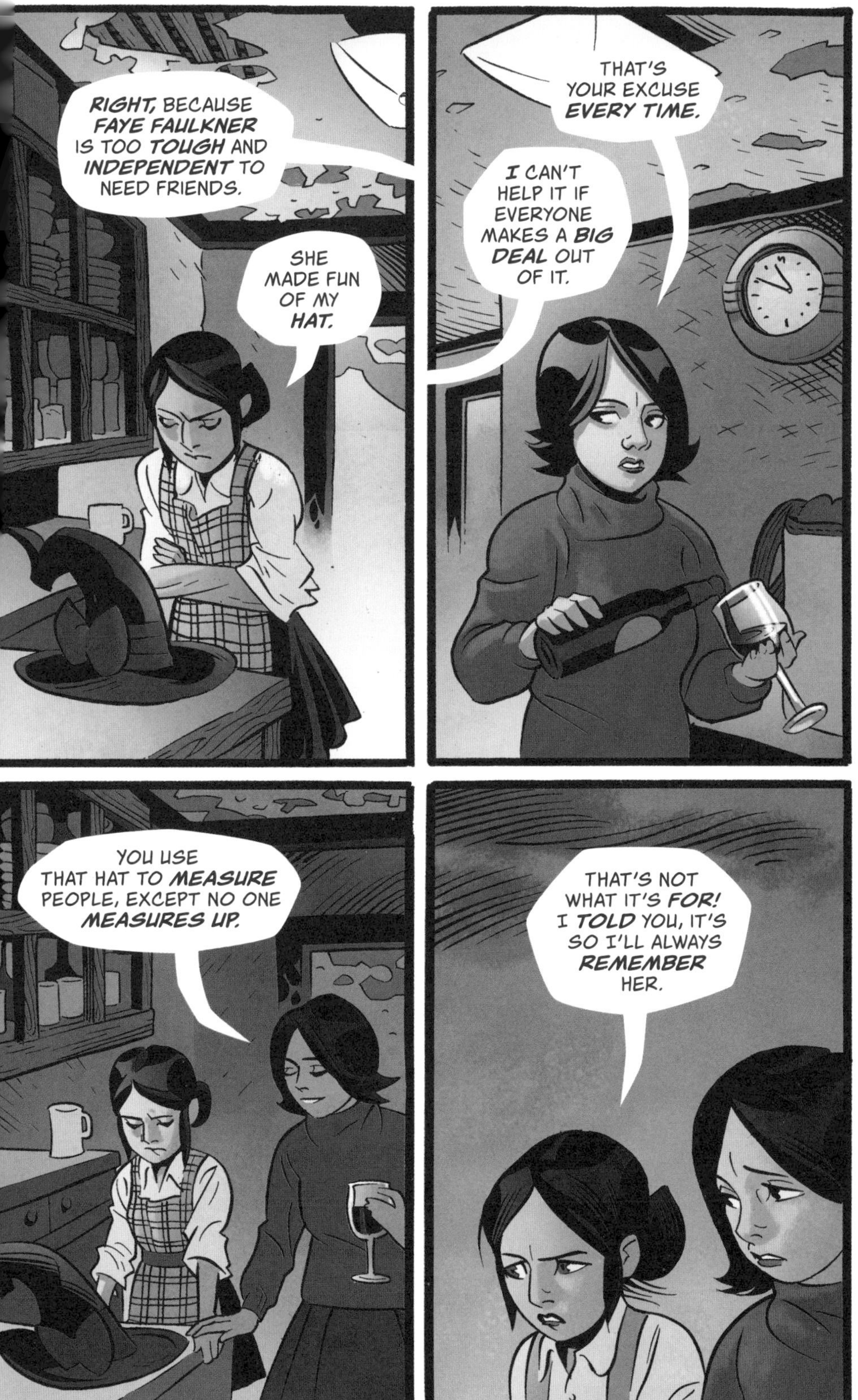
RIGHT, BECAUSE FAYE FAULKNER IS TOO TOUGH AND INDEPENDENT TO NEED FRIENDS.
SHE MADE FUN OF MY HAT.
THAT'S YOUR EXCUSE EVERY TIME.
I CAN'T HELP IT IF EVERYONE MAKES A BIG DEAL OUT OF IT.
YOU USE THAT HAT TO MEASURE PEOPLE, EXCEPT NO ONE MEASURES UP.
THAT'S NOT WHAT IT'S FOR! I TOLD YOU, IT'S SO I'LL ALWAYS REMEMBER HER.

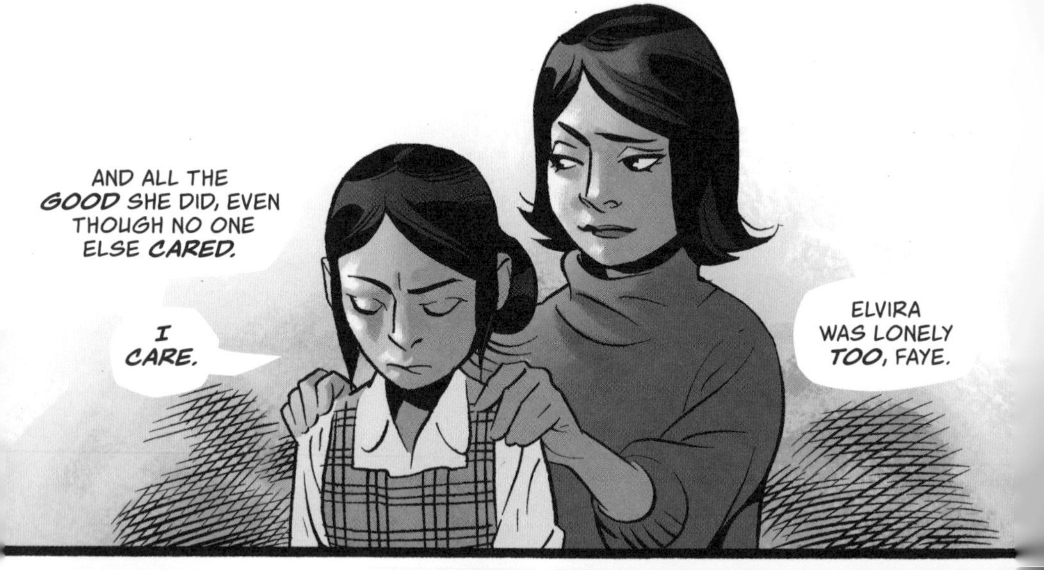
AND ALL THE GOOD SHE DID, EVEN THOUGH NO ONE ELSE CARED.
I CARE.
ELVIRA WAS LONELY TOO, FAYE.

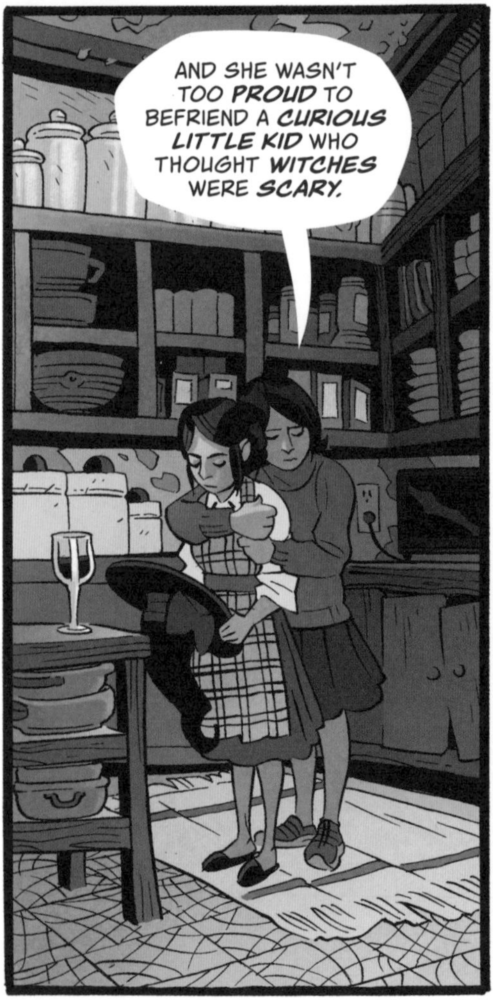
AND SHE WASN'T TOO PROUD TO BEFRIEND A CURIOUS LITTLE KID WHO THOUGHT WITCHES WERE SCARY.

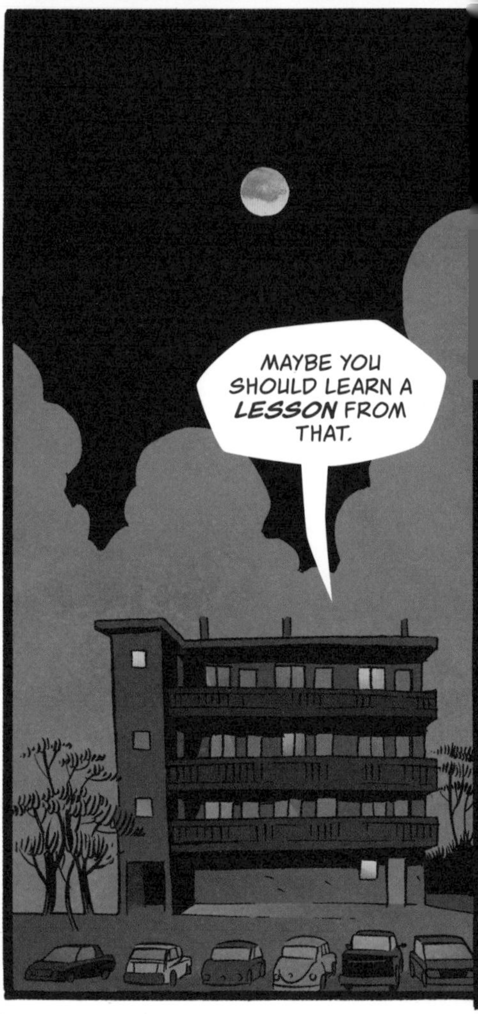
MAYBE YOU SHOULD LEARN A LESSON FROM THAT.

JÚLIO?
YOU OKAY? HAVE
YOU SEEN HER?

I . . .
I DON'T
KNOW WHAT
TO *SAY.*

HAH!
THAT'S A
FIRST.

OH GOD!
I WISH I DIDN'T
EXIST!

ST. MARY'S
HOSPITAL

EMERGENCY
ENTRANCE

TRAUMA
CENTER

CHILL OUT!
OBVIOUSLY,
CODY WOULDN'T
AGREE.

SHE
MUST *HATE*
ME!

ALL RIGHT, DRAMA BOY. LET'S *DIAL IT BACK* A LITTLE. NOBODY *HATES* YOU.

YOU HAVE NO *IDEA.* YOU WOULDN'T *BELIEVE* ME . . .

ACTUALLY . . .

. . . I'M PRETTY SURE I *WOULD.*

shy_shelbi
Kill yourself, loser.

'YOU'RE NOT THE *ONLY* ONE.

I . . . I COULDN'T *TELL* ANYBODY.

YOU DON'T KNOW WHAT IT'S *LIKE* TO FEEL THAT *ALONE.*

oh, *C'MON!* REMEMBER WHO YOU'RE *TALKING* TO?

AND YOU'RE *NOT* ALONE, OKAY?

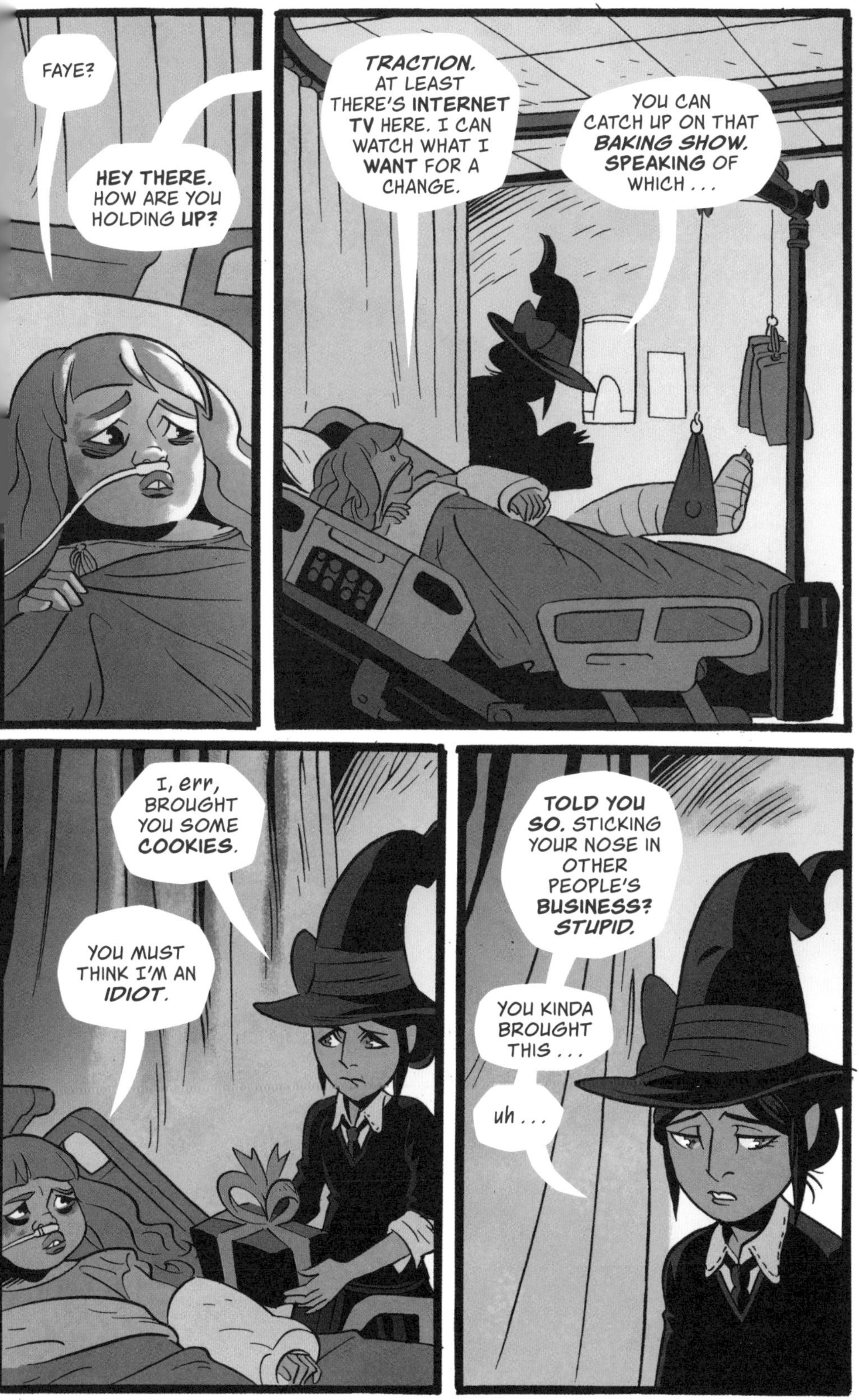
FAYE?
HEY THERE. HOW ARE YOU HOLDING UP?
TRACTION. AT LEAST THERE'S INTERNET TV HERE. I CAN WATCH WHAT I WANT FOR A CHANGE.
YOU CAN CATCH UP ON THAT BAKING SHOW. SPEAKING OF WHICH . . .
I, err, BROUGHT YOU SOME COOKIES.
YOU MUST THINK I'M AN IDIOT.
TOLD YOU SO. STICKING YOUR NOSE IN OTHER PEOPLE'S BUSINESS? STUPID.
YOU KINDA BROUGHT THIS . . .
uh . . .

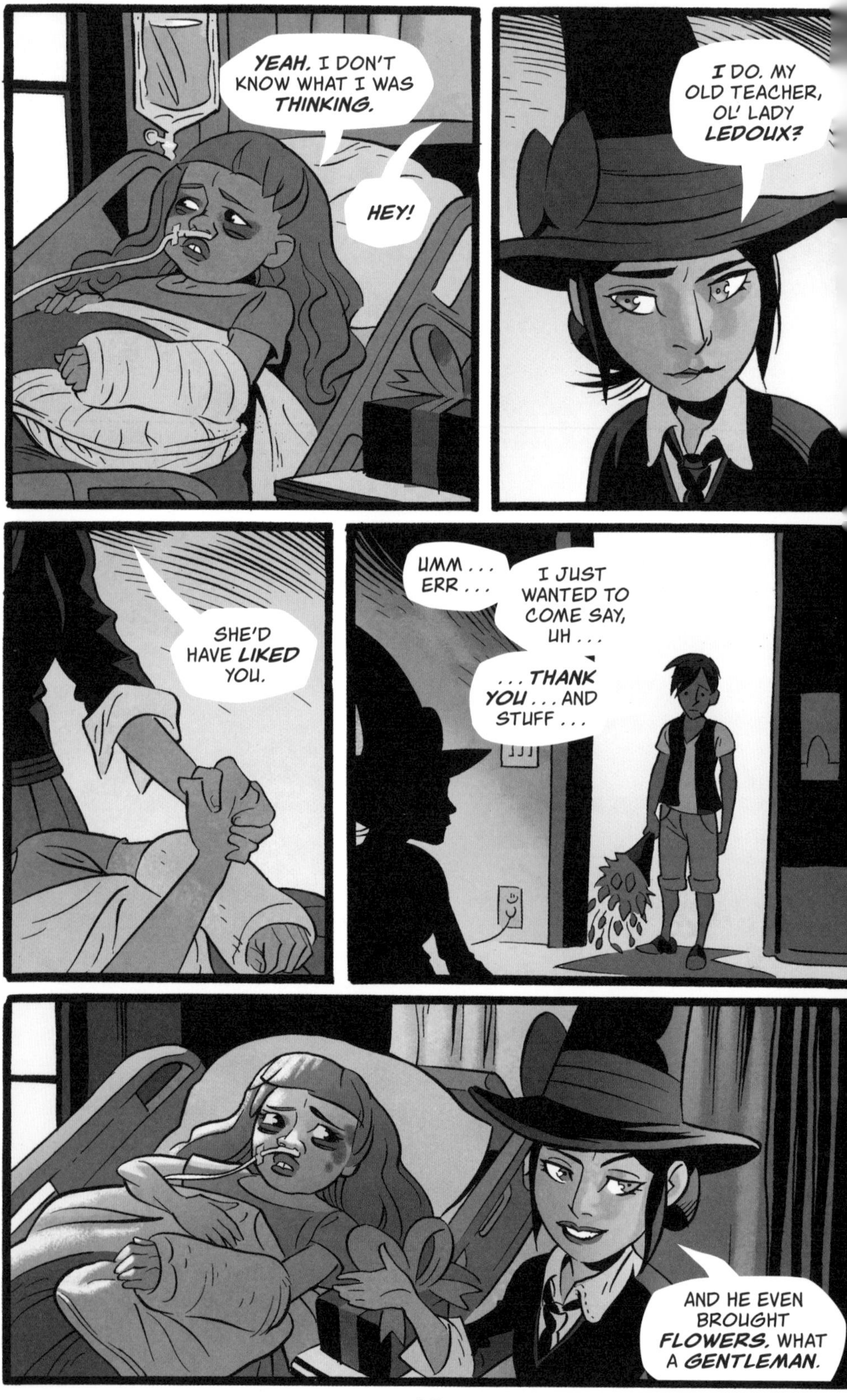
YEAH. I DON'T KNOW WHAT I WAS THINKING.
HEY!
I DO. MY OLD TEACHER, OL' LADY LEDOUX?
SHE'D HAVE LIKED YOU.
UMM . . . ERR . . .
I JUST WANTED TO COME SAY, UH . . .
. . . THANK YOU . . . AND STUFF . . .
AND HE EVEN BROUGHT FLOWERS. WHAT A GENTLEMAN.

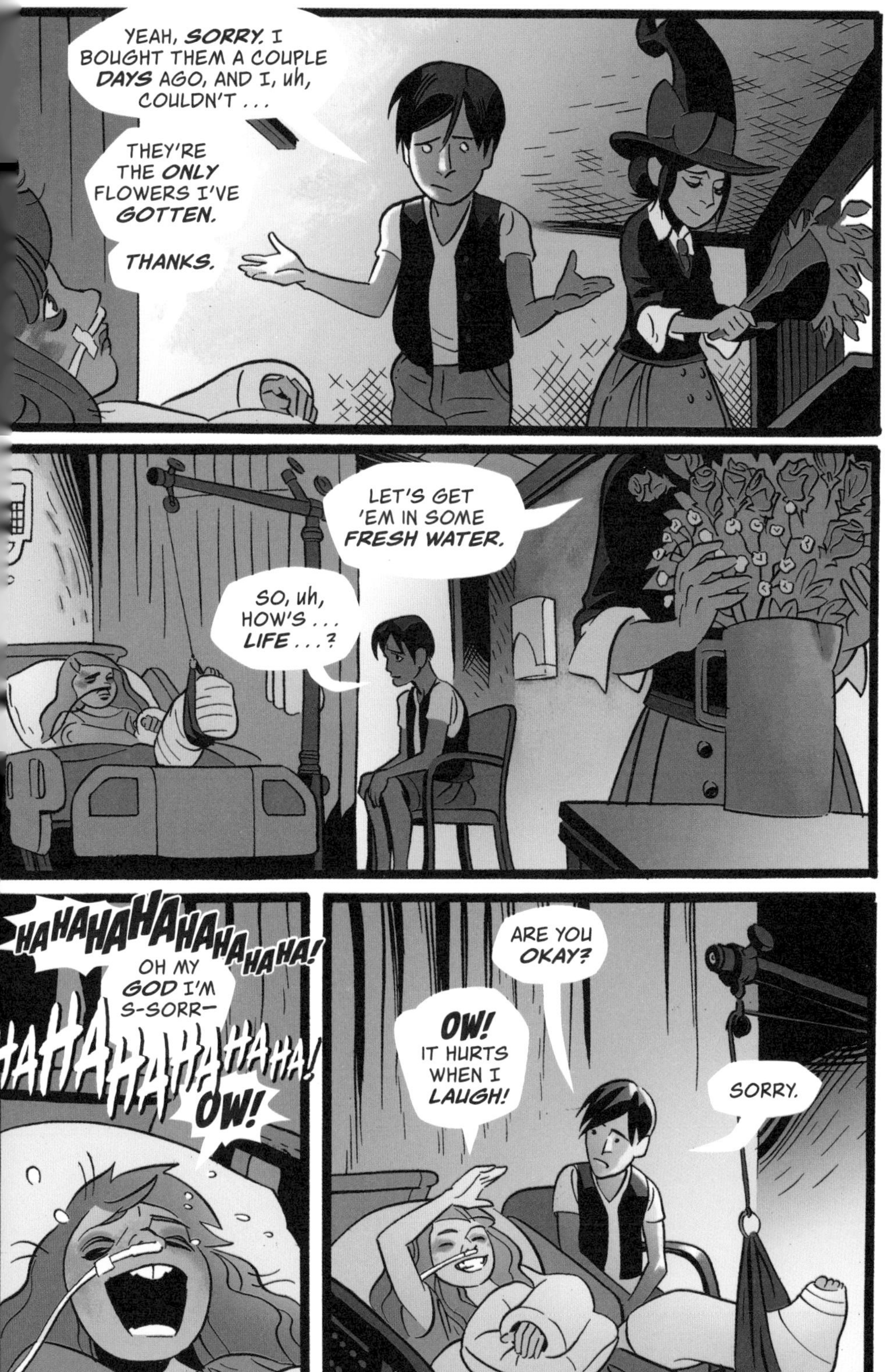
YEAH, SORRY. I BOUGHT THEM A COUPLE DAYS AGO, AND I, uh, COULDN'T . . .
THEY'RE THE ONLY FLOWERS I'VE GOTTEN.
THANKS.
LET'S GET 'EM IN SOME FRESH WATER.
SO, uh, HOW'S . . . LIFE . . . ?
HAHAHAHAHAHAHAHAHA!
OH MY GOD I'M S-SORR—
HAHAHAHAHAHAHAHA!
OW!
ARE YOU OKAY?
OW! IT HURTS WHEN I LAUGH!
SORRY.

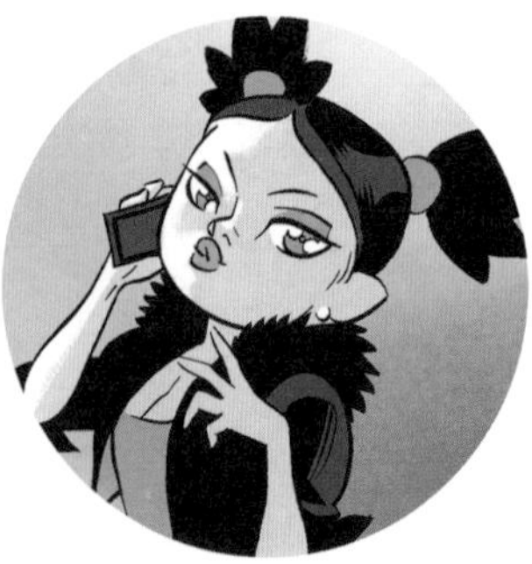

the shy_shelbi program

Step 5: Alphas Don't Run in Packs

The higher you climb, the more people will drag you dow trying to ride your coattails. Cut them loose. It's lonely at the top, but the view is worth it. Step 5, there's only one first place. Make sure it's yours . . . more

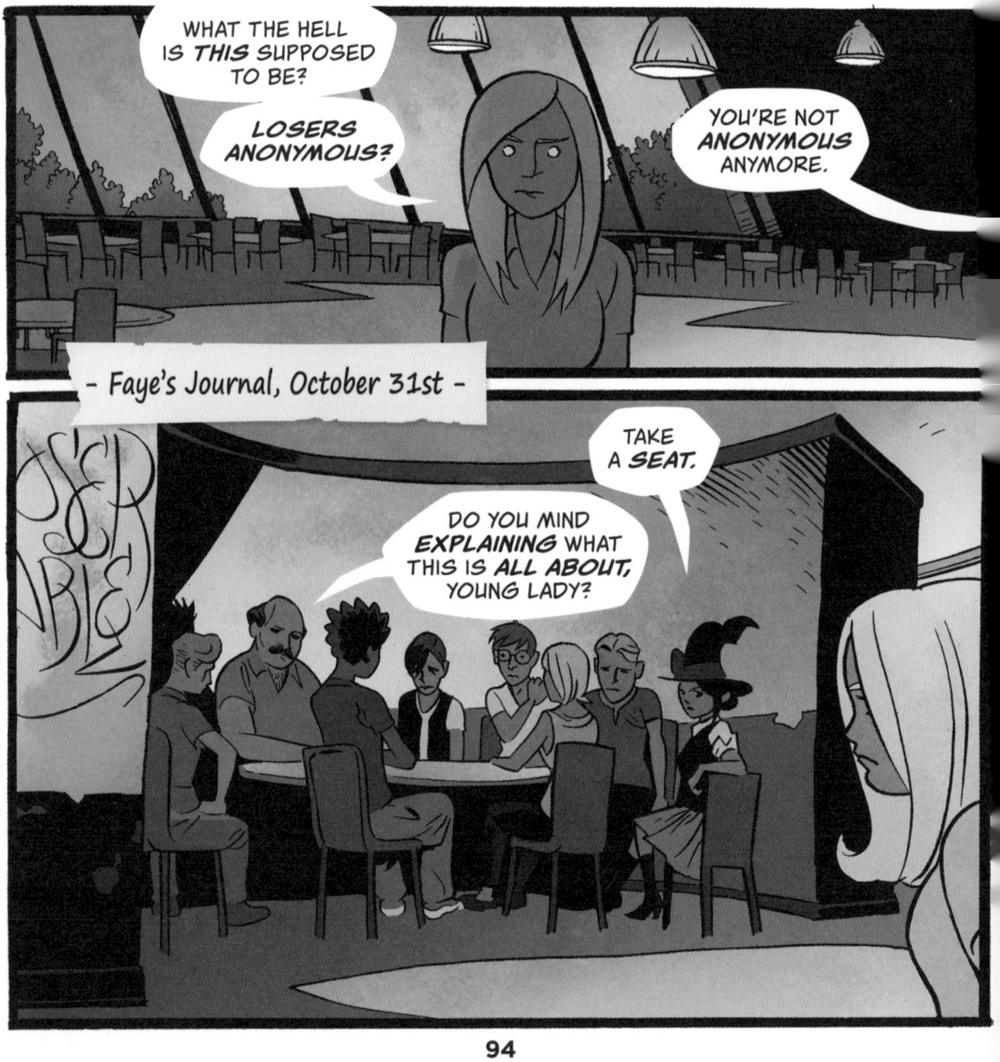

WHAT THE HELL IS *THIS* SUPPOSED TO BE?
LOSERS ANONYMOUS?
YOU'RE NOT *ANONYMOUS* ANYMORE.
- Faye's Journal, October 31st -
TAKE A *SEAT.*
DO YOU MIND *EXPLAINING* WHAT THIS IS *ALL ABOUT,* YOUNG LADY?

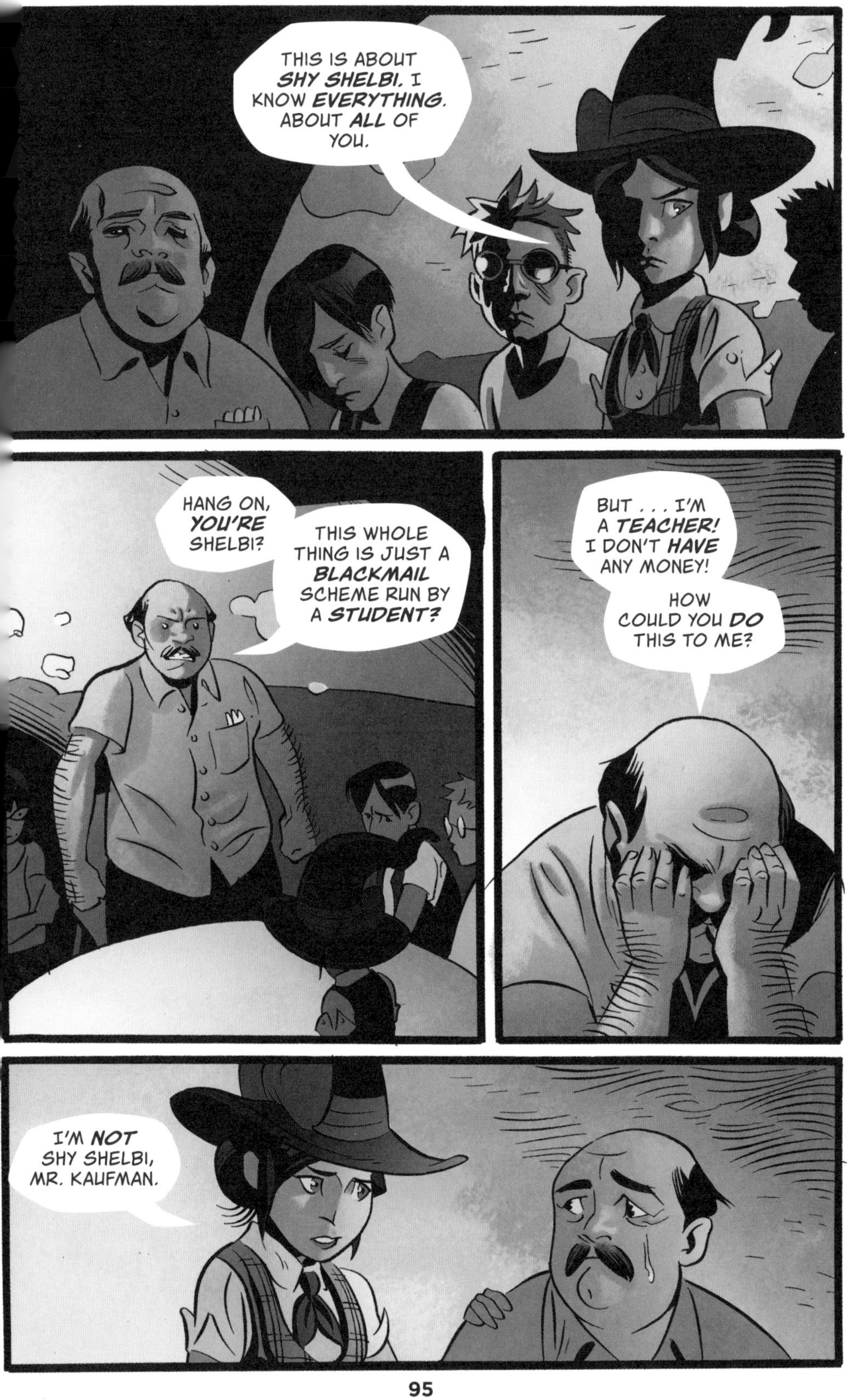

THIS IS ABOUT SHY SHELBI. I KNOW EVERYTHING. ABOUT ALL OF YOU.
HANG ON, YOU'RE SHELBI?
THIS WHOLE THING IS JUST A BLACKMAIL SCHEME RUN BY A STUDENT?
BUT . . . I'M A TEACHER! I DON'T HAVE ANY MONEY!
HOW COULD YOU DO THIS TO ME?
I'M NOT SHY SHELBI, MR. KAUFMAN.

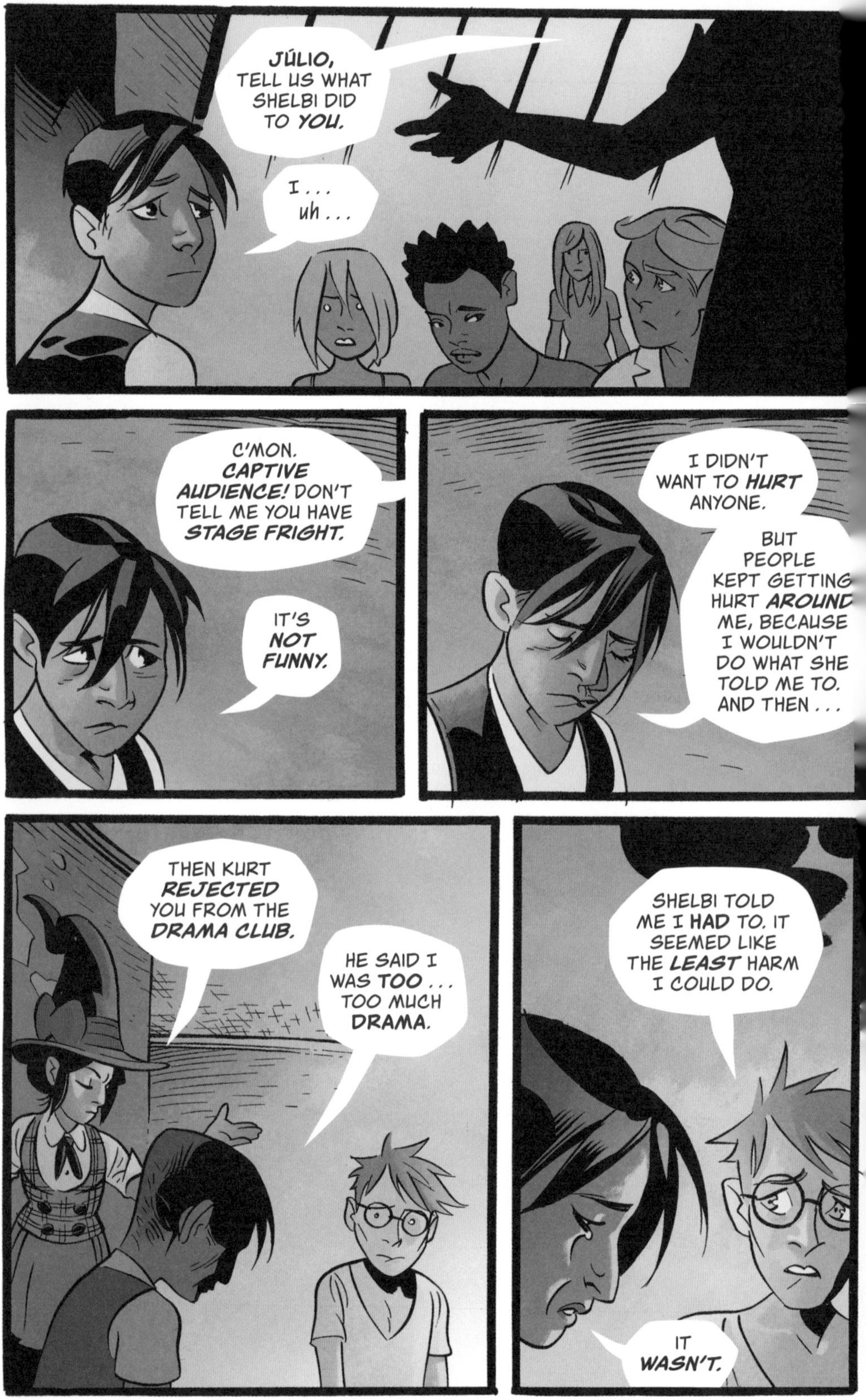
JÚLIO, TELL US WHAT SHELBI DID TO YOU.
I . . . uh . . .
C'MON. CAPTIVE AUDIENCE! DON'T TELL ME YOU HAVE STAGE FRIGHT.
IT'S NOT FUNNY.
I DIDN'T WANT TO HURT ANYONE.
BUT PEOPLE KEPT GETTING HURT AROUND ME, BECAUSE I WOULDN'T DO WHAT SHE TOLD ME TO. AND THEN . . .
THEN KURT REJECTED YOU FROM THE DRAMA CLUB.
HE SAID I WAS TOO . . . TOO MUCH DRAMA.
SHELBI TOLD ME I HAD TO. IT SEEMED LIKE THE LEAST HARM I COULD DO.
IT WASN'T.

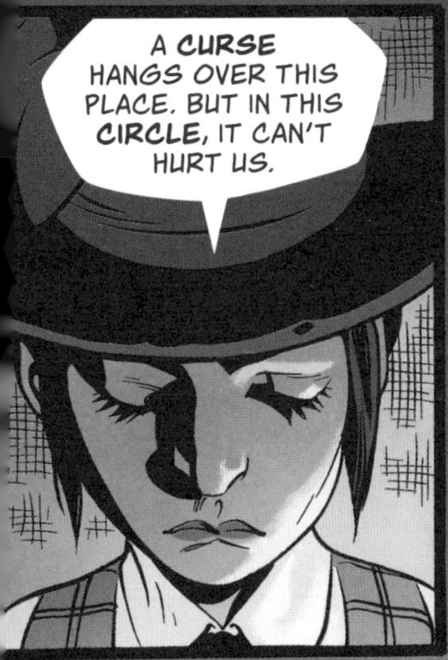
A CURSE HANGS OVER THIS PLACE. BUT IN THIS CIRCLE, IT CAN'T HURT US.
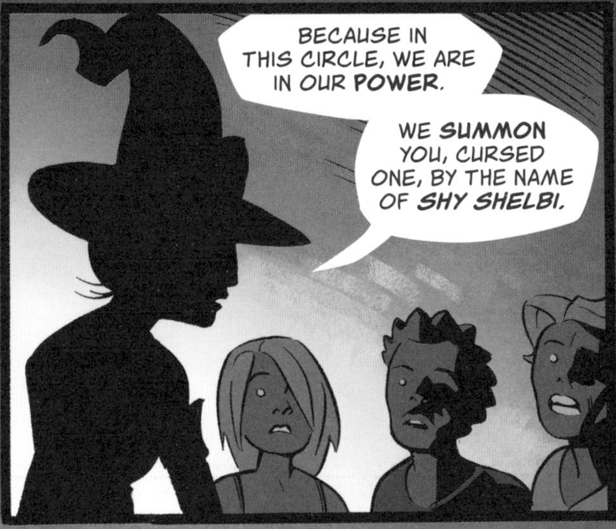
BECAUSE IN THIS CIRCLE, WE ARE IN OUR POWER.
WE SUMMON YOU, CURSED ONE, BY THE NAME OF SHY SHELBI.
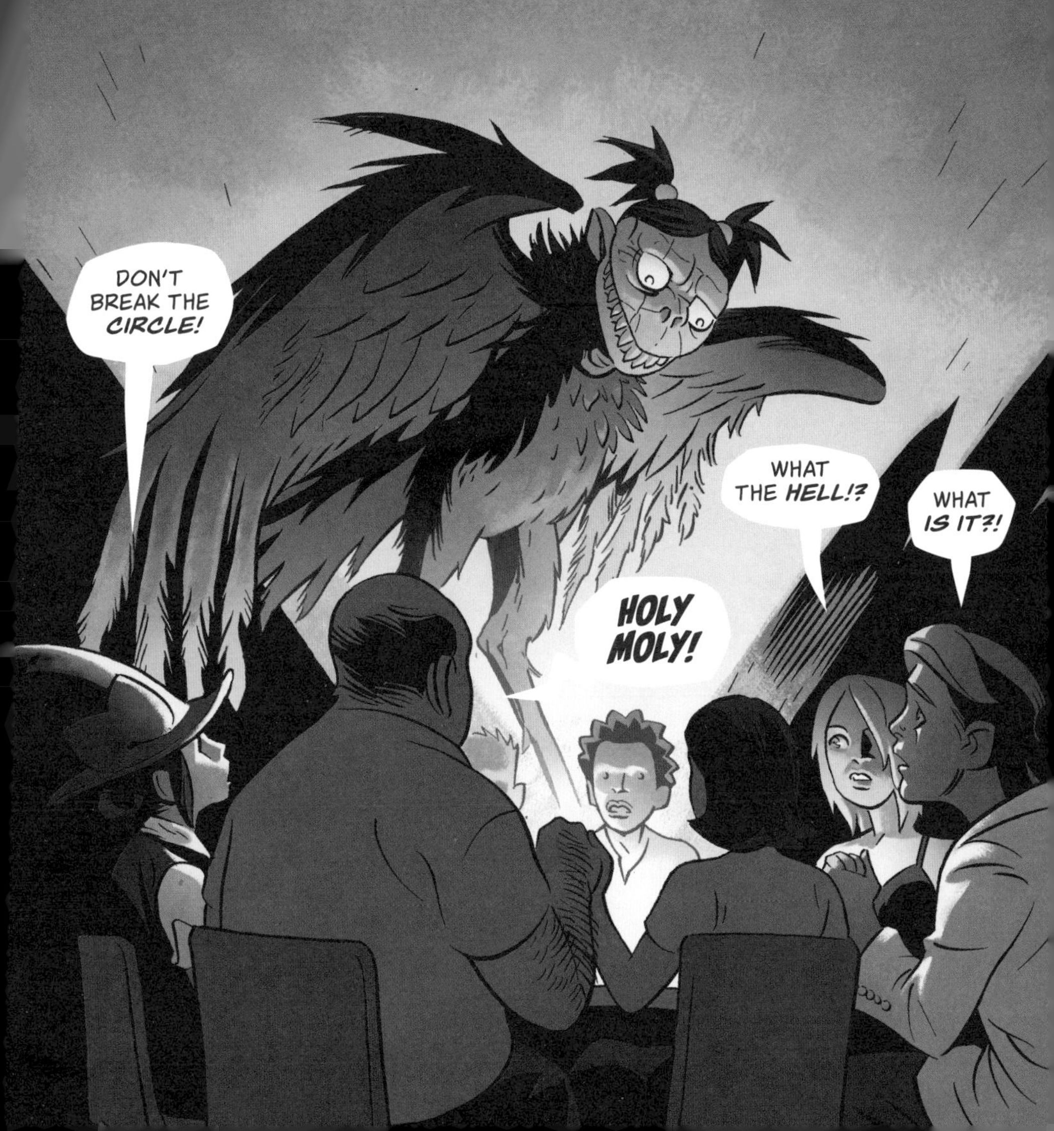
DON'T BREAK THE CIRCLE!
WHAT THE HELL!?
WHAT IS IT?!
HOLY MOLY!

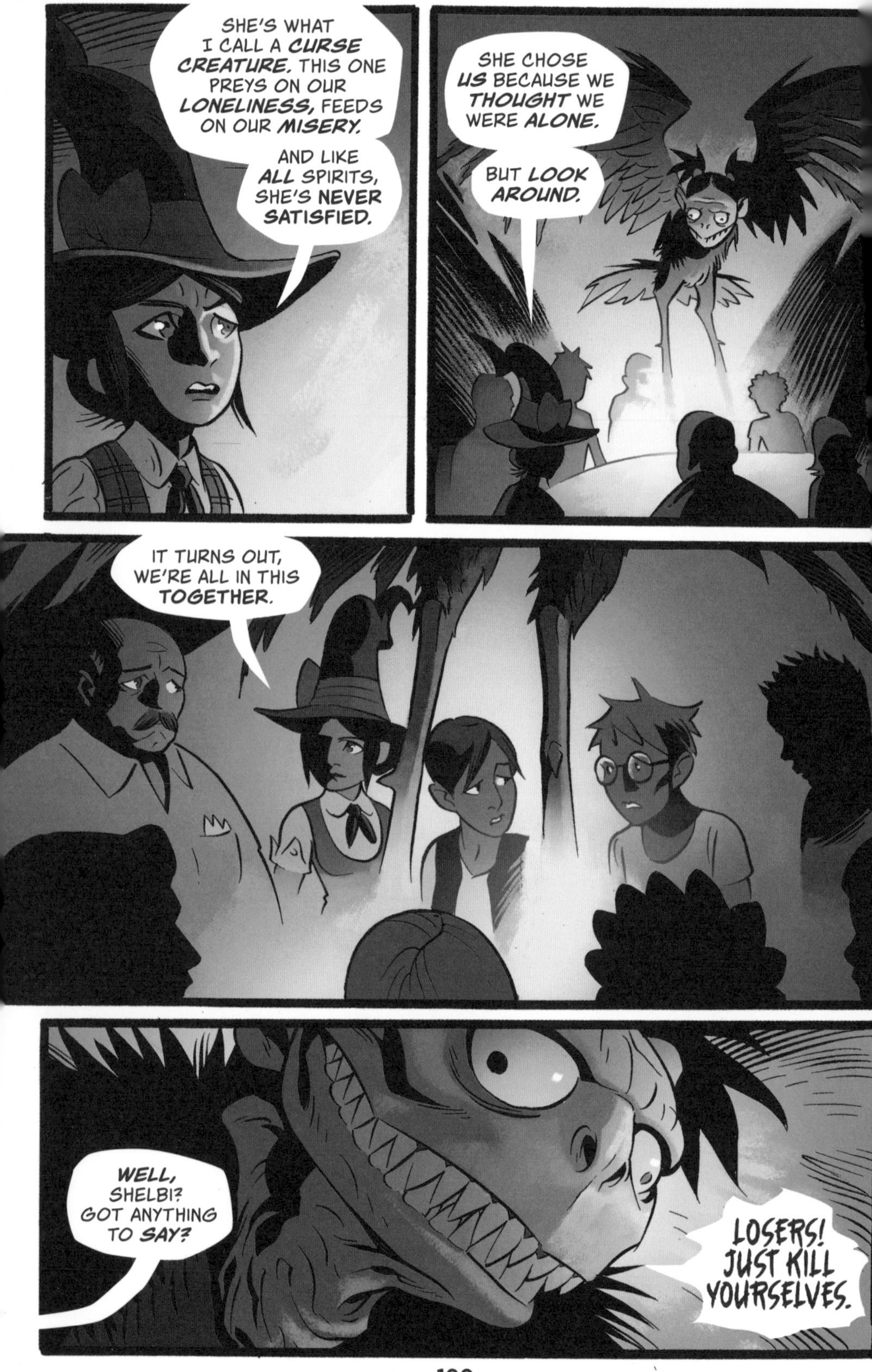
SHE'S WHAT I CALL A CURSE CREATURE. THIS ONE PREYS ON OUR LONELINESS, FEEDS ON OUR MISERY.
AND LIKE ALL SPIRITS, SHE'S NEVER SATISFIED.
SHE CHOSE US BECAUSE WE THOUGHT WE WERE ALONE.
BUT LOOK AROUND.
IT TURNS OUT, WE'RE ALL IN THIS TOGETHER.
WELL, SHELBI? GOT ANYTHING TO SAY?
LOSERS! JUST KILL YOURSELVES.

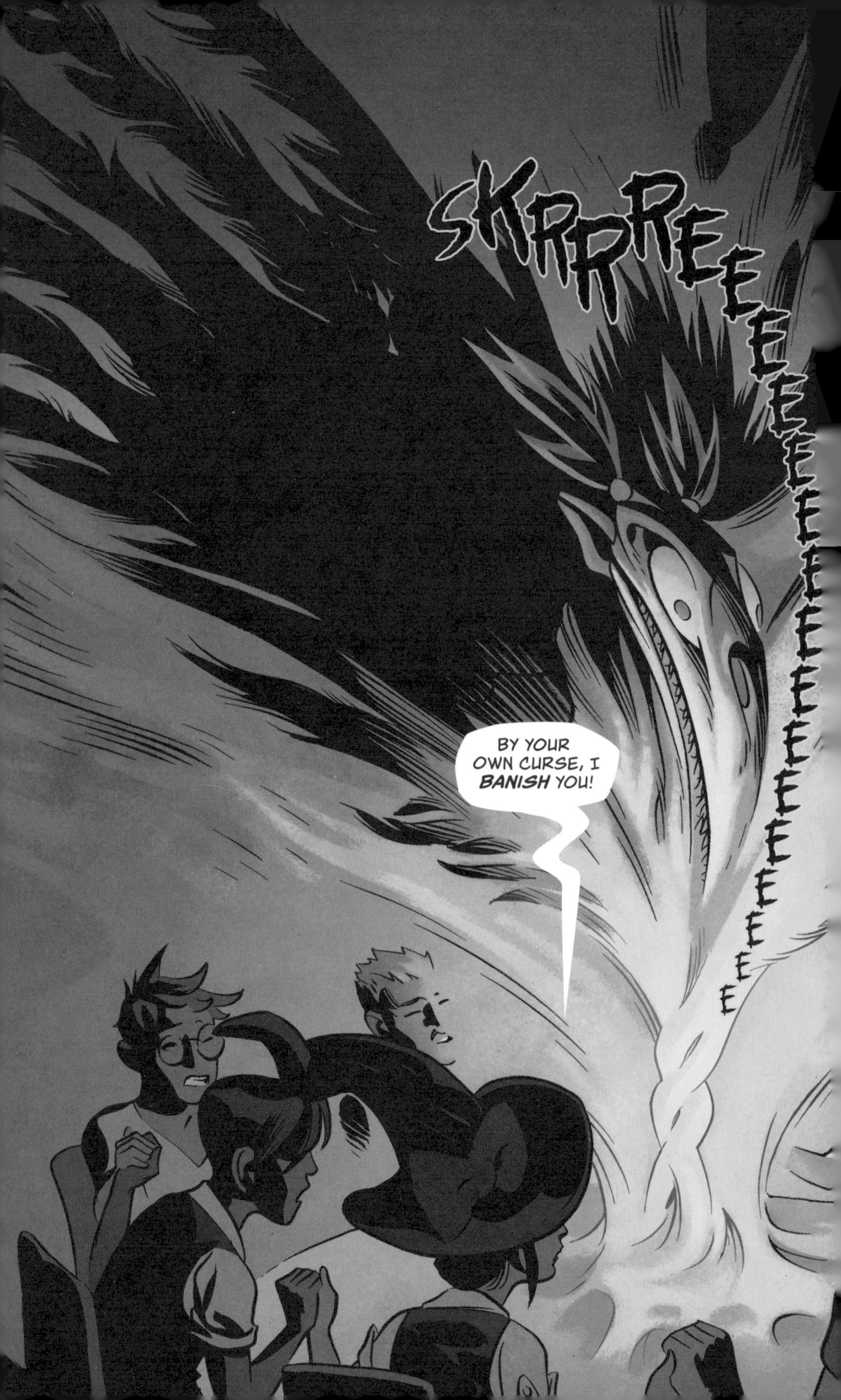
SKRRREEEEEEEEEEEEEEEEE
BY YOUR OWN CURSE, I *BANISH* YOU!

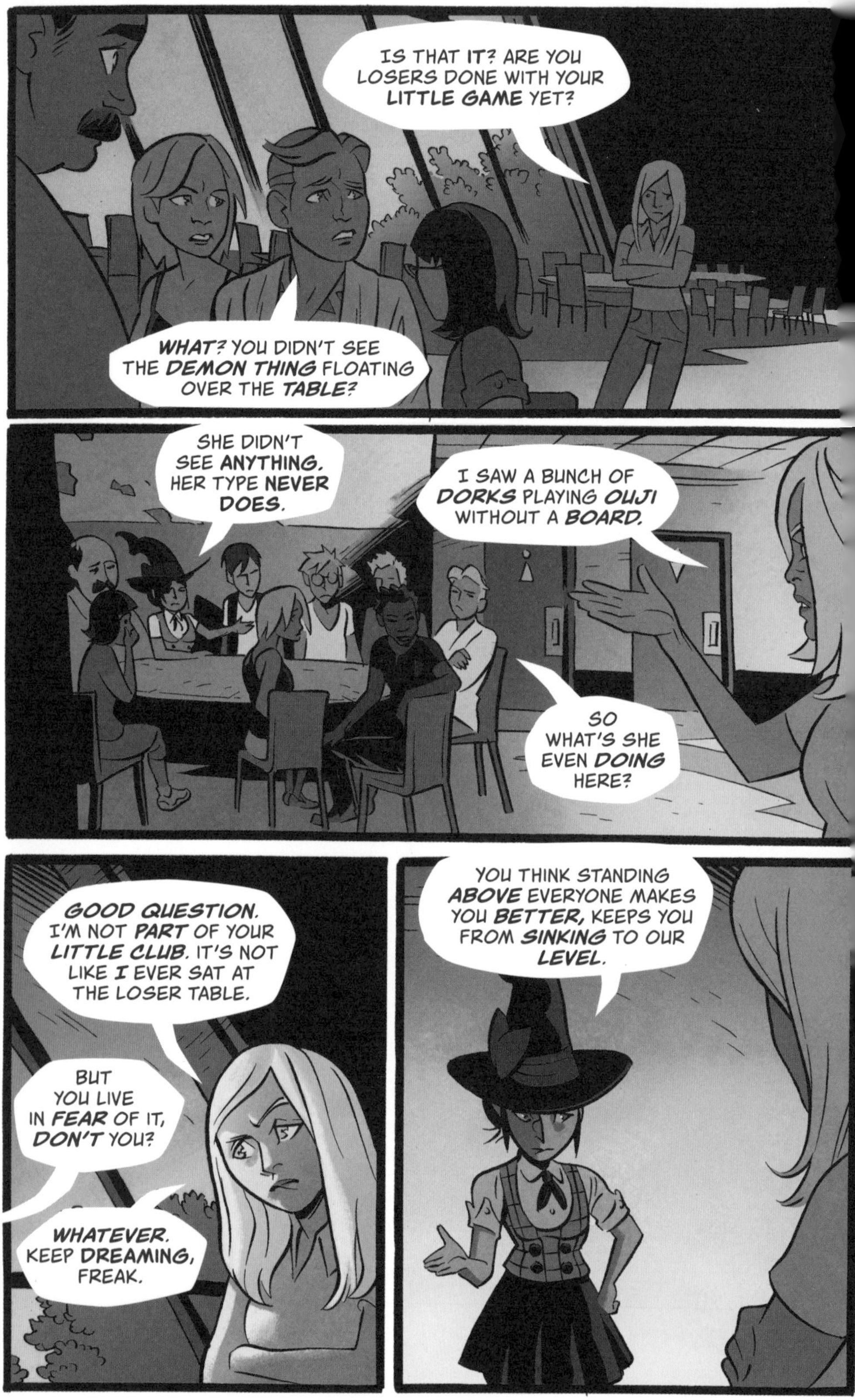

IS THAT IT? ARE YOU LOSERS DONE WITH YOUR LITTLE GAME YET?
WHAT? YOU DIDN'T SEE THE DEMON THING FLOATING OVER THE TABLE?
SHE DIDN'T SEE ANYTHING. HER TYPE NEVER DOES.
I SAW A BUNCH OF DORKS PLAYING OUJI WITHOUT A BOARD.
SO WHAT'S SHE EVEN DOING HERE?
GOOD QUESTION. I'M NOT PART OF YOUR LITTLE CLUB. IT'S NOT LIKE I EVER SAT AT THE LOSER TABLE.
BUT YOU LIVE IN FEAR OF IT, DON'T YOU?
WHATEVER. KEEP DREAMING, FREAK.
YOU THINK STANDING ABOVE EVERYONE MAKES YOU BETTER, KEEPS YOU FROM SINKING TO OUR LEVEL.

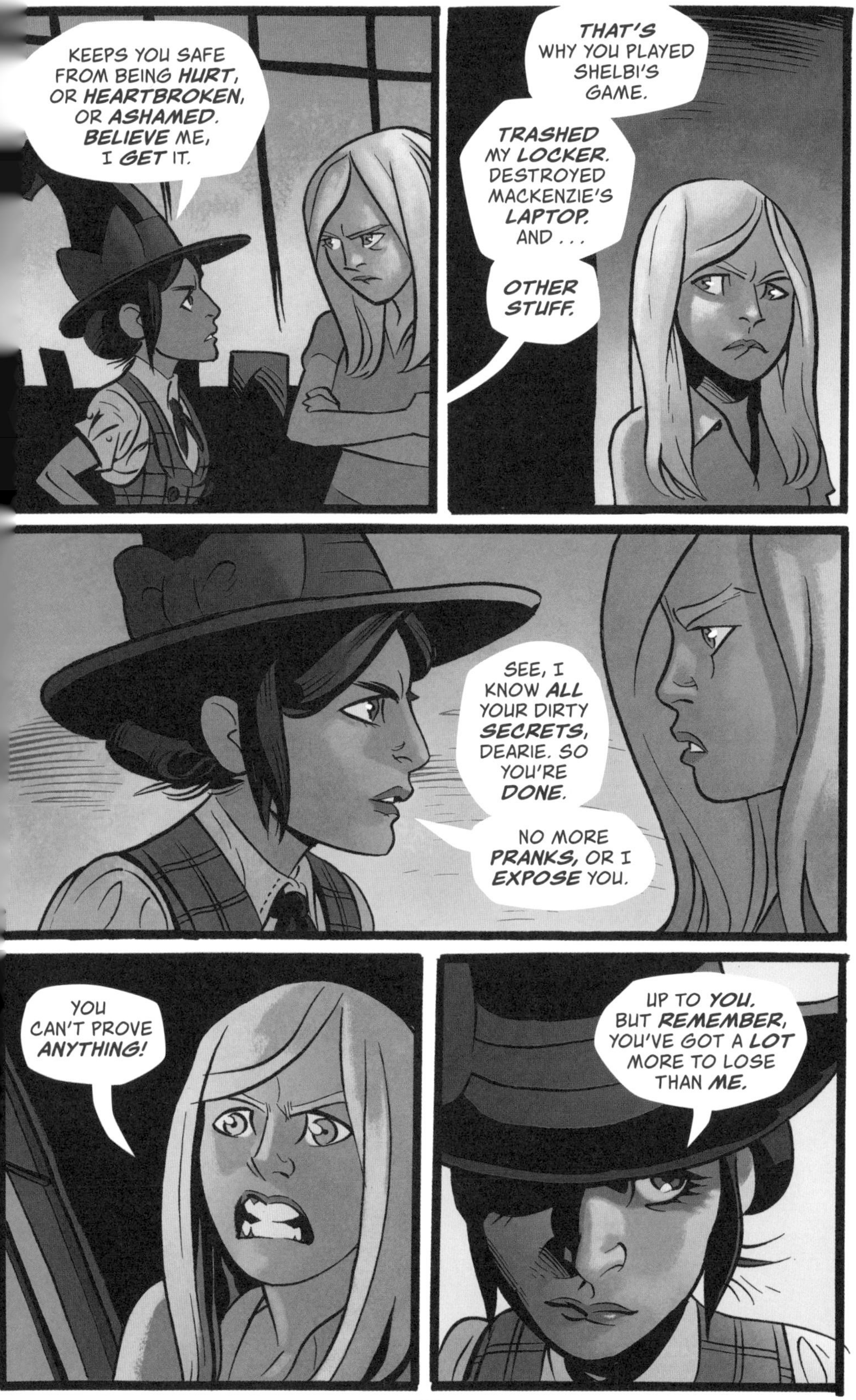
KEEPS YOU SAFE FROM BEING HURT, OR HEARTBROKEN, OR ASHAMED. BELIEVE ME, I GET IT.
THAT'S WHY YOU PLAYED SHELBI'S GAME.
TRASHED MY LOCKER. DESTROYED MACKENZIE'S LAPTOP. AND . . .
OTHER STUFF.
SEE, I KNOW ALL YOUR DIRTY SECRETS, DEARIE. SO YOU'RE DONE.
NO MORE PRANKS, OR I EXPOSE YOU.
YOU CAN'T PROVE ANYTHING!
UP TO YOU. BUT REMEMBER, YOU'VE GOT A LOT MORE TO LOSE THAN ME.

WE **FEW,** WE **HAPPY** FEW, WE BAND OF **BROTHERS** . . .

FOR HE TO-DAY THAT SHEDS HIS **BLOOD** WITH ME SHALL **BE MY BROTHER—**

- Faye's Journal, November 1st -

OR **SISTER!**

THAT'S JUST HOW IT WAS **WRITTEN,** STEF.

AND GENTLEMEN IN ENGLAND NOW A-BED SHALL THINK THEMSELVES **ACCURSED** THEY WERE NOT HERE . . .

AND HOLD THEIR MANHOODS **CHEAP** WHILST **ANY SPEAKS** THAT FOUGHT WITH **US** . . .

I'd gotten so used to it, so used to having no one . . .

WELL, IF YOU GUYS WANT TO **STAGE** THIS, WE NEED TO **DISCUSS** SOME THINGS.

HE'S **NOT BAD,** THOUGH. SMUG LITTLE **TWERP.**

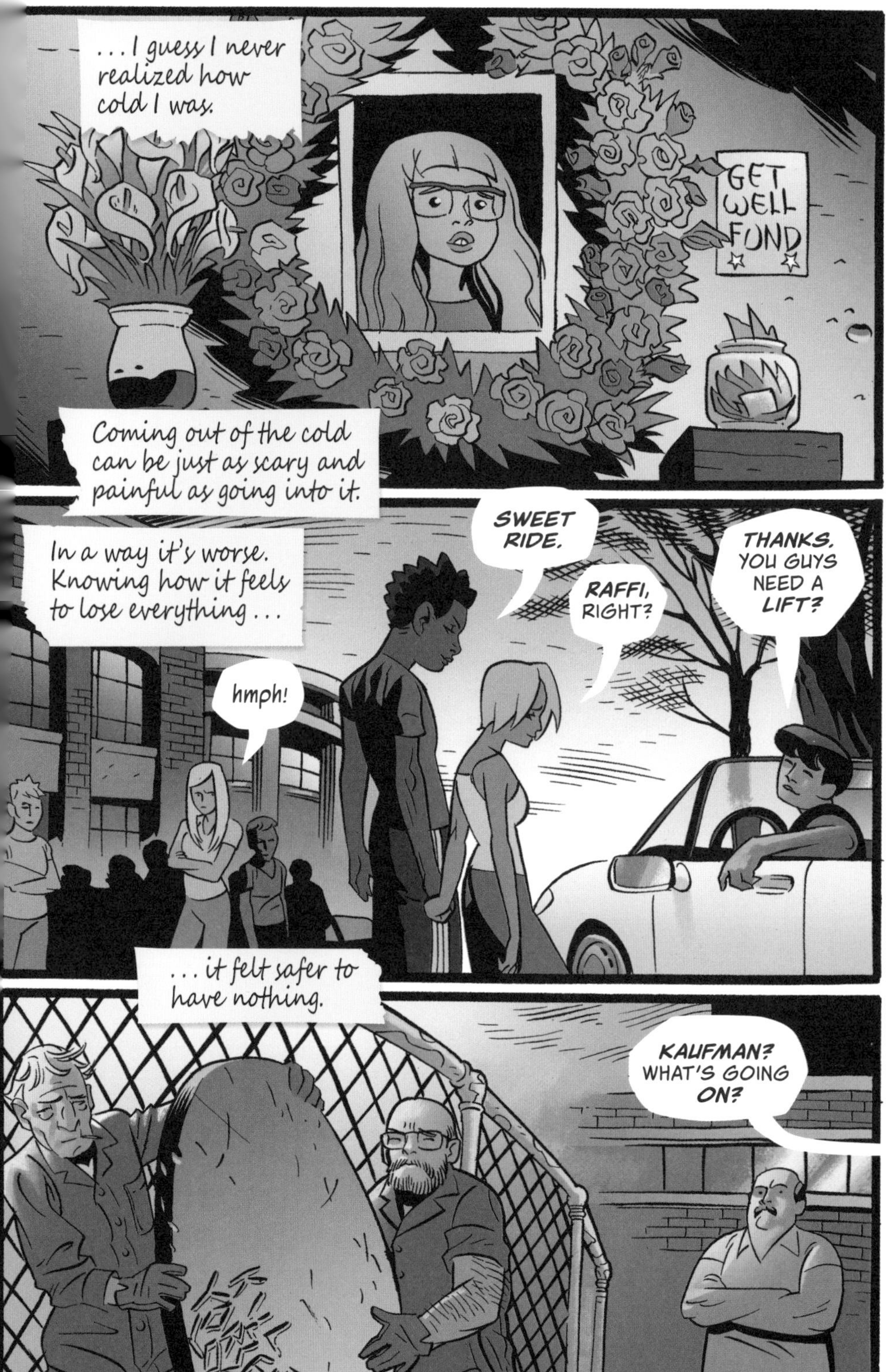
. . . I guess I never realized how cold I was.
GET WELL FUND
Coming out of the cold can be just as scary and painful as going into it.
In a way it's worse. Knowing how it feels to lose everything . . .
SWEET RIDE.
RAFFI, RIGHT?
THANKS. YOU GUYS NEED A LIFT?
hmph!
. . . it felt safer to have nothing.
KAUFMAN? WHAT'S GOING ON?

IT WAS *YOU*, huh? THIS IS MY *SHOCKED* FACE.

MY DAD HAS A LOTTA *PULL* ON THE *SCHOOL BOARD*.

SO I GUESS I'LL SEE YOU *AROUND*. OR MAYBE *NOT*.

IT'S FOR THE *BEST*, I SUPPOSE. A *SCAPEGOAT* MEANS *SHY SHELBI* LOSES ANY LINGERING *MYSTIQUE*. ONE MORE *NAIL* IN HER *COFFIN*.

BUT HERE'S THE THING ABOUT CALLING SOMEONE'S *BLUFF*, BRYCE.

SATAN'S LITTLE HELPER

SLAM

YOU BETTER BE *DAMN* SURE THEY'RE *BLUFFING*.

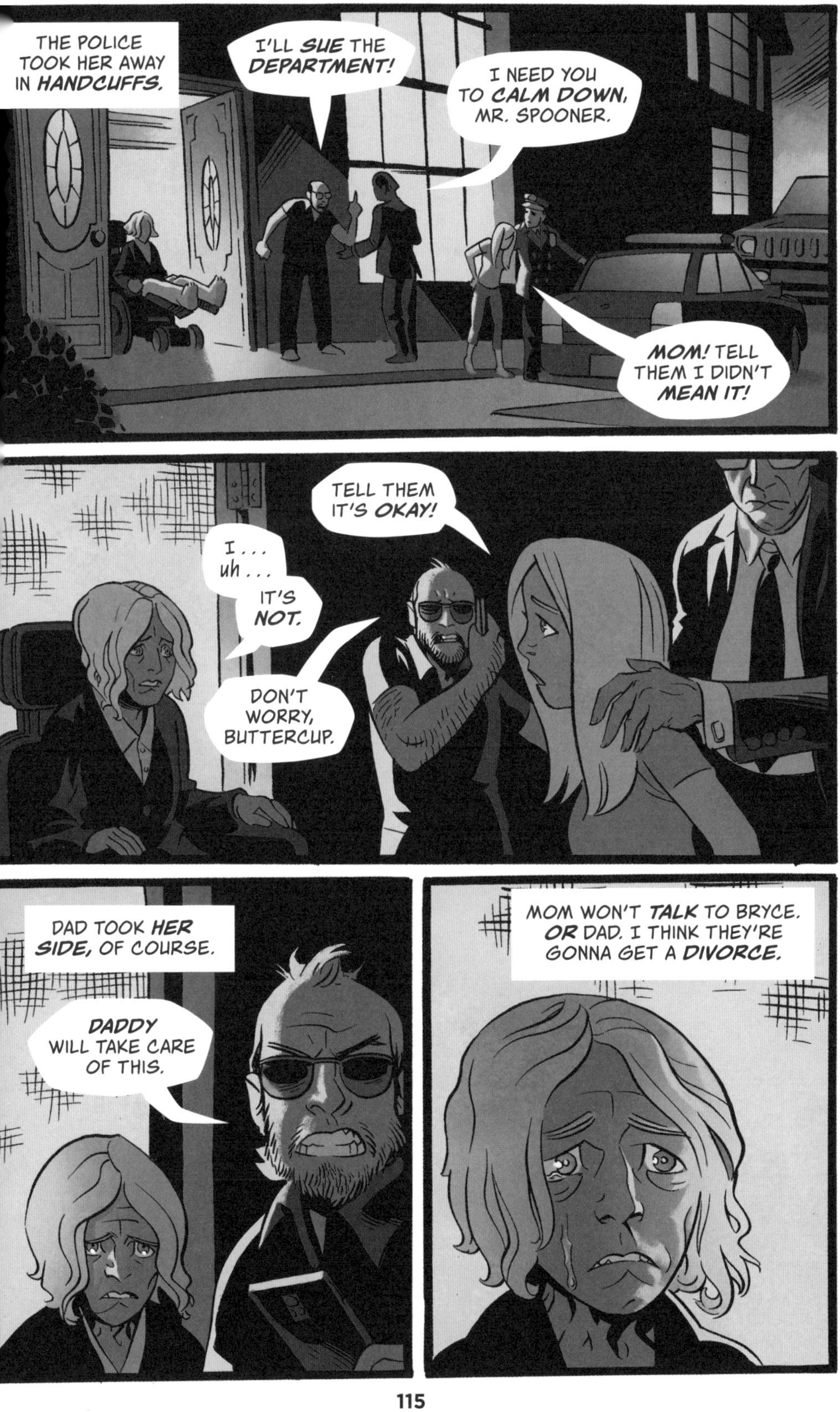
THE POLICE TOOK HER AWAY IN HANDCUFFS.
I'LL SUE THE DEPARTMENT!
I NEED YOU TO CALM DOWN, MR. SPOONER.
MOM! TELL THEM I DIDN'T MEAN IT!
TELL THEM IT'S OKAY!
I . . . uh . . .
IT'S NOT.
DON'T WORRY, BUTTERCUP.
DAD TOOK HER SIDE, OF COURSE.
DADDY WILL TAKE CARE OF THIS.
MOM WON'T TALK TO BRYCE. OR DAD. I THINK THEY'RE GONNA GET A DIVORCE.

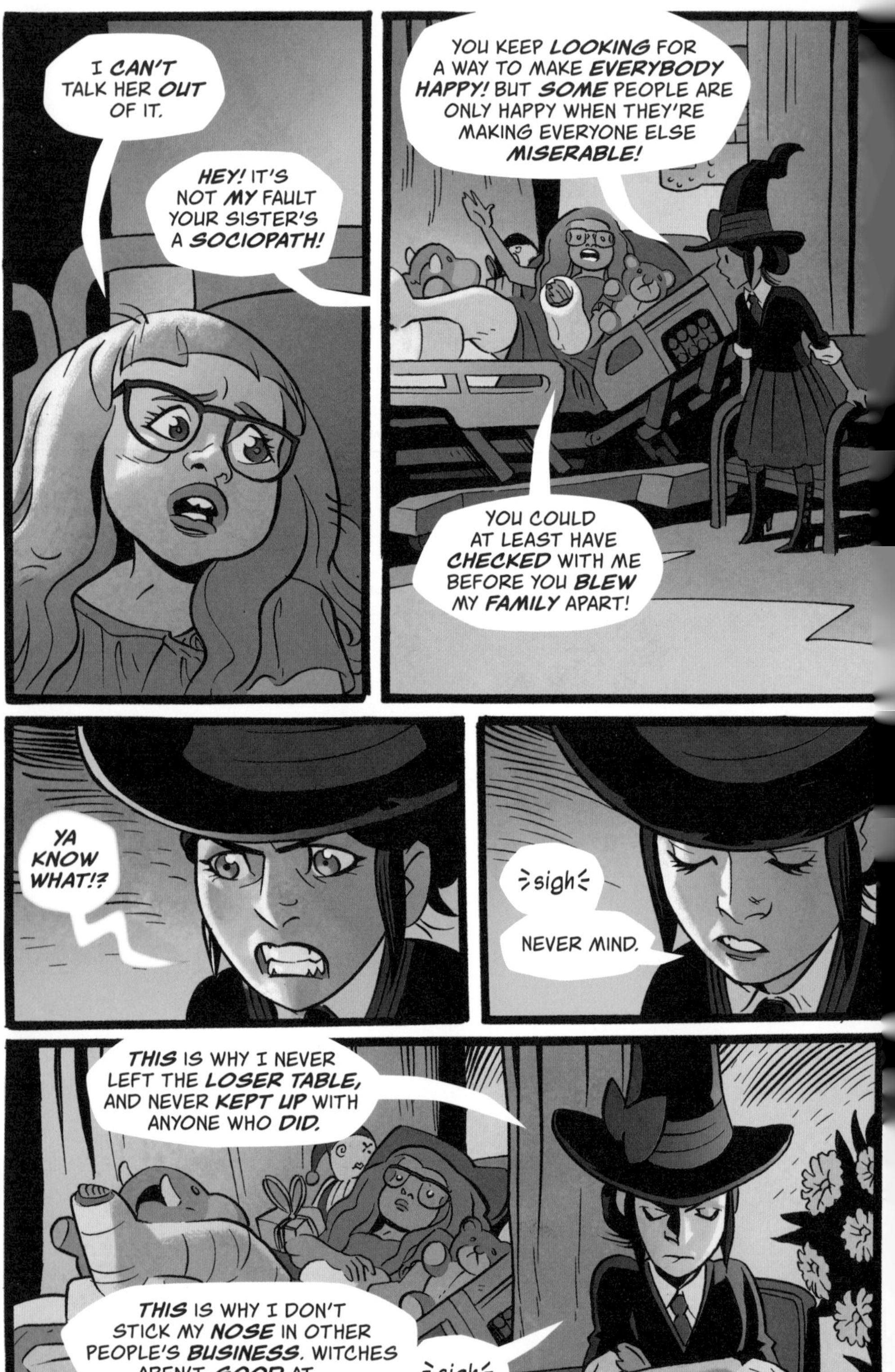

I CAN'T TALK HER OUT OF IT.
HEY! IT'S NOT MY FAULT YOUR SISTER'S A SOCIOPATH!
YOU KEEP LOOKING FOR A WAY TO MAKE EVERYBODY HAPPY! BUT SOME PEOPLE ARE ONLY HAPPY WHEN THEY'RE MAKING EVERYONE ELSE MISERABLE!
YOU COULD AT LEAST HAVE CHECKED WITH ME BEFORE YOU BLEW MY FAMILY APART!
YA KNOW WHAT!?
sigh
NEVER MIND.
THIS IS WHY I NEVER LEFT THE LOSER TABLE, AND NEVER KEPT UP WITH ANYONE WHO DID.
THIS IS WHY I DON'T STICK MY NOSE IN OTHER PEOPLE'S BUSINESS. WITCHES AREN'T GOOD AT . . .
sigh

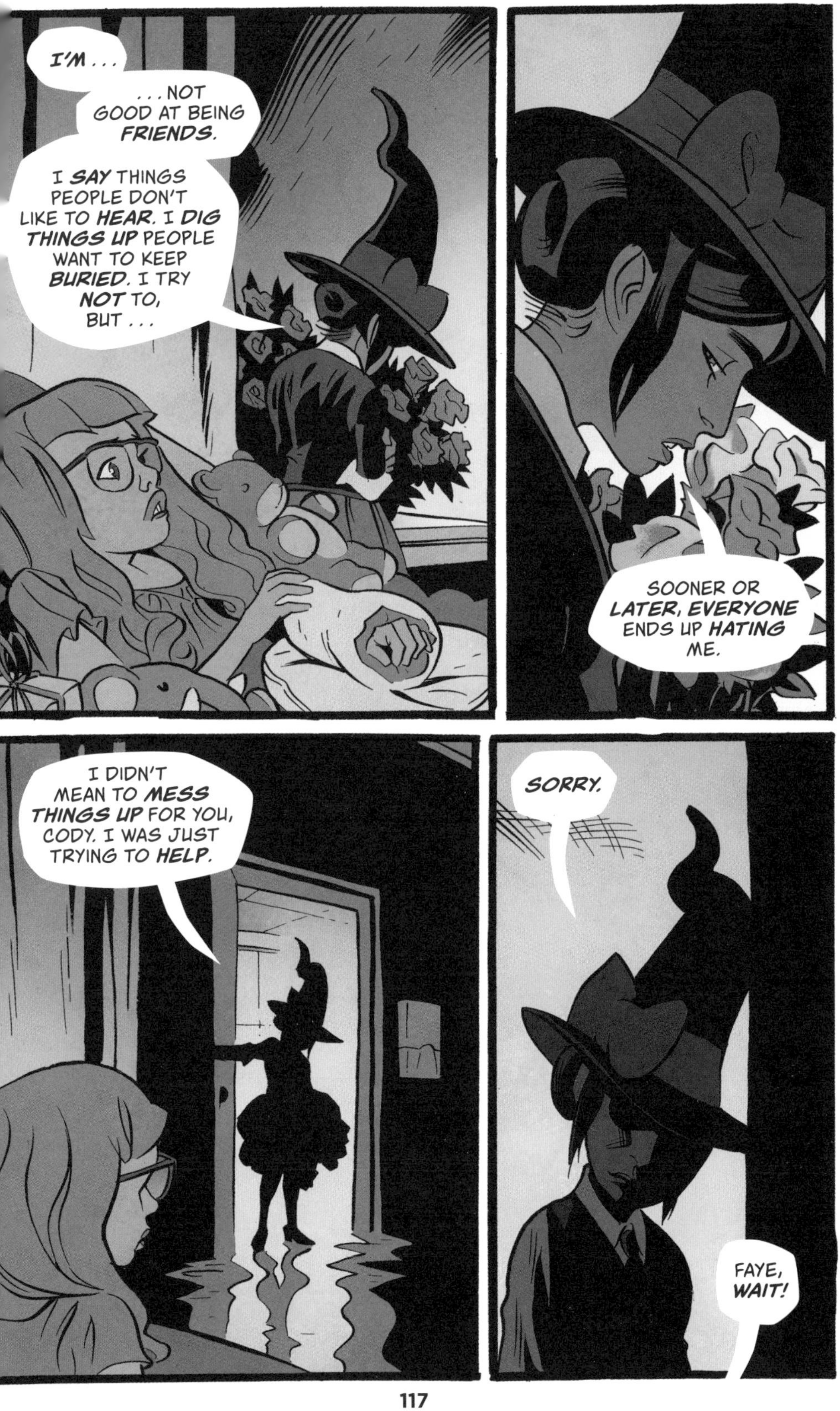

I'M . . .
. . . NOT GOOD AT BEING FRIENDS.
I SAY THINGS PEOPLE DON'T LIKE TO HEAR. I DIG THINGS UP PEOPLE WANT TO KEEP BURIED. I TRY NOT TO, BUT . . .
SOONER OR LATER, EVERYONE ENDS UP HATING ME.
I DIDN'T MEAN TO MESS THINGS UP FOR YOU, CODY. I WAS JUST TRYING TO HELP.
SORRY.
FAYE, WAIT!

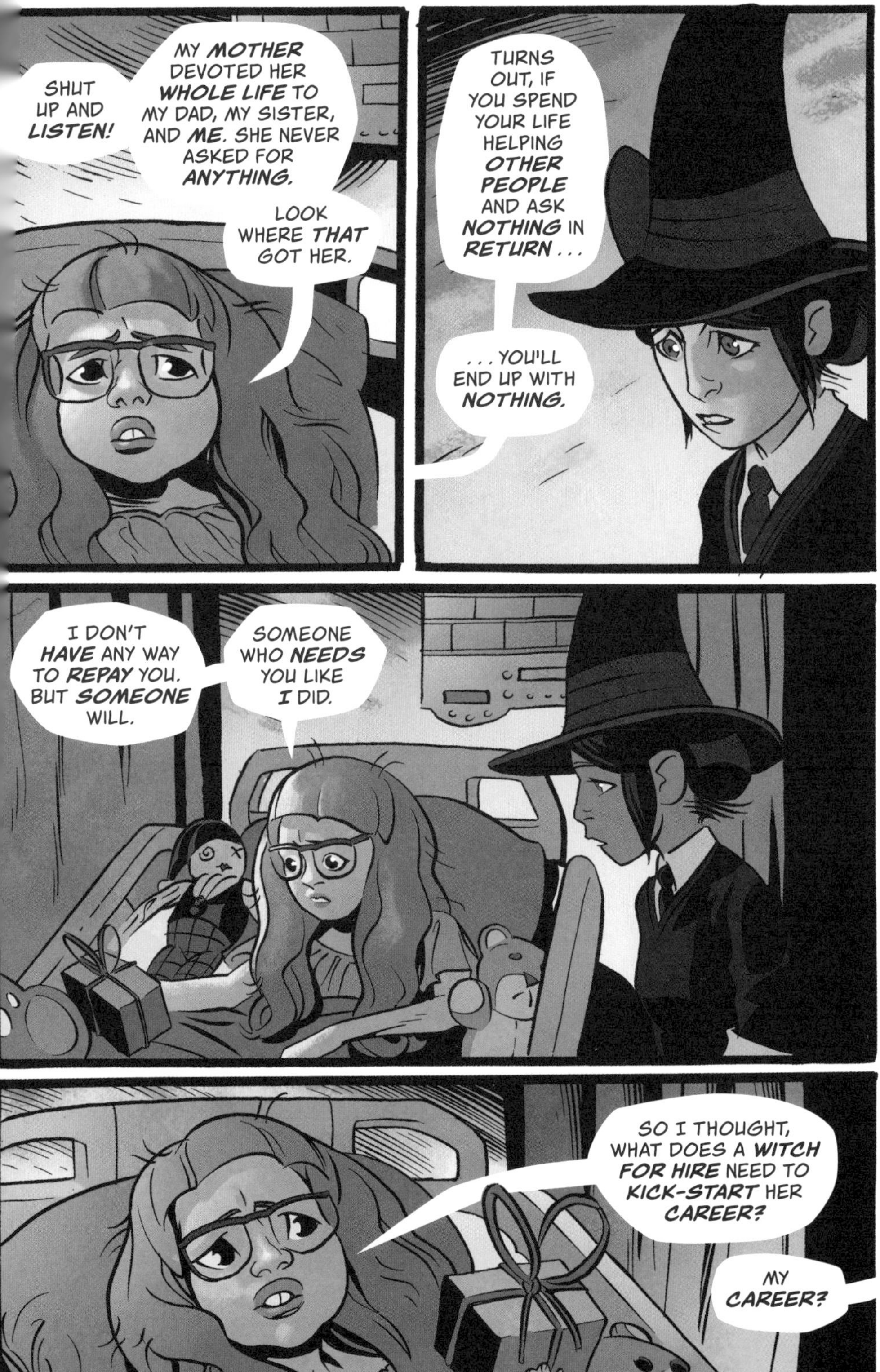
SHUT UP AND LISTEN!
MY MOTHER DEVOTED HER WHOLE LIFE TO MY DAD, MY SISTER, AND ME. SHE NEVER ASKED FOR ANYTHING.
LOOK WHERE THAT GOT HER.
TURNS OUT, IF YOU SPEND YOUR LIFE HELPING OTHER PEOPLE AND ASK NOTHING IN RETURN . . .
. . . YOU'LL END UP WITH NOTHING.
I DON'T HAVE ANY WAY TO REPAY YOU. BUT SOMEONE WILL.
SOMEONE WHO NEEDS YOU LIKE I DID.
SO I THOUGHT, WHAT DOES A WITCH FOR HIRE NEED TO KICK-START HER CAREER?
MY CAREER?

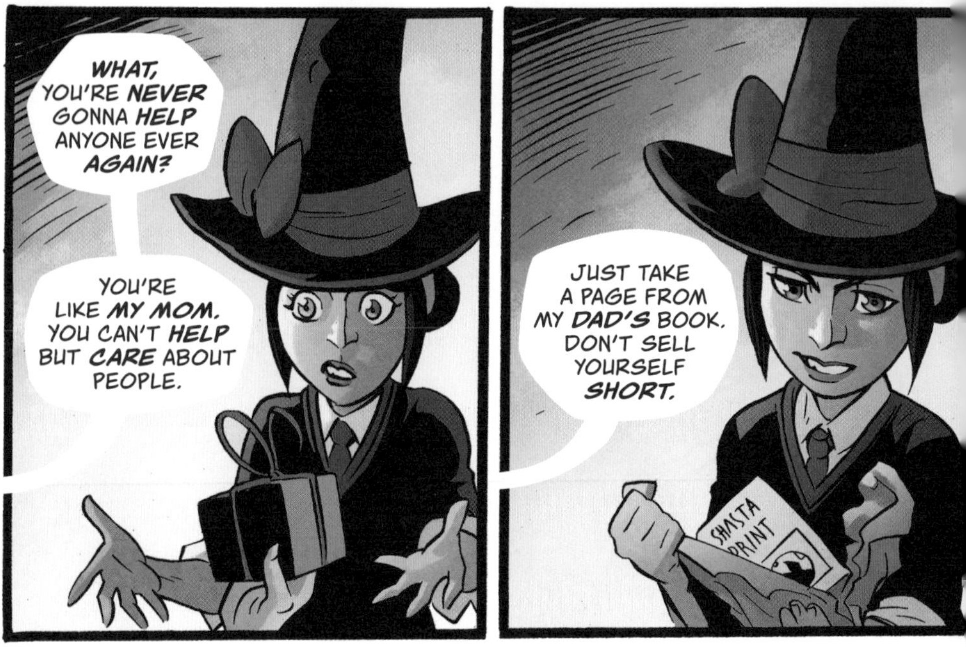
WHAT, YOU'RE NEVER GONNA HELP ANYONE EVER AGAIN?
YOU'RE LIKE MY MOM. YOU CAN'T HELP BUT CARE ABOUT PEOPLE.
JUST TAKE A PAGE FROM MY DAD'S BOOK. DON'T SELL YOURSELF SHORT.
SHASTA PRINT

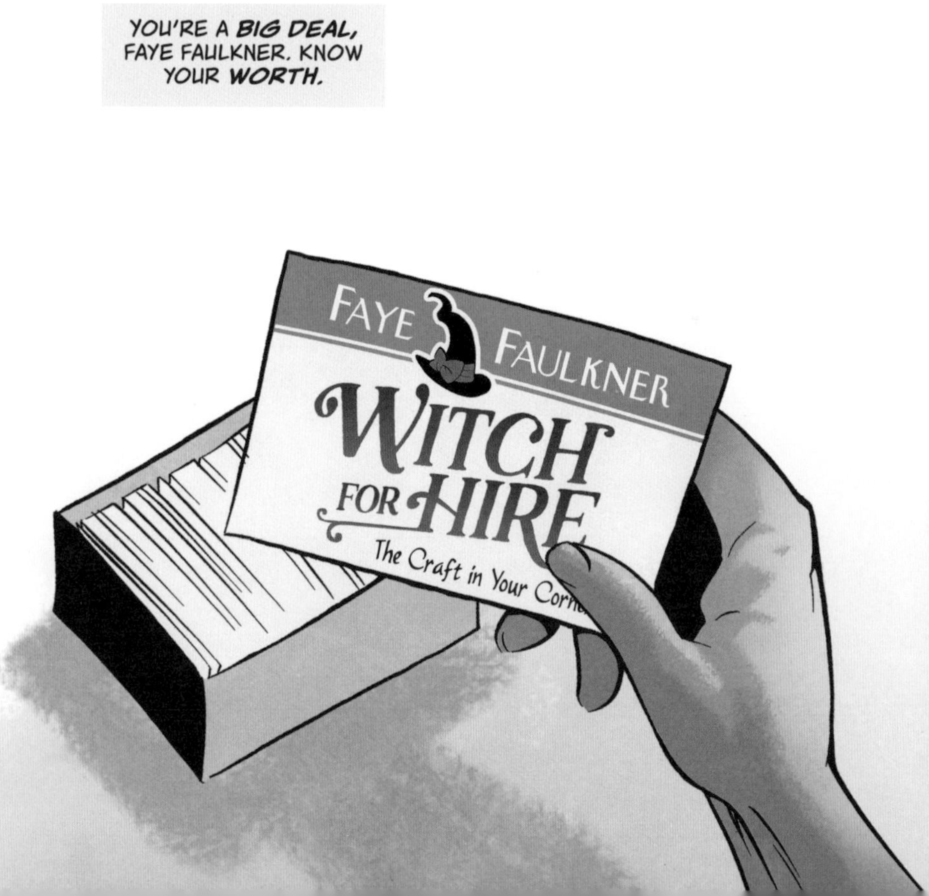
YOU'RE A BIG DEAL, FAYE FAULKNER. KNOW YOUR WORTH.
FAYE FAULKNER
WITCH FOR HIRE
The Craft in Your Corne

Thanks to Charlotte, Kay, and everyone at Abrams
for believing in this project.

Thanks to Scott Zoback for having my back and
Alan Spiegel for being a warm, friendly presence
at Comic Cons since forever. You guys are the best.

Thanks to Paget, Azmeer, Anne-Claude, and everyone
else who let me talk their ear off about this project.
Sometimes you just need to hear the ideas out loud
and good feedback is priceless.

Thanks to Jessica and Brian Berlin, Melanie,
Barbara, Jen, Lesley, and all my beloved community
for moral, emotional, and spiritual support.

Thanks Mom and Dad for always believing in my work.

As ever, thanks to Kelly Crumrin.